JFK CONSPIRACY THE MISSING FILE

JIM BOWLES

Jim Bowles

2-18-09

CONTENTS

FOREWORD

The assassination of President John F. Kennedy is a tragedy indelibly etched in the minds of most people. The legend lives because of the awful nature of the crime. However, the legend is clouded by the unending beliefs of some 85% of the population, world wide, that the assassination and its aftermath are the consequences of conspiracy.

The assassination has become the most intensively investigated crime in history. With so many minds working almost a half century, and finding no proof of a conspiracy it would seem the conspiracy notion would cease. But it hasn't and it isn't likly it will!

The conspiracy theory is largely sustained by feelings of disbelief. Most people find it impossible to believe that such heinous crimes could have been committed so casually by such total misfits. How could such a great person's life be wasted so simply by such a nobody? And how could the assassin in turn be assassinated by still another nobody?

It just won't add up! Even though the evidence refutes "conspiracy," human emotions won't, no, can't accept the idea! There must be more to it than that!

As a Dallas police officer during that era, I contributed to the investigation. As a result, seldome a month passes that I'm not interviewed by people from all walks of life. asking questions, mostly dealing with their "conspiracy" views. Having worked with dozens of authors on dozens of books both pro and con regarding conspiracy views, I developed an idea:

Since most people believe there was a conspiracy, why not "give" them their conspiracy?

This novel hopes in that manner to settle the conspiracy question for some. It is pure fiction, but based of pure facts, except for the conspiracy angle. Where necessary, true names are used. However, in the interest of privacy, the names of living officers are not used. The conspiracy characters are fictional and refer to no one, living or dead. It is my intention, through a fiction format, to weave a conspiracy into the true accounts of the assassination. Hopefully, readers seeing how impossible it would be to organize, develop, control, finance and conduct such an undertaking, they will then be able to finally acknowledge: It just didn't happen!

PROLOGUE

David Wright had been a Dallas Police officer for some thirty-five years. As well as a fellow officer of mine, he had been a lifelong family friend. A few years after retiring, he became ill with cancer and was near death. His nurse phoned me late one night to say he needed to see me and that it was urgent.

That worried me, as I had not seen nor spoken to him for more than a year. What could he want that was so urgent? I got out of bed and made an anxious run to his bedside. What I thought would be a consoling visit with an ailing friend became a life-changing event. I became an unwitting messenger in the murder of a president.

During our late-hour visit, Dave gave me a large sealed envelope. He swore me to its safekeeping, giving me permission to open it after November 2007. I gave him my assurance, then visited with him for a while. His nurse came to sedate him and asked me to leave. Returning home, I complied with his request, placing the file in a box with other papers in my attic. Shortly thereafter, Dave died and I forgot the incident. November 2007 passed without notice.

Recently I sold my home, and in clearing the attic, I removed the storage box and set it aside. Later, while organizing things in my new home, I discovered Dave's long-forgotten package. I left it out and finished moving. Some time later, I read Dave's file.

At first, the date November 2007 hadn't registered with me. On opening the file it was immediately obvious. The date coincided with the forty-fourth anniversary of the assassination of President John F. Kennedy. Dave had been involved. He had been a conspirator, one of several. He had trusted into my safekeeping his written account—a diary of events. It amounted to his confession.

This is his story.

CHAPTER ONE

En Route to the Lodge

The side road that branched off from Farm Road 12 was isolated. Driving slowly, I passed through remote and undeveloped pastureland dotted with scrubby stands of oak. This was part of the Old Man's property, and it was deliberately uninhabited. The Old Man was not a recluse, but he valued his privacy. He was not a jolly person, neither was he drab. Humor was usually expressed with a thin smile and a pleasant grunt. He was fairly tall, a little more than six feet, and a bit rotund, with two rows of white hair framing a shiny pink dome that was usually covered with a rumpled fedora. To me, he was a look-alike of the 1940s actor Sidney Greenstreet. While he was a very private person, he was unhesitating when it came to taking a public stand on world issues. However, when possible, he preferred to withdraw from public view. He often said, "My best security measure is not being noticed." His home in town was too conspicuous for business purposes so he acquired this lodge as his retreat through quiet purchases of unused farms and pastures in this isolated area. He now had more than 2,000 acres to which he could retreat and still be only an hour or so from the city. As I drove along en route to the lodge I reflected on how all this had come to be, where it had started, how I had become involved. I was reluctant to be going to the lodge this time, and that was reflected in my driving. I hadn't exceeded thirty miles per hour since I left my home. For a reason I couldn't describe, I really didn't want to attend this night's meeting. But the Old Man had called the group together, so that's how it would be. We, the group, would meet the Old Man at the lodge at seven o'clock. Many things had changed since the early fifties, but that hadn't. The Old Man was quiet but persuasive. He wasn't demanding. He just had a way of asserting his will. People, at least certain people, felt compelled to cooperate, to respond to his wishes. The fact that he was one of the wealthiest men in the world didn't really seem important; his appearance and mannerisms belied his wealth.

As I neared the lodge, my reluctance became foreboding. The lodge was a private place along a creek in an unused area of the huge ranch. Screened off by trees and far enough from the main house, its existence was known only to those who had been personally invited there by the Old Man. It was a pleasant place, cool and quiet in its desolate surroundings. I am certain the others in the group shared my memories of good times at the lodge, even though our usual reason for being there was to conduct careful strategy sessions. While the work was harrowing, we remember our visits for the general comfort and companionship we felt there. The Old Man had a rule about drinking. You didn't. He served wholesome meals, and the accommodations were simple yet comfortable. The lodge was an example of the wealthy old man's way of avoiding extravagance without sacrificing quality.

I was beginning to feel a bit old myself, sooner than expected. I was six feet, one inch tall, one hundred and ninety pounds, and starting to gray, but I still presented a decent profile. Maybe it was time to be showing my fifty years. I had joined the police department in 1938, and now, in my twenty-sixth year with the department, I was a lieutenant in the Criminal Investigation Division.

As I drove on, en route to the lodge, I reminisced about my earlier assignment to Washington, D.C., as an investigator for Senator Estes Kefauver's Organized Crime Committee, and how that assignment changed my point of view, then my whole life. Before World War

II, I was an ordinary officer in an ordinary police department. Before the war, Dallas was a peaceful city of little more than one hundred thousand people. Most of them had been born and raised in the area. They were a law-abiding and industrious working people. They had little concern for world affairs. They were more concerned with whether the Dallas Rebels would take the Fort Worth Cats in the Sunday doubleheader. They knew a little about Hitler and his Nazis, and they had heard of the Mafia or the Black Hand, and some had heard about the revolution in Russia, about Uncle Joe Stalin and Communism, but few comprehended what it all meant. That was something happening on the other side of the world. It couldn't concern them.

The war changed things for Dallas. The war brought in new and bigger industry; it tripled the population and introduced new lifestyles. Our simple prairie community became a full-grown city. People, new residents, and returning service personnel had a lot of catching up to do. That occupied their minds more than crime and communism. After all, the Mafia was up in New York and Chicago, and Russia had become an ally, or so we thought.

Things changed for me, too. The police department had enlarged with postwar growth and there were many new faces. And with growth came opportunity. I made detective shortly after I returned from my hitch in the Air Corps. That was a new field for me, but I think I fit in okay. During the next five years, I gained a lot of experience, met a lot of people and was content.

Dallas' growth had attracted outside interest. The Mafia's crime syndicate recognized the community's worth and considered Dallas virgin territory ripe for expansion. But before they could organize and control operations they had to make connections with local politicians and law enforcement officials. The chief of police learned of the syndicate's intentions. In cooperation with the sheriff, they decided to set a trap. I was tagged as bait to attract the syndicate's envoy. The plan worked. The syndicate conducted their business with me; the transactions were recorded and their intentions were exposed. The syndicate failed to penetrate Dallas. I didn't know it at the time, but that assignment was the door opener for the Washington assignment. I had met with and handled the Mafia's ambassadors so I was considered to be an authority on organized crime's activity. Maybe it was only natural for Senator Kefauver and his Organized Crime

Committee to look my way. It turned out to be a real twist of fate. For a few years my life had been devoted to solving burglaries. Then a chance undercover assignment, which could have been handled by any one of a dozen other detectives, changed everything. That started me on the unbelievable trip that brought me once again to the lodge.

Then my mind drifted to Joe Kervin, who is now retired from the Secret Service. He was not your typical secret service agent. He wasn't your tall, slim, shorthaired man in a dark blue suit, wearing sunglasses. He was a good four inches shorter than the rest of our group, about five-eight or -nine, balding just a bit, with the start of a spare tire around his waist. While he did wear dark suits, he shunned dark glasses.

Although Joe had been in Washington with the Presidential Detail during the early fifties while I was with the Crime Committee, he didn't become acquainted with the rest of the group until about the middle of 1960. His late arrival as a member of the group, however, didn't limit his role.

For nearly ten years, some of us, various members of the group, had met casually on random occasions. At first we met for general discussions about law enforcement or politics. Seldom were more than two or three of us able to get away at the same time for a few hours. The conversations eventually turned to the insidious and encroaching nature of communism in America. We worried about how socialism in the form of public welfare had gone unrecognized as a means whereby lazy people could be made dependent upon the labor of the industrious. We worried about how their dependents would raise a second, a third, and even a fourth generation of welfare dependents. We worried about how Senator Joe McCarthy had seen his anticommunist program scuttled by the skillful undercover commie pros and communist dupes. We worried about how fast and how far the communists and their fellow travelers had flooded into the vacuum created by McCarthy's defeat. Each subsequent gathering seemed to find things in worse condition than before. We discussed ways of dealing with the growing crisis, but that was the limit of our activity—talk. That had been our limit until we allied ourselves with the Old Man. Until then we had merely been well-intentioned, reasonably well-informed civil service workers. We had no means for action. If we spoke out too loudly or publicly, it could end our careers.

I became acquainted with the Old Man in early 1958. As president of the Police Officer League, I had often spoken out against the tide of liberal politics and creeping socialism. Eisenhower had done a credible job as President but what could he really be expected to do without a clear majority in Congress? His position was like rowing upstream with a broken paddle. Everywhere you looked, new groups were beginning to protest against our American way of life. People were coming out against all our old institutions and traditions. Student protests, not too uncommon in unsettled foreign countries, were becoming more frequent in the United States. It was frightening that the Washington political crowd was running scared. They were afraid to take a stand for normalcy because they might lose a few votes.

I had attracted the Old Man's attention during that period, and after he had me carefully checked out by his confidential assistant, he contacted me. We became well acquainted, and developed a mutual respect because we shared almost identical views and beliefs.

The Communist Manifesto declared that a democracy required the social stability afforded by the institutions of family, church, school, local government, and local police.

Communism promised to destroy the unity of the family, the effectiveness of public education, and the peoples' confidence in the ability of local governments to serve and the local police to protect the populace.

I was a frequent visitor of the Old Man, and he in turn visited me. He addressed meetings of the Police Officer's League. It was after one such meeting that things started to happen. The conversation went like this.

"I appreciate your taking the time to attend tonight's meeting, sir, and what you said really needed saying," I began.

"The pleasure is mine," the Old Man assured me. "I only wish we could meet more frequently and with more people. But that's not the solution, Dave. These small meetings are important, but it's like fighting a big dog with a small stick. You might make an impression, but you can't win."

I looked at him in a way that showed I agreed but was at a loss for words. Then I said, "I follow your thought, sir, but what can we do? We aren't that big and almost anything we do is subject to civil service scrutiny."

He answered, "No, I wasn't thinking in terms of you and your organization, Dave. God knows there isn't much that they can do. It is important that they learn as much as they can and that they pass the word to as many as will listen and trust them. But that simply is not enough. We need an organization, Davey boy! We need some well-selected people in a variety of places who believe in what must be done. We need people who can get around. We need trained observers and investigators, people who can find out who are involved and the things in which they are involved. We need an intelligence network. We aren't going to achieve results just hassling a few bellyachers. Neither can we accomplish anything by cracking the heads of those protesters. We must educate a whole population.

"People just don't seem to understand it, Dave. There is an unseen enemy force in our land. They are well trained and committed to their purpose. That purpose is the overthrow of this country!"

"Do you mean Communist agents have infiltrated the country to that extent?"

"Infiltrated the country? Dave, they've infiltrated *the government!* They're well up into government. McCarthy told them. At least he tried to. Just look at what they did to his Un-American Activities Committee. Those people are good. They are real pros. They have the experience, and McCarthy was a babe-in-the-woods by comparison. He was outclassed from the start. He never stood a chance."

"But what about John Birch," I asked. "They're active and seem to be making a headway."

"They'll never make it," the Old Man replied. "They've got some good ideas, and good people, but look what's happened. Like I said, our unseen enemies are sharp. They don't stand out in front of the opposition and fight! No, they're too smart for that. They have dupes! They spend time and money teaching dupes to do their fighting. They've been here for years, Davey. They've starved the Russian people at home so they could finance their people over here. They haven't starved themselves, however. They don't practice what they preach. They take the cream off the top. They've cheated the common people, the workers they are supposed to support. They've kept them poor and hungry for two reasons: one, so the common people can't fight back; and two, so they can raise money to send over here to finance their activities. They know very well that for so long as there's a strong and functioning U.S.A., they'll never be able to dominate the free world. All anybody has to do is look at us and see what free enterprise in a democratic republic can do. Given a choice, nobody would choose communism! And the communists know that! They know we're strong. They know that unless they break us from within they'll never take us. Not head-on."

"I should have guessed what you would say about the John Birch Society," I replied. "I've had a few guys around here kid me about that. Things like, 'Hey, Dave, seen any pinkos today?' Or 'Have you gone *Bircher* or something?' I guess that's to be expected. Policemen are for the most part ordinary people. It's the work that's different. But when they have the chance, they're just ordinary people. So they think just like anybody else, or at least pretty much like them."

"You've got the picture now, Dave. You just said what I've been saying. Even people who ought to know better don't seem to realize what's happening right under their noses!"

I paused a moment to be sure the Old Man had finished his thought and to think about what he said, "What can we do, then, those of us who can?"

The Old Man smiled his cherubic smile. Then grinding out his cigar with satisfied moves he said, "You can do anything you have the conviction to do, Davey. I have some ideas but no immediate plans. Let's do this. You think back. Think of a few good men such as yourself. Think of some men with conviction; men with some smarts; men with some capabilities. We need a close-knit group of thinkers who have an unyielding love for this country. We need a group who knows the meaning of commitment; some men who aren't afraid to work, to take a chance. My God, man, those communists aren't afraid to die if they have to! What can Americans hope to do in opposing them if they are afraid to get involved? Too many Americans have become so satisfied with their lives of plenty that the thought of a little work, scares all reason out of them. God forbid that they should take any risks. No, Dave, the people we need can't be ordinary Americans. They must be extraordinary! They must be as though they were cut from the original stock!"

That conversation had taken place almost six years ago. Now, driving to the lodge, I could remember the exact words and expressions as well as I would if the conversation had occurred that very afternoon. I had gone home that evening after our meeting with a sudden feeling of total fatigue. I couldn't remember having been so tired. But I couldn't sleep. Thoughts of the Old Man's conversation echoed through my mind again and again. What, exactly had he meant? How far would he go? I know now that my most exaggerated estimate of the Old Man's potential missed its mark completely. If there had been any way for me to imagine what the Old Man was going to do, my heart would have frozen in mid-beat.

* * *

I turned off the main highway and headed east down State 27 for its junction with Farm Road 12 a few miles ahead.

My next thoughts turned to the realization that, at first, I couldn't think of a single person who fit the Old Man's criteria. What had the Old Man meant? Whom could I consider? What would be expected of them? The Old Man even spoke of the communists' willingness to die for their purposes. Surely that wasn't what he had in mind.

It wasn't until I was well into a sleepless night a week later that I considered how Charlie might fit in. Charles Evans was an early member of the group. He was an FBI agent I had known well for years. He had spent twenty-two of his forty-four years with the Bureau. He wore his store-rack suits and his 195 pounds equally well. We had met while we were both assigned to the Organized Crime Committee investigations. Charlie, the younger of us, was the Bureau's liaison with the committee. I had privately wondered why such a brilliant young lawyer as he had decided to go with the Bureau rather than private practice. He was a sharp attorney who could have made a mint on the outside.

Later, I asked Anthony Amatta to become another early member of the group. Tony was a political science major, a former first lieutenant in the Office of Strategic Services. He was the oldest and the shortest member of the original group. An olive complexion, Roman nose, and wavy black hair complemented his fluent Italian. He had been heavily involved in OSS activities behind the German lines in Italy and had become well acquainted with the inroads of communism there before the Germans retreated. Continuing in the intelligence field, Tony joined the Central Intelligence Agency and was trained as a specialist in Mafia affairs. It didn't matter that he was a third generation member of a well-established, well-respected family. Being Italian, it was presumed he would know about the Mafia. Accordingly, that became his specialty.

As I made my last turn onto the lodge road, my immediate recollections of past events seemed so remote as to have been someone else's memories from another lifetime. But they were not. They were mine, and they were real. I had known and worked with those and other intimate friends. In fact, I had often worried that too many were involved for our own safety. Regardless of the risks and the improbability of the odds, we succeeded. God, did we ever succeed! Our initial objectives were to combat lawlessness and communism. In the end we assassinated the President of the United States.

CHAPTER TWO

AT THE LODGE

I found that I had arrived at the lodge first. The building was situated in a well-wooded hollow on a winding creek. Its comfort was reflected in its outward appearance. The rough-hewn cedar planks and beams had faded out to a satin-like silver hue. There was just enough antique brick trim to accent the wood tones. A veranda reaching across the front width of the lodge was furnished with several comfortable lounging chairs. Over the years, I had sat there for uncounted hours looking out over the creek, relaxing in serious mediation. This had to be one of the most restful settings anywhere; no problem was so weighty that it couldn't be lightened while sitting on that veranda. I had hoped I would arrive early so I could relax while I waited for the others.

Sitting down and leaning back, I returned to my thoughts of the events that had brought me to this evening. My mind drifted back to an innocent after-dinner discussion in a suburban Dallas steak house. The group's consideration of criminal matters had given way to the greater crisis of an increasing communist influence in this country. We considered the growing views of liberal versus conservative philosophy in national politics, and of how we might move against those things and inform the people that their freedom was at risk.

I think I can remember the first conversation when we got into politics. It was in early 1960.

Tony started the conversation. "Well, Eisenhower might not be rated as one of the top ten Presidents, at least not for a few years, but—"

Charlie interrupted, "It usually takes at least ten years for an administration's true worth to surface, doesn't it? There are too many variables for a short answer."

Tony answered, "You have to consider how long the President was in office, whether his party controlled Congress, whether the President's party had succeeded itself in office, world affairs, the economy, and myriad other things."

I agreed, saying, "As a rule, it does take a few years. On the other hand, if the Democrats get Kennedy in, come November we'll learn to appreciate Ike a helluva lot faster!"

The Old Man had sat back listening to his associates. He was waiting for the exact time to speak. "Don't say 'if' Kennedy, say 'when,' because they are simply too powerful and too well-organized. It would be a tough enough fight if it were just the Kennedy machine we had to contend with. There's the Kennedy name, the Kennedy family, his war record, his political record. He even makes a good-looking candidate. He's making it well with labor, he's making it well with the Negroes, and he's making it well with all the women. The older ones want to mother him and the younger ones—well; they look at him the way girls used to look at Sinatra. When you figure that Democrats generally outnumber Republicans, and how big he is back East, and when you consider all those special interest groups he has in his camp, I can tell you now, we're in an uphill battle that we will most likely lose. But then there's another reason."

I asked him, "Do you mean the election is really all over? Do you mean Nixon doesn't have a chance?"

Charlie exclaimed, "My God! If it's all over but the shouting, why are we concerning ourselves?"

The Old Man paused to relight his after-dinner cigar, then he smiled his thin, reassuring smile, and continued. "Nothing is ever absolutely certain, my boys, except as you know, death and taxes. It will be a race, a very close race. And we've got to take a stand; take our licks at 'em. We certainly can't lay down and play dead. Not at all! We have to give them a run for their money. We've got to show as much strength as possible. They've got to know they've been in a fight. Then, if we lose, or more accurately, when we lose, it won't be because we didn't make a case. It'll be because they outgunned us. But they must be made to know that we are a serious factor that must be considered."

I said, "I can't believe that the American voters are so irresponsible. Before now, I always thought we were among the best-educated people in the world. How can smart people be so stupid when it comes to voting?"

Drawing on his own schooling, Tony rejoined the conversation. "People vote or don't vote for some unbelievable reasons. Would you believe that there are two simple reasons that account for the most votes in any election? Some people always vote for 'the party' with no earthly idea why; they just do so because they always have. Then there's a great number who look at an election much as though it's a sporting contest. They handicap the election. They want to be sure they're on the winning side. They vote, not for a candidate's position on the issues but for whomever the media, the polls, and odds-makers predict will win."

I agreed. "Yeah, I guess there's a tremendous amount of stupidity in voting. There will be those who will vote for Kennedy because he's a Catholic just like there will be some who'll vote against him for the same reason."

Adjusting his chair for a better position before the group, Charlie asked, "Where does that leave us, sir? I'm a sore loser. So if I'm going to lose I'm going to do something to make our losing easier, or at least more acceptable. I'm not going to sit back and just let it happen."

Looking more pleased than before, the Old Man said, "I'm glad you've brought that up. If you noted, I mentioned earlier that the Kennedy machine wasn't the only reason he'd likely win. There's another reason. Gentlemen, the unseen enemy has never been busier. The communists and their sympathizers and fellow travelers certainly will have a hand in determining the outcome of the 1960 election. Not only do the communist front organizations that support Kennedy, they are hard at work running Nixon down. They have ample money and subtle ways of hurting a candidate. And when it's done, who

JFK CONSPIRACY - THE MISSING FILE

would ever suspect it was a communist plot? In fact, if you even suggest that, they will make you look like some kind of a fool."

I thought for a moment, then asked the Old Man, "Sir, I don't doubt you, not at all. But how can the communists sway votes to Kennedy and against Nixon, and why?"

"Good question, lad. Now let me answer you. Take a look at those student groups at the colleges. Who do you suppose trained the spokesmen who stir up the rest of the students? Who do you suppose saw to it that card-carrying communists have become tenured professors in even the best of our colleges and universities? When McCarthy was trying to expose those people, who do you suppose stopped him? And take the racial situation. Who do you suppose financed the training for their leadership? How do you suppose the demonstrators can keep eating and meeting expenses when they aren't working? And don't forget the propaganda value of our vast entertainment industry. If a popular comedian makes a joke about Nixon, there are many people who will repeat it as if it were the truth because of that comedian's popularity. One-time jokes aren't so bad, but they become destructive when hateful jokes about a candidate become the *in thing*. The sarcasm is always directed toward the candidate the communists oppose and never toward their chosen candidate. Our people just don't realize that they are being manipulated when they are being bombarded daily by radio, TV, stage, and motion picture propaganda that advances the communist-socialist dogma and makes a joke of our philosophy or makes it seem hypocritical and wrong. If you think back, it was the entertainment people and the media people who knocked McCarthy out of power. His investigations were striking too close to the heart of their movement. Given a couple of more years and a little backbone from some gutless politicians, McCarthy would have dealt a death blow to communism in America. Then those liberal politicians who are so dead set to redistribute the wealth of the workers, to give the wealth of the working class to a bunch of loafers who should be out looking for jobs, would be out of office.

The conversation continued a while longer on the same subject. Then, as we left to go our separate ways, I spoke to Charlie. "I guess that 'bout wraps it up for us, don't you think? If it's so probable that Kennedy's going to beat Nixon, we can't really do anything but gut about it."

Charlie shrugged, and I could see that he agreed. Then he added, "I guess so, but the thought of that sends a hot flash up and down my spine. God knows, somebody ought to be able to do something."

I reached my car first, said my good-byes to Charlie, and waved to Tony who was still within sight walking the Old Man to his car. I thought about how strange it was that the Old Man, for all his wealth, still did his own driving. No limousines or chauffeurs for him. He had an older model, nondescript sedan that he drove himself. It wasn't even air conditioned.

Pulling from the parking lot, I wondered whether our little group would ever get together again. Why would they? If Kennedy beats Nixon, and it appeared that he would, and assuming Kennedy would be reelected, that would take things to 1968. And what if Bobby Kennedy managed to succeed him in office, and what if he managed two terms, too? God! That would carry us into 1976, sixteen years ahead. And then there's Teddy. I couldn't know whether any of our group would be alive then, much less be able to have any influence on the presidency.

CHAPTER THREE

POLITICS—1962

As I sat on the veranda waiting for the others, I thought about how accurately the Old Man had predicted the outcome of the 1960 election. Senator Kennedy had beaten Vice President Nixon, but only by the slightest margin. Less than 1% percent of the voters had made the difference. But consider the results. Whatever Eisenhower's administration had been able to achieve had been lost. The Democrats were back—back and in strength.

It didn't take long for Kennedy to get going either. He started with a challenge for Americans: "Ask not what your country can do for you but what you can do for your country." Then he started on social programs as if there would be no tomorrow. Much of that insanity and there *would be* no tomorrow in the opinion of conservatives.

While I sat there waiting, I thought back to a strategy meeting with the group at the lodge

JFK CONSPIRACY - THE MISSING FILE

in the fall of 1962. Joe Kervin had become a familiar face in the group by then. The Old Man had become distressed with events during the President's first year and a half in office. He felt that it was time to start planning for the next election. How were things stacking up? What had happened so far, and what was likely to happen next? Moreover, what could happen between then and 1964? What were our options?

The Old Man had started that visit with, "Let's take a look at what's happened and how might we use those things to our advantage."

Charlie started the answer: "Well, unemployment isn't so bad, what with the space program. That's kept people working, but it stands to play the devil with the value of the dollar. You can't pay for government spending by running the printing presses overtime in the basement of the Treasury Department. The idea that a debt you owe yourself really isn't a debt is a lot of hooey. Kennedy's already started running up a debt for my grand kids!"

The Old Man agreed. He said, "A good observation. Not only is unfunded indebtedness a liability to our successors, there is an ironic side to the issue. The illusion of prosperity creates euphoria in our people. They feel like rejoicing in their seeming good fortune, and they consider their assailant to be their benefactor."

I listened carefully, then meekly asked, "Could you explain that for me? You went over my head."

"Certainly, Davey. What it means is that by the simple process of printing more money to pay their bills the government hasn't truly made the people more prosperous. They simply have more paper money passing through their hands. But the government has nothing with which to back that money. Eventually, there'll be a day of reckoning. All these 'good old days' will come back to haunt us. We will have inflation the likes of which our people have never known. The dollar as we know it today will hardly be worth the cost of its printing. But because, for the time being, many people have more money coming through their hands than ever before, they feel well off. They feel that they owe their good fortune to the President because he got all these good things going. They feel that he's done them a favor. They feel fortunate without realizing that the short-term favor he's bestowed on them today is in reality a long-term debt that they, their children and their children's children will be paying off for years to come. In fact, they will only be paying on the interest. The indebtedness will snowball at such a rate the principal can never be paid off. Can you imagine what unborn generations are going to say about us?" This time he concluded without his usual smile. Clearly he had given that considerable thought; he meant everything he had said, and the truth of it distressed him very much.

"Well, everything hasn't come up roses for Kennedy," Tony chimed in. "Consider the Cuban missile crisis and the Bay of Pigs. The missile crisis created quite a scare. He had people out buying and installing bomb shelters and stockpiling emergency supplies. That didn't give me a feeling of euphoria!"

"No, but you've got to admit that when he was faced with it, he stood up to the Russians," I mentioned. "He blockaded Cuba and made them haul those missiles away."

The Old Man shook his head slowly, indicating mild disagreement and said, "He actually came away a bit the better for this. He showed that we don't feel the Monroe Doctrine is dead, and he reacted in such a manner as to cause the communists to believe we meant business so they backed off. At least, it seems they backed off. Without some onsite inspection capability we can't be positive just who and what was removed, and who and what remained. I'm reasonably sure some communist 'technicians' stayed. And there's no way of knowing what kinds of military hardware and ordinance the Cubans still have."

Tony, feeling the time now appropriate, said, "This much I can tell you. All the Russians are not out of Cuba. We aren't sure of just how many or what kind of long-range ordinance is there, too. And the President, yes, he got some good press for standing up to the Russians and for holding the line on Castro. But it isn't all peaches and cream. The Kremlin boys are in a real lather. They surely didn't enjoy backing down, but they weren't quite ready to risk war. You might say it's a role reversal of the U-2 bit. Then, they were in the driver's seat for a while and we had to eat crow. Now, we've called their hand on the missiles and got them to back off. I can assure you that Premier Khrushchev is furious. He's in a rage."

Charlie, feeling that Tony's CIA connections might provide the answer, asked, "Well, Tony, what can you tell us about the Bay of Pigs fiasco?"

"That's just what it was, Charlie, a fiasco. You should try to get someone to accept some blame." Then Tony stood up as if to make his further response more emphatic. "What happened is the CIA was supposed to set the deal up with the

Cuban exiles and they were supposed to pull it off. The air cover didn't show up, and that left the land troops flat-footed on the beach. There are some who say the problem involved missed signals, and there are some who say it was a scheduling error. Well, whatever the truth, the B-26s never did show. They were ordered off, and I understand those orders came from *him, from Kennedy!*"

That floored me. I looked surprisingly at Tony and asked, "You mean he got cold feet?"

"I don't know what he got, I only know that the B-26s got ordered back while en route. Even if they had been late, it would have been better than nothing! As it is we, the U.S. government, let those poor S.O.B.s down. We left them flat-footed on the beach."

I shook my head in disbelief, and said, "I'll bet they love us."

"That isn't the half of it," Tony said

The Old Man entered the conversation, "Could you be more specific with us, Tony?"

Tony paused a moment as if considering the propriety of his answer. Remember he was CIA. He had to wonder what would happen if his confidence in the group was betrayed. Not deliberately. After all, we had trusted each other on many occasions over the years. Still, he seemed to be feeling a bit queasy. But if he couldn't trust the guys in the group, whom could he trust? He wasn't all that sure about his associates in the Company. He had said that several times before. Then he relaxed a bit and said, "You almost need a scorecard to keep the record straight. Don't breathe a word of this. I know I don't have to remind you, but this couldn't come from just anybody. You know what I mean. Anyhow, here it is. We've talked about how angry the Russians are because of the missile deal. And the Cuban exiles are plenty hot over the Bay of Pigs. Now, here's some more. The Mafia is hot because of Bobby's attitude since he was appointed Attorney General. But it gets worse. Try this one on. The President put out a contract on Castro! The idea was in the works at the time he was elected. He inherited it, and has gone along with it so far."

Our reaction was, "What the—" in a chorus.

"You heard me." Tony confirmed. "I don't have all the details, but it adds up to this. The President wants Castro off his back door so he got the Company to approach the syndicate. To make a long story short, the syndicate wants to control the action in Cuba when Castro is out, and the President wanted some kind of deal. It went so far, and then there was a leak. Castro got wind of it, and the whole deal went sour. So you can add Castro to the hate list because of the efforts to have him assassinated. And you can add the syndicate to the list too because they didn't get their deal. They cooperated but things didn't click so they got left out, and now, Bobby's out to put 'em all in prison if not out of the country!

"And there are crowds in D.C. who are unhappy because Kennedy wants out of Vietnam, and the military-industrial complex is most unhappy."

Then Charlie reminded us, "So far as it goes, you can add 'labor' to your 'hate-the-President' list because Bobby's made a bunch of them mad, too.

Joe, who typically was silent, spoke up. "It stands to reason that you'd know about the assassination plan, but God, it sounds weird to hear us talking about it. It doesn't sound real. I wonder who all knows about it. Kennedy has a bad habit of confiding in too many people. He's forever bouncing ideas off different people. But really, I don't think it's so much 'trust' as it is 'carelessness.' It still leaves me with a chill when I hear things that I have no earthly right or reason to hear. And that's partly why I feel so guilty hearing these things."

I mustered up a sardonic smile and added, "It just might be easier to make a list of who *isn't* mad at him. With a slate of enemies like that, I'd hate to be the investigator if somebody killed him. The suspect list would be too long. You're better off to start with *no* suspect than *too many*. The conservatives could trigger the idea, the Agency could arrange things, the mob could do the hit, it could be set up to blame Castro, a patsy could take the fall, and with the Russians out of the deal, it wouldn't start World War III. Man, what a deal!"

I didn't know then that my that my little hypothetical reference stimulated a profound consideration. My casual and innocent observation provoked the Old Man into a frightening scheme. The President would be assassinated.

CHAPTER FOUR

THE PLOT

That episode prompted my recall of our next meeting, early in December 1962. By a quarter to seven we had arrived at the lodge and moved near the blazing fireplace and out of the biting chill. The housekeeper from the main quarters, a little more than a quarter mile from the lodge, entered with the evening meal in insulated containers. He moved invisibly into the kitchen area, served coffee, set out the meal and departed. Would you believe that in all those years I never knew of that little guy ever saying a word? When he finished, it was like a signal for the Old Man to enter and extend greetings to us as he made his way to the dining area and took his usual place at the center of the long table, facing the cheerful fire.

That night he seemed particularly quiet, almost troubled, an unusual condition for him. Taking our cue, we ate our meal in a strange silence. Several times I thought he was about to speak but if that had been his intention, he decided against it. Within a few minutes we were hoping someone would break the silence, but there was an unspoken understanding that the opening of conversation was at his discretion.

After the meal, we returned to the main room, a large congenial area furnished and arranged for comfort and conversation. We had another round of coffee and wished for something more potent as we sat in our customary seats. The Old Man settled into his chair, opened the wrapper from his cigar, prepped it, then clenched it in his teeth for a few moments without lighting it. Then, removing it, he spoke.

"Gentlemen, I'm pleased that you were able to join me this evening. While I didn't want to make an issue of it, I was most anxious for the entire group to assemble tonight.

"I've given much careful thought to the manner in which the political situation is shaping up and quite frankly I'm more than alarmed; indeed I'm frightened. We are more than halfway through this administration, and two things are obvious. He hasn't made the kind of mistakes that would be self-defeating; in fact, public opinion, deluded as it is, appears to be growing more favorable daily. And he has a tremendous skill with the media, hence they are more strongly in his grasp than ever before. The second problem is one of opposition candidacy. Nixon has effectively removed himself from future consideration.

"That leaves us in a quandary, lads. The opposition grows stronger while we grow weaker."

Joe broke tradition and spoke. "I agree fully with your observations, sir." After a brief conspicuous pause he continued. "Things are bad, but are we without options? Do you think it's impossible for Senator Goldwater to win?"

Not waiting for an answer, Charlie added, "It seems much worse than it was during the last campaign. Tough as it was in 1960, with Nixon there was at least a thread of hope. Some big money is making Vietnam a bad issue for Goldwater, branding him a 'warmonger.' No one seems interested in the real issue."

The others voiced their agreement but I don't remember what anyone said specifically. In later years, not one of us could accurately say who had made the first reference to the death of the President. Perhaps it was a merciful eclipse of our minds. It was more like a spontaneous thing; it was being discussed with out actual reference to *murder* being suggested.

I consider myself to be a trained observer. But I could only recall that someone else had said something about "options" to which someone commented about the list of people who might wish to see him dead, and how convoluted a plot it could be with everybody being suspect. Perhaps it is best that we lost the identity of the initial speaker considering the nature of the subject and the eventual outcome.

The best I can remember, Tony had said that none of those who might actually wish to see the President dead could be approached on the subject. To that, Charlie had asked, "How could it be done like you said so it would appear that one of those people or groups did it?"

Tony had shifted in his chair, a gesture of thoughtful response. "I don't know offhand," he said, "but it certainly can't be out of the range of possibility."

"Such a possibility has to be considered," I countered. "Somebody just might do it, or at least try." I was considering 'someone else,' *not us,* as possible actors.

Then, Tony had smiled at me and said, "That's the way ordinary people would consider it, Davey. But that isn't the way the pros do it. Not only must you manage the act, you must manage or at least manipulate the investigation."

Next, Joe spoke up and organized the conversation. "You're saying then, that we, or some one, would need to find a hit man, find an opportunity, plant the evidence to throw suspicion on someone else, and then watch the investigation so that it goes the way it was planned."

That's where I got scared. "My God, wait a minute. You guys are talking about this like it was some sort of planning-training exercise; you write a lesson plan and the students carry out their assignments and everybody lives happily ever after. What the—"

But the Old Man cut me off. "Gentlemen, extraordinary problems have always required extraordinary people to perform extraordinary deeds. As uncommonly strange and forbidding as this is, it appears to be obviously necessary. Suppose some 'evil' German had assassinated Adolf Hitler before 1932, or even 1939? I do not propose that we consider Mr. Kennedy in the same light as Mr. Hitler. I only suggest that, uncivilized as it might seem to ordinary sensitivities, we are in a history-shaping crisis. We cannot survive as a people if he survives.

It is better for one man to fall than a nation. Rather than dwell on this in general terms, I feel that we should discuss various possibilities and evaluate them. We should only consider pursuit of the matter if and when it appears that we have between us the essentials for success, and the unalterable necessity to pursue that end. And let me remind you, it will not be without risks. One or all of us could suffer serious and irreversible consequences if we are not absolutely cautious."

"What's been said already could land us in prison!" I reminded them. "That's what we're talking about."

Charlie tried to lighten the conversation. Straightening his body to the erect position, he spoke. "Like I've always heard, the bigger the prize, the harder the fight. You don't win big pots with small stakes."

Then, the Old Man again assumed the role of discussion leader with a question. "I suppose the 'who' would be the first thing to consider, wouldn't it? Who should be considered for the task? Who should we look for, and where might we find him?"

He was answered with a minute or so of silence. Nobody had been willing to assume the initiative. No doubt we were humbled and horrified by the enormity and audacity of the topic.

Then Tony spoke. "What do you think of including a patsy, someone selected and groomed to be the suspect, but who would know absolutely nothing about the plan?"

"I'm certainly not experienced in this business," Joe offered, "but wouldn't that be rather obvious? He would certainly deny his guilt. Then what happens?"

Tony then responded, "It isn't all that simple, Joe. You not only set up the patsy, you might have to take him out, too."

Joe seemed genuinely startled. "Take him out, too?" he cried. "My God, what are we talking about?"

I remember, Tony didn't waste a second with his answerer. "Losers, Joe, plain and simple, losers. We're talking about taking out the main hit as the primary objective with some loser as an insulator. Face it, Joe, it might be the only significant thing the poor stooge ever does for humanity."

Joe started to say, "But it sounds so cold, so callous—"

But Tony interrupted, "We aren't talking about playing cops and robbers, Joe. We're talking about one of the most serious things we are ever likely to do."

Charlie moved uncomfortably in his chair before he asked the next obvious question. "Do you have anyone in mind for this patsy, Tony?"

"No, not off hand. How about you?"

"Not really. Not that easily—"

"We should be able to find someone from the past. Someone who has 'doubled' between us and the communists."

Joe sat up straight and responded to Tony. "With all the confab between anti-Castro and pro-Castro Cubans, and all those exiles that have come into the U.S., we shouldn't have any trouble finding one, should we? But that's outside my field. I was just thinking that one of those people might be easy enough to line up. You've already said how they, some of them, hate the President."

The Old Man leaned into the group with uncharacteristic intimacy. "Tony, Charlie, why don't you make some discreet records checks? Joe, you might keep your ears alert as well. I'm certain that there are any number of candidates.

I would say our next task is to identify them, locate and check them out, and then make our decision." Then he retracted into his wingback chair, unapproachable again.

The meeting had ended shortly after that. The Old Man believed in turning in early. He always related mental health with ample rest. The group was exhausted, if only mentally. No one objected to going to bed, but it's doubtful that anyone actually slept.

* * *

About two weeks later the group of nefarious conspirators trekked back to the lodge. The intervening progress had been as unbelievable as our task. Several potential candidates were discussed and dismissed or put on a reserve list. Then one candidate stood out as more clearly suitable than the others.

Tony bolted straight up, "You've got an ideal candidate for the job right here in Dallas. His name is Oswald, Lee Oswald. And here's what we've got on him: he was a marine who, after his discharge, defected to Russia, denounced his citizenship, applied for Russian citizenship, married a Russian girl, and started a family. Pretty soon he supposedly changed his mind and asked the State Department to help get him and his family back into the U.S. We felt sure he was coming back as a Russian agent. But really, that would be too obvious. They knew we would watch him like a hawk. And we've kept pretty close tabs on him but he seems to be going straight. And can you believe it? He's in Dallas. Conveniently, right here."

Joe suggested, "Maybe he's really had a change of heart. Maybe he really wants to be on our side. His gratitude—"

I interrupted, "And maybe he owes us. We let him back in, even let him bring his Russian family, so—"

Charlie cut me off. "Forget it! Those people don't know gratitude. But he might be scared to death of being sent back, or maybe worse, his wife and kid. Sounds like a good candidate. Any ideas about his backbone? Can he be scared?"

The Old Man assured us, "Anyone can be managed, Charlie. The strong-willed have always mastered people of little will. Leverage is the thing. We learn his limit and go one step further. We can manipulate this person if he meets our criteria, and it seems that he does."

After a few moments for consideration, the Old Man continued, "I think you should arrange a local check on this person. Can you manage that?"

"No problem," I answered.

"Very well. Let that be our next activity. You can get on it right away, can't you, Davey?" He asked, but he spoke in a tone that said it was not really a question.

I replied, "Oh, yes, sir, no problem." What else could I have said? Turning to Tony, I said, "Can you fill me in on the details?"

His reply, "You'll have them, Buddy."

A few friendly chuckles and some nervous chatter closed the dialogue.

* * *

I completed my investigation during the next week and communicated my findings privately to the Old Man. It was only a couple of days before Christmas, but none of us had noticed. Reflecting on my report and information from Charlie, the Old Man was satisfied. We had found our patsy.

CHAPTER FIVE

OSWALD THE PATSY

It wasn't easy to cultivate and harvest a patsy. As the Old Man had said, you must identify and exploit his weakness, but that was far easier said than done. It is most essential that as you set him up and begin to carve away, he must never suspect his ultimate role. You must virtually destroy his right to self-determination but at the same time cause him to believe that he's in charge of his circumstances, and that he's off on the grandest, most important adventure in his life.

I found Oswald living in quiet poverty. He and his family rented a poorly furnished flat, no washing machine, scant clothing and irregular, low-paying jobs. Nothing in his present conduct reflected his past protest and defection. If he had, in fact, become a communist, it was a carefully concealed secret. Joe had suggested that it would be hard if not impossible to make a realistic deportation threat based on his behavior since his return to the States. Tony reminded Joe that circumstances could be managed and that was what they would have to work out with Oswald.

Strategy was developed around a two-pronged attack. Charlie arranged for Oswald's case agent to pay a routine visit. The renewed interest of the FBI worried and angered Oswald just as Joe had anticipated it would. Tony, meanwhile, had arranged for a New Orleans area contact to become acquainted with Oswald. The man from New Orleans, a rumpled, gangly, Latin male referred to only as Freddie, was not a member of the group. He was paid on contract to perform a task. He was to pose as a Castro sympathizer, win Oswald's confidence, and be the group's liaison with Oswald's progress. Because the Cuban situation had offered a good cover to our plans, we decided to establish a Cuban connection. We used the pro-Castro approach assuming that Oswald hadn't completely vacated his Marxist sympathies.

If Oswald would take the bait, we figured we would have him back on the pro-communist, anti-American side of the ledger. That would give us, or at least it would suggest that we had, the necessary leverage for threatening to deport his family, should the need ever arise.

Freddie, while conversant in Marxist issues, had no personal interest in the politics of the

U.S.S.R. He found Oswald a willing subject, eager to discuss Marxist-Leninist doctrine. Freddie flattered Oswald by letting Lee "instruct" him through his keen knowledge of the topic. Lee still felt that the government establishment exploited the poor, and he saw himself as a living example. To Freddie's surprise, however, Oswald expressed admiration for President Kennedy. Freddie had countered by reminding Oswald that the plot to invade Cuba had Kennedy's endorsement. Oswald agreed that Kennedy should not have permitted the Bay of Pigs operation, and he didn't follow through on the mission. More importantly, the President had initiated numerous social reforms. He was an outspoken champion of minorities, the poverty-stricken, and the elderly. President Kennedy while not perfect, had made a favorable impression on Oswald. The group agreed that we could have a problem. It all depended on our Freddie at this point. And we didn't really know him.

After a casual first encounter followed by more frequent meetings, Freddie became as close a friend as one could be to Lee. This was quite an accomplishment because Oswald wasn't ordinarily sociable. Once Freddie had Lee talking more openly about communism than he had at first, he brought up the name of a pro-Castro association and discussed working with a group. Freddie also noted that Oswald was more concerned with Marxism than with communism, a distinction Freddie didn't truly understand.

Oswald was intrigued with the idea of working with the "Fair Play for Cuba Organization," and he was eager for the opportunity of active involvement. Freddie was surprised at how readily Oswald had jumped on the FPCO idea, but it made his task much easier. In a very brief period, Oswald underwent a metamorphosis from a quiet, moody, retiring individual into a visible and outspoken pro-Marxist, pro-communist, pro-Castro closet-activist.

During January 1963, while Freddie was cultivating Oswald's friendship and confidence, he persuaded Lee to purchase a weapon "for his protection." Oswald obligingly ordered an old Italian army rifle, a Mannlicher-Carcano, and an old S&W revolver through out-of-state mail order ads. Freddie cautioned him to buy them under an alias, but he avoided advising him about using his traceable address. Oswald had them sent to a post office box rented in his own name. He had no real need for weapons, but the group did. And it was necessary that they be traced to Oswald while it appeared that he had tried to conceal the purchase.

At Freddie's suggestion, Lee began taking frequent target practice so that, should the need arise, it could be shown he would have been able to make efficient use of the obsolete weapons. On the night of April 10, 1963, Freddie took Oswald out for a more serious test with his rifle, a test which, had the group known, it would never have approved. Perhaps that is why Freddie never discussed his plan with us, nor did he report the matter to us afterwards. Freddie drove Lee to the home of an ultra- right-wing patriot, General Edwin Walker, "so he could demonstrate his newly developed skill." He fired a shot through the window at the figure of the former general working at his desk. Although he missed the General, Lee Oswald had taken a major step toward his infamous role in history. In Freddie's mind, he had locked Oswald in for keeps. Lee had committed a crime, had demonstrated his ability to kill if necessary, and Freddie was a witness. Oswald was trapped.

Two weeks later, Oswald left Dallas for New Orleans. The group, on learning of his departure and that he had become an activist in the FPCO, assumed that was his only objective. We considered it strange that he made such a sudden exodus, but Freddie felt the need to get him out of Dallas. Actually, he wanted him away from the attempted assassination of the former general.

While we were discussing the New Orleans move, we considered how it might affect our plans. We had never considered *where* the President would be hit, only that he *would* be. Joe provided the key for decision. Looking to the 1964 elections, it was inevitable that, at the urging of the DNC, Kennedy would come to Texas, but not when or where. It couldn't hurt to have Oswald out of the way for a while. Letting him decide whether to go allowed him to exercise some autonomy. We could not have planned it better. Later it would seem that Providence was shepherding our destiny.

Information from Freddie to Tony was sparse through the spring and summer. Oswald stayed busy with his FPCO work while his wife remained in Dallas. Freddie felt this would work to our overall advantage as Oswald was developing a track record away from the prying eyes of local officials. Besides, Freddie had some more work to do. He needed to work out a means of throwing further suspicion on Oswald when the time was right.

A September news report scheduled the President for a visit to Texas for November the twenty-first or twenty-second. This put Freddie's plan into motion. He would have Oswald go to Mexico City and stay out of sight while he, Freddie, arranged for it to appear that Oswald planned to leave the country again. An advance plan to leave would make it look like he was planning his escape. Freddie's plan was simple enough, but in later years the Warren Commission never did figure it out.

Upon completion of his visit, Oswald returned to Dallas, but not to his family. Freddie had carefully explained the need for him to stay out on his own. They had much to do and little time for doing it. So it was that Oswald rented a small apartment on North Beckley Avenue. about five miles away from his wife Marina, from whom he was becoming increasingly estranged. At that time there was no active communist front work for him. Although he and Marina visited on weekends and, through the kindness of Marina's new landlady, became involved with a local Russian Club, that didn't satisfy his need for involvement or Marina's need for stabilizing her marriage. While he attempted to devote some attention to his family, Lee retained his interest in pro-communist activity. Freddie visited Lee a few times and suggested that Lee establish a FPCO in Dallas.

While these things were being planned, the need for the presidential visit to Texas was under discussion in Washington. What had at first sounded like a windfall opportunity now might not happen. Joe's position with the Secret Service would permit him only chance information regarding developments. That information was reinforced by an occasional rumor. While he had no opportunity to influence decisions, he tried to keep informed on events as they were discussed. However, the business of politics was too fluid. Sometimes things changed hourly. Although a tour of Texas would be beneficial if not critical to President Kennedy's re-election plans, at times it seemed that it might not take place. Several key advisors were anxious for him to stay away from Texas. Next, if the visit was made, it might very well bypass Dallas.

John Connally, the governor of Texas, had been involved in a re-election campaign of his own. Although a Democrat like Kennedy, it wasn't wise strategy for him to involve himself too deeply in the President's campaign as Kennedy had not been widely received in Texas, and especially not in Dallas. But as the titular head of the State Democratic Party, Connally would have to be involved. To further cloud the issue, Kennedy's visit would also seek to raise funds for his forthcoming campaign. Maybe

Connally felt more time should be allowed to pass between paying the cost of his re-election and efforts to tap the till for the President again. Also, there were some statewide party problems between Texas Democrats. There was a growing rift between "liberals" and "conservatives." Many Texas Democrats had crossed party lines and voted for Eisenhower in 1952 and 1956. In 1960, Kennedy had carried Texas, but only by a very narrow margin.

Kennedy would have to face the obstacles presented in Texas. Having Lyndon B. Johnson for his vice president hadn't benefited him as much as he had hoped. In fact, there were problems between Johnson and both Kennedys, Jack and Bobby, as well as those with the state party structure. The President needed party harmony and unity; he needed money; and his successful intervention in the Texas squabble would enhance his national image while adding to his strength in marginal states. The only question seemed to be: when and where President Kennedy would visit Texas.

CHAPTER SIX

TIGHTENING THE KNOT

With events falling rapidly into order, we were still concerned regarding who would actually commit the act. During a meeting at the lodge, this had been the subject of a soul-shaking discussion. In a combination of guilt and nervous fear, first Joe, then Charlie and I confided that while we accepted the assassination as inevitable and did not oppose it, we didn't have the ability to carry out the act.

With a great feeling of relief we found that our misgivings were understandable and acceptable to each other. However, our sense of relief didn't lessen the problem at hand: who would do the actual hit?

The Old Man eased the tension. "Lads, I really didn't expect that any of you would or even could perform such a deed, and I respect that decent quality in each of you. This requires the services of a person with certain special qualifications. Less than that would be far too risky. Not only do we need to be as certain as possible of success, we need to isolate ourselves completely from the incident. Tony, tell us where we are in that regard."

"Yes sir." Pausing a moment to contemplate his statement, Tony stood and ambled toward the empty fireplace. He then turned and said, "We have access to a professional. He is good— the best. And he's experienced. What's more, he's so skillful he's completely unknown to the authorities. He's never been a suspect. Of course, you'll have to trust me with the entire contract. It's best that the rest of you have absolutely no knowledge of him, not even where or how I secure his services. That way there can be no accidents. For our discussions he will be referred to only as John. That's all."

"That's how it will be," the Old Man concluded, and that closed the discussion.

Tony knew that without further word the task of actual negotiation was his. He would settle the price, the means for payment, and to some extent, how the mission would be carried out. This could not be the ordinary "contract." We determined that the assassination should be done in such a manner as to place suspicion completely on Castro, the Cuban communists, and Lee Oswald. No investigation should ever suggest that anyone else was involved. Not the Company, the mob, nobody. Otherwise, some investigator might stumble onto a shred of evidence that could lead back to our group. John knew the consequences of error in his work.

We figured a collateral benefit would be a death blow to communism and social liberalism in the United States. The elimination of the man who was such an unimaginable threat, a clear and present danger to the American way of life, was the primary objective. However, we felt that the public's outrage would surely lead to a full-fledged invasion of Cuba and the end of Castro and communism in this hemisphere. To accomplish such a significant public service would make all the risks and the act, as heinous as it was, fully worthwhile.

Joe had reported that the Texas trip was confirmed and that the dates November twenty-first through twenty-third were the most probable. I mentioned that the news reports still reflected official ambivalence, and that the police department had not been alerted for final preparations. He assured me that all the folderol was to stimulate publicity and to increase attention and public awareness. He added, "The more publicity, the larger the crowds. You wouldn't get the same public reaction if today's

news said, 'The President will come tomorrow.'"
While the exact itinerary had not been settled, the
President would be in Dallas in late November.

Tony emphasized the importance of
determining specifics at the earliest date, and
Joe promised that he would provide regular
reports and updates.

In the intervening time, Tony was busy with
shaping alternate and contingency plans and
covers. I explained how parades and motorcades
traditionally assembled at Dealey Plaza, the
open area at the west end of downtown and
the courthouse, and how they moved eastward
along Main Street through the business district.
While my estimate of what would happen was
grossly in error, I made a fortunate reference. In
mentioning the staging area, I had unwittingly
focused attention to a key location: Dealey Plaza.

Through his contact with the Russian-American
group in the Dallas area, Tony learned of a possible
employment opportunity for Lee Oswald at the
Texas School Book Depository, a firm located
on the northwest corner of Elm and Houston
Streets, overlooking Dealey Plaza. In an effort to
avoid causing visible interest in Oswald's behavior,
Tony had arranged for the job suggestion to be
made through one of Oswald's Russian-American

friends. Lee applied for and obtained the job under his correct name. However, Freddie had urged him to rent his apartment in an assumed name and to remain incognito, but he hadn't said why. Actually he hadn't needed to say why, as Lee seemed to enjoy a sense of importance with all the mystery and intrigue.

In all other respects, Freddie had urged Lee to keep a low profile, which he did. He didn't even tell his wife of his new address or of his assumed identity. Freddie had determined that Lee had secreted his rifle at his wife's place of residence in Irving. That had worried Freddie until Lee satisfied him it was safer there, out of the sight of his landlady. So far as Lee was concerned, things were in limbo. He had cooperated with Freddie's suggestions as to the identity and his residence, but he had no idea why. Aside from that, an acquaintance had directed him to a new job, one that wasn't all that bad. It didn't pay so well, but he felt he would be able to get into better financial shape pretty soon. Perhaps he would be able to buy Marina the washing machine she had wanted for so long. She certainly needed it, and it might help smooth out some of their problems. He had become so wrapped up in his interests, he had sorely neglected his family.

* * *

Tony covertly entered the School Book Depository one night to photograph and sketch careful plans of the upper floors, stairs and elevators, entrances and exits and the absence of an alarm system. He then furnished the details to John. As specified in his contract, John reserved the right to finalize plans. Since success or failure rested on him, the final execution plans must be his. All that remained was confirmation of the President's itinerary. That was not long in coming.

In our last meeting at the lodge prior to the President's arrival, Joe briefed us on the tour plans available at the time.

"The President and his party will arrive in Houston on November twenty-first. While there, he will attend a dinner honoring a retiring Democratic congressman. Afterwards, he will go to Fort Worth for the night. The morning of the twenty-second he is to receive an honorary degree. Just before noon, he will arrive in Dallas. The schedule for Dallas isn't settled yet. There's a question as to whether the luncheon and address should be at the Women's Building in Fair Park or at the Trade Mart in the Industrial District. I can't say just when I'll be able to get the last word on that. It's tied up on a security question. Some of the bright boys want the Women's

Building because it would be easier to secure. If the truth were known, I'll bet the real reason is political. Fair Park is in South Dallas. It isn't the nicest place, but it's mostly black down there, so some prefer that location. But the President is holding his own with blacks so I'm betting on the Trade Mart. First, that's what Connally wants because they can get more fat cats in there. Second, it would permit the motorcade to go through a better class neighborhood all the way. That would give them wider exposure to a larger number of a middle-class people. Those are the people he really needs to attract. Of course, that wouldn't be without risks because that's the class of people who have been showing up with anti-administration posters. But there's nothing to keep them from showing up at Fair Park, too, so there you have it. That's why I'm betting on the Trade Mart."

The Old Man then asked, "Davey, what route would be the most likely for a motorcade if they go from Love Field to the Trade Mart?"

I replied, "Well sir, there's any number of routes. I would say we should anticipate the route that best serves the President's purpose. If he expects to draw a crowd, he will have to go through downtown. That means he will have to enter from the east and go through to the west.

While he could turn north before he reached the west end of the central business district, it isn't likely. The probable route would be through town and then north either on Industrial Boulevard or Stemmons Freeway."

"Wouldn't that include Dealey Plaza, Davey?"

"Yes sir, it would, but it would mean exiting from the west end of town rather than assembling there. In fact, the motorcade would in all probability be in a parade formation from Love Field to town and through town. Going through in parade formation is inevitable, and it limits the time the motorcade will be at any given point. Motorcades, especially those involving high security consideration, move at a fairly rapid pace."

"Let's look at it this way," Tony suggested. "We plan for the least advantage. If that's how it turns out, we won't be disappointed. If it turns out better, well, we take advantage of any breaks we get."

The Old Man straightened up in his chair and added, "Well put. If your man can do his work during the period the motorcade is passing through Dealey Plaza, that's all we could hope for. That's all we really should need. After all, they aren't staging this for our benefit."

Tony closed saying, "I think our man can handle it. I'll get with him and get his feelings. If there's any problem I'll get back to you. Meanwhile, if you can turn anymore information on the visit, especially the motorcade, Joe, get it to me quickly."

Although the time was drawing close, for the next few days nothing happened. It made waiting unbearable.

CHAPTER SEVEN

THE COUNTDOWN

In mid-November, Joe contacted Tony to consider the latest particulars on the President's visit. The itinerary was as firm as it could be at the time. Extenuating circumstances could prompt changes but, for practical purposes, the plans for the President's visit were set. The entourage would arrive at Love Field shortly after eleven. It would form into a motorcade that would leave the field and proceed south on Lemmon and west on Turtle Creek Boulevard and Cedar Springs to Harwood Street, then south to Main Street and west on Main to Stemmons Freeway, then north on Stemmons to the Trade Mart. On Main, just beyond Houston the motorcade *would* be passing through Dealey Plaza.

Tony thought things over, then contacted John. He was concerned whether John would have the necessary time in that brief opportunity between the downtown congestion and Stemmons Freeway. He had been afraid he probably would not. This put him in a quandary. Now he wondered whether he could set up a new location in so short a time. The route would be checked and rechecked before and during the motorcade. Even though it was common knowledge that complete protection was impossible, he didn't want to leave anything to needless chance. Murphy's Law would surely apply. Wouldn't it be just their luck to have some agent or even a random citizen see something he shouldn't at the last critical instant? But that's what Murphy said: "If there's a chance for something to go wrong, it will." Tony didn't want that chance. We had come too far. We were long since committed. It had to be done, and in the manner planned. If John were discovered, they would know the Castro Cubans had nothing to do with it. Even if the President were not harmed, there would be an investigation the likes of which the world had never known. No, we had to take risks, but not unnecessary chances.

Tony came to me with a question. "Could the department influence the conduct of the motorcade in such a manner that it could stall or at least slow down as it approaches Dealey Plaza?"

I answered, "Yes and no. Anything like a staged street crowd or a vehicular accident could slow it down, but that would put the agents on guard. That could cause the whole thing to be diverted. It never fails. The closer you get, the tougher it gets." I needed more time to study the problem, but Tony reminded me that time was a precious commodity.

I checked a couple of maps of the area and found nothing. Making myself inconspicuous in the afternoon traffic I drove several times through the area, then along the motorcade route. A possible answer became clear. I noticed they couldn't turn north onto Stemmons from Main Street unless the motorcade jumped the median, bridged it, or had it removed. The through streets, Elm, Main, Commerce, run parallel at that point, and each street is separated from the next by a paved median strip about ten inches high and from three to ten feet wide. If the vehicles traveled west on Main Street and the median went unchanged, they would have to go north on Industrial Boulevard, some distance west of Stemmons Freeway. Or they would have to make a U-turn onto Elm Street and travel back in an easterly direction for several hundred feet, then make a very difficult left turn to get onto Stemmons. It was obvious to me, although I had never worked traffic, that it would be more practical to re-route the motorcade at Dealey Plaza. It should turn right from west on Main to north on Houston Street for one block to Elm Street, then turn left to go west on Elm Street. That would permit direct access to the freeway immediately west of the triple underpass where the three streets merge to pass under a series of railroad tracks. More important, that detour would bring the motorcade past the front door of the Texas School Book Depository *at a very slow speed!* What a break that would be! That ought to do it, I thought. Things couldn't have worked out better had we been asked to plan the whole thing.

My elation was brief because I didn't know how to get the idea across to the traffic people. It was of no operational concern to me, so I had no normal opportunity to mention it. And if I did stick my nose into the matter, someone might remember later and start asking questions. I considered that since it was such an obvious problem with an obvious solution, the traffic people would surely see it and make the change. But I still worried about what would happen if they didn't. I felt I couldn't afford to leave it to chance. It was such a simple solution, but I could do nothing to make it happen.

As before, Providence came to my rescue two days later. While I was having a beer in the POL lounge with several officers, the conversation naturally got around to the approaching Presidential visit. I casually dropped the problem of the median into the conversation. That's how I learned that the traffic planners had already run into that and that the motorcade would be detoured by way of Houston and Elm. The information sent a chill down my spine. I hurried to tell Tony.

* * *

Tony was as excited about this turn of events as I was. Somebody "up there" certainly must be looking out for us. Things were really starting to shape up. Then, instead of worrying about whether we could bring things together, we felt a flash of apprehension because it was all beginning to be too easy. Was that a portent of problems ahead?

Later that day, Tony reminded Freddie that it was essential for Oswald to bring his rifle to the book depository on Friday morning when he reported for work. Freddie had developed a compatible relationship with Oswald. He would have to get him to do this. Could Lee pick up his rifle and get it into the warehouse without anyone knowing? Would he need any help? We left that problem with Tony and Freddie.

Lee was so smug in his confidence, so pleased at being asked to do something for a change that it never occurred to him to ask or even wonder why. That next Thursday, a day earlier than usual, Lee asked for a ride to where his wife lived in Irving. He had frequently sought the ride on Fridays so he could spend the weekend with his family. He explained that he needed to pick up something he would later describe as "curtain rods."

As the Warren Commission would find out, that evening went normally for Lee, other than the question of why he had changed his schedule. He didn't go for curtain rods because there weren't any. Notably, his rifle disappeared from its hiding place between the folds of a blanket in the garage.

That evening, after eating and visiting for a while, Lee excused himself from the gathering and went to the garage that was attached to the house. He was there for a brief period, then he retired to the bedroom without encountering the others in the living room. Friday morning arrived with a chilling rain. Lee dressed and departed without waking anyone. For a reason never made clear, Lee left his wedding ring and some money on the dresser. I wonder what he might have been thinking.

Walking a short distance, he returned to the companion who had driven him there the evening before and who would now return him to the book depository. When the companion asked about the brown paper package he was carrying, Lee explained that it contained some curtain rods; he had bought some curtains for his apartment and he wanted to hang them that weekend. It didn't seem too strange that Lee took the package with him when they left the car and entered the warehouse because he would go home that evening as usual on the bus.

Inconspicuously but hurriedly, Lee entered the Texas School Book Depository Building at Elm and Houston Streets that Friday morning, November 22, 1963, carrying an inconspicuous brown paper package up to the sixth floor warehouse as Freddie had instructed. He hid the package as he had been told and went about his usual business without wondering why he had made the curious delivery. It worked to our advantage that he took the package upstairs as he did, and that he left the paper wrapper, as that would become further evidence against Oswald as the infamous assassin.

So far as Lee had known, he was the only person present on the sixth floor that fateful noon. He never saw John.

CHAPTER EIGHT

The Assassination

For me that day seemed to last for years, but during the events, time compressed into thousands of brief moments. A police sergeant informed the dispatcher that Air Force One was on the ground. The dispatcher acknowledged this information at 11:37 a.m. The sun had broken through the clouds; the streets were drying out from the earlier rain. November twenty-second had the makings of a beautiful day.

President Kennedy departed the aircraft and walked with his wife, Jackie, to meet the local dignitaries. Next he greeted the overflowing crowd and then entered SS100X, his shiny black Lincoln limousine, taking his traditional position in the right rear seat. Mrs. Kennedy followed, sitting in the left rear seat. Governor and Mrs. Connally were seated on jump seats toward the center and a bit lower and in front of the President and Mrs. Kennedy. Agents and advisors had recommended a closed car, or that he at least authorize the use of the protective bubble over the limousine. But Kennedy refused. He had work to do. He was going to work the crowd the way he did so well. The President's entourage took seats in their assigned vehicles and moved out on their date with destiny. It was then 11:50 a.m.

The motorcade proceeded along much the same as others had, both for the President and the police department. The most notable thing with this procession was the huge crowd and the enthusiasm with which they greeted their guest. I wondered if this was the problem Dallas presidential advisors had wanted to avoid. It was hard to believe that this was where crowds had rudely shoved Vice President Lyndon Johnson and had struck at Ambassador Stevenson with a cardboard sign during their recent visits. This couldn't be the same place. The Kennedys commented on how jubilant the crowd was. That was what the President was seeking. That was what he needed if he expected to bolster his position in Texas. The Kennedy charisma was at its zenith. He had entered Dallas, a proverbial lion's den, and was winning decisively. The lions had become boisterous, cheering lambs.

At the intersection of Lemmon and Lomo Alto, a group of schoolgirls held up a sign asking the President to say hello to them. He couldn't resist the invitation. Stopping the motorcade, President Kennedy honored the young ladies' request, each receiving a personal thrill from the act. It was then 12:05 p.m.

The motorcade continued along Lemmon Avenue and turned west onto Turtle Creek Boulevard, then onto Cedar Springs Road where they passed under the MKT Railroad overpass at 12:14 p.m. They were unable to maintain the speed necessary to make their scheduled arrival at the Trade Mart at 12:30 p.m. The chief urged the escort to step it up, "three or four miles an hour faster—let's try it." The dispatcher announced, "12:15 KKB364." In my unmarked police car, I cruised a route nearby and approximately abreast of the motorcade, listening intently to every word.

The President reached Harwood and turned south. A lead car cautioned that the crowd was even heavier near Ross Avenue and Harwood. They were on the northern fringe of the downtown area. It was 12:20 p.m.

Reaching Main Street the motorcade turned west toward St. Paul then Ervay, then Akard, then Field. It was 12:26 p.m. They were at least five, maybe ten minutes behind schedule; they should have been on Stemmons by now. While they would be late, it wasn't too bad considering the tremendous press of the crowds. Then they were crossing Lamar Street. It was 12:28 p.m. The Main and Houston Street intersection was in sight. Within another thousand or so feet they would reach Dealey Plaza. I had been driving west on Pacific between Lamar and Houston. I pulled to the curb and stopped, unable to drive further due to the crowd. I walked the rest of the way to Dealey Plaza. Never in my military or police career had I felt such raw fear.

As the motorcade units turned onto Houston Street off Main, the large clock in a Rent-A-Car advertisement on the roof of the Texas School Book Depository showed 12:30 p.m. The police chief had turned west on Elm. The President was close behind. The crowd was still heavy at that point. Everything appeared to be in order. On the railroad tracks over the triple underpass leading to Stemmons and the last leg of the parade stood a couple of men who were not supposed to be there. But the assigned officers were there, too, and everything seemed all right. It's strange now how much concern that caused later. Chief Jesse Curry and Sheriff Bill Decker made references on the police radio to the overpass, to the hill, and to the railroad yard, because they saw people, not because they saw anything suspicious. They couldn't see back behind them, up in the parking lot and warehouse area. Chief Curry later told me his comments were just a spontaneous outburst that really meant nothing.

The presidential limousine completed its turn to follow in behind the chief and the escort motorcycles. The President was visibly pleased, Mrs. Kennedy and Nellie Connally commented to him regarding the crowd's apparent approval of him. They were within a few yards and mere seconds of the end of the crowd and the motorcade precession. The escort supervisor was watching for the chief's signal to pick up speed. In another few seconds, they would be on Stemmons Freeway, hurrying north to the Trade Mart for lunch and a brief rest. It had been a tiring assignment what with all the crowds and the cheering. They were ready for a break.

A few seconds later, at 12:31, they were on Stemmons Freeway racing north. But they did not stop at the Trade Mart, and no one got a break. Something had happened back in Dealey Plaza. Now, the motorcade was racing to Parkland Hospital. The President had been mortally wounded. I was numb with fear. We had passed the point of no return: we had crossed over the line.

Even now those three shots still ring in my ears.

CHAPTER NINE

THE FLIGHT

Months later, Tony filled in the missing details concerning John's actions inside the school book depository. Those events, added to what I knew or had assumed, made the picture complete. On Thursday night, November twenty-first, John had secretly entered the sixth floor and set about arranging to carry out his assignment. First, he needed a secure hiding place. Within a pile of stored corrugated boxes of books, he arranged a small opening and placed two empty boxes end to end so that they appeared to be part of a stand of boxed-up books. Next, he took three empty cartridge cases from his package, shell casings from cartridges that had been fired in Lee Oswald's rifle during a target shooting session in the woods and carefully recovered by Freddie. The remainder of the package he placed in his hideaway. It contained some bread, some cheese, and a bottle of water. The nourishment would sustain him for the next few hours and the emptied bottle would substitute for a urinal. Last, he stacked a row of cartons in such a manner as to screen his chosen window from the rest of the warehouse should anyone intrude the next day. He wore surgical gloves to avoid leaving his fingerprints.

Before retreating into the confinement of his packing case home, John checked and rechecked the rifle he had assembled from his valise. It was an exquisite instrument, custom made in Switzerland and smuggled into the United States with no record of its origin or its owner. It had been designed and constructed exclusively for this kind of work: John's trade.

From his concealment, John had watched Lee bring his rifle in that morning and hide it. He then curled up again, trying to be patient while he waited for the next few hours to pass. Don't you know how much he would have loved to stretch out full length? Lee Oswald remembered Freddie's instructions, and he performed well. Freddie had told Lee to hang around the sixth floor for a while until after the noon hour. If anyone came to eat their lunch and watch the motorcade from the sixth floor warehouse, he was to attempt to discourage them, suggesting that they all should go down to the front sidewalk for a closer look from the curb. That failing, he was to suggest that they watch from the west end of the building. Had that occurred, John's appalling contingency plan was to kill any who remained. It would wreck the original plan but he was no martyr. He intended to carry out his contract and then get the hell away.

Oswald had been carefully instructed that he was to remain in the building, or immediately return should he be required to leave. He was to prevent or at least discourage anyone from going upstairs; then he should remain out of sight. To assist in this, Oswald had the elevator sent upstairs where he jammed the door shut so that it would be unavailable to anyone else. People probably wouldn't bother to climb the narrow stairway should they want to come upstairs. By 12:15 p.m., Lee had performed his assignment with complete success. He did hazard a quick look outside the front door to see the President. That caused some people to assume he was downstairs for the entire episode. He then went back inside to the snack room. No one was there; they were all outside, except perhaps his supervisor. Oswald had been busy for the past half-hour and had not yet eaten. He stepped over to the soft drink machine, deposited a dime, opened his bottle of Coke and drank from it.

Looking up, he saw a Dallas police officer approaching him with a service revolver pointed menacingly in his direction. The officer was with Oswald's boss, who readily vouched for Oswald's presence at the location. They left Oswald and started upstairs.

In the preceding moments, John had carried out his contract exactly as planned. Slipping from his nest without disturbing its arrangement, he quickly retrieved Oswald's rifle. Wearing his surgeon's gloves, he opened the package, removed the weapon, checked it, inserted a live cartridge into the breech, and then placed it between some boxes so it would appear to have been hidden, but in such a manner that it was sure to be found without too much difficulty. He did not want a thorough search of the warehouse lest his hideout be discovered. Next, he pitched the three shell casings on the floor near the window from which he would fire. He knew it shouldn't take more than a few minutes for investigators to locate the window, spot the casings, find the rifle and hopefully draw the obvious conclusion: the assassin had used that weapon to fire the three shots, had hidden the weapon and had escaped before their arrival.

John checked the motorcade from his window behind the screen of boxes, watching the President complete his turn onto Houston. He was less than two hundred fifty feet away. John calmly removed his surgical gloves, put them in his pocket, picked up his rifle, sat down on his packing box, and rested the rifle on another box placed as a bench rest. He looked through his telescopic sight.

As the President started west on Elm Street, his upper torso filled the lens, the crosshairs centering on the back of his head. At this distance, John couldn't miss. But he remembered that he would have to fire three shots at a slow interval. These thoughts had uncharacteristically distracted him for an instant, and just as he squeezed off his first shot a tree branch disrupted his field of view. He had noted the presence of the tree and had determined that he could get his first shot off in time. He flinched, not wanting to believe it, but certain that he had wasted his first round. Cursing his carelessness, he promptly recovered his composure. The scope was instantly trained back on the President's head. The second round was discharged with uncertain results. John squeezed off shot number three. Through the lens of his scope he saw the President's head explode. He had fulfilled his contract, now he must cover his tracks.

Bending down away from the window he picked up his spent cases, put them in his pocket and returned to his nest, disassembling his rifle en route. He snuggled back into his packing cases and waited, hopeful of being overlooked.

* * *

Lee, while not the most brilliant of men, was not completely dense. He had hidden his rifle upstairs in the warehouse just as he'd been instructed. People knew he had brought in a package that he could not now remove. He had discouraged bystanders from the sixth floor. He had been told to stay out of sight as much as possible and to stay in the building. Just after the President had passed the building, he had heard three shots. And then he was confronted by an armed policeman. His reasoning was astute. *My God, someone shot the President, and they'll blame me! Sure as hell, they'll blame me!*

It's likely that Oswald had but one thought, or more accurately, an impulse: *Get out of here!* Having been caught in total surprise, Oswald apparently had no plans, as evidenced by his irrational escape. He reacted instinctively. He made his way through the crowd and boarded a city bus, paid his fare, and took a seat as he had done almost daily since taking employment at the book depository. Then he realized his mistake. The bus wasn't going anywhere in that crowd.

He left the bus after asking for a transfer slip and walked hurriedly toward the Greyhound bus station where he found a taxicab. He must have considered whether "they," whoever "they" might be, would know he had escaped and might follow him home, because he gave the cabbie a block number on Beckley different from his own address. Then becoming nervous as he neared the original destination, he suddenly said that the present location would do and asked to be let out there. He paid the driver and walked the short remaining distance to his apartment while nervously looking about for any sign that someone might be looking for him.

Meanwhile the plans at the book warehouse unfolded. I regained control of myself returned to recover my car and parked it near the building. I could see other officers enter first. I need to follow developments, but I preferred to be inconspicuous. My first information was encouraging; the early search had found the shells and the rifle. But from that point, our plans had deteriorated.

Contrary to what John had thought, that the assassin would have been presumed to have escaped, our plan was for Oswald to be discovered and accused. While his co-workers watched the motorcade, it was to appear that he had gone to the sixth floor where he had hidden his rifle, and that he shot the President. He could deny it, but who would believe him? Perhaps he would keep quiet if it were suggested that his wife and children might be deported. Time alone would indicate which way it would go. All that Oswald could have insisted was that he was innocent, but he could produce no supporting evidence. He could name Freddie, but that wouldn't work; that was an alias, and Freddie had left no trail. There was no "Freddie" but the one in Oswald's mind. Oswald could offer no proof that Freddie had ever existed, much less that he had coached him in a plot to assassinate the President of the United States. Oswald was the pro-Castro Marxist who might even have become an agent while in Russia posing as a defector. He ordered weapons under his FPCO alias. He didn't know it, but when he was in Mexico City Freddie had laid the groundwork that would make it appear that he had plans to leave the country unannounced. He stood a snowball's chance in hell of convincing anyone that he had been framed. Patsy? They would come looking for a killer: for the man who had assassinated the President of the United States.

But he had escaped. I couldn't immediately assess the situation. Why had Oswald run? What could he know? Where would he go? A roll call of the employees at the warehouse determined that he was absent. Not certain of the advisability of so readily naming Oswald as a fleeing suspect, I gave only his physical description for radio broadcast but I didn't identify myself over the radio as the source. I was hopeful that in the confusion this would go unnoticed. It was a minor detail. In my haste, however, I made a serious blunder. I gave a pretty good description of Oswald when I had no explainable reason for knowing it.

Then my reasoning began to function more effectively. I assumed that Oswald would rush home, perhaps to change clothes, get some money or the like, and then he would try to go God knows where. Returning to my car, I headed for the neighborhood of Beckley and Zang Boulevard while trying to think of a plan of action. The obvious thought kept returning to me. *I've got to find him and kill him. I've got to kill him. It's too risky to let him have a trial. If I can kill him while he's trying to escape, there will be no trial.* A new wave of fear and dread surged through me. I knew I'd have to make it look justified. And just as I thought about that, I rejected the idea. That would bring the investigation too close to the group. Besides, I had never killed anybody, not in my line of work, or even in the war.

CHAPTER TEN

OSWALD AND TIPPIT

I probably got J.D. Tippit killed.

The dispatcher, in checking the distribution of available police officers in the Oak Cliff area, asked Squad 78 to state his location. That was officer J.D. Tippit. He was an older, experienced officer whom I had known well for a long time. He had been one of the first officers to join the POL when membership could be dangerous to an officer's career. City government considered league membership tantamount to labor union membership, and they were strenuously opposed to officers joining even though state law permitted it.

J.D. gave his location as Lancaster and Eighth, just a block away from me. It was then 12:54 p.m. Rushing there, I spotted J.D. a block ahead. Catching up with him, I sounded my horn and motioned for him to stop. J.D. walked back to my car and exchanged greetings, then asked

JFK CONSPIRACY - THE MISSING FILE

the obvious question, "What's goin' on?" Radio information was unclear; a transmitter was bad.

My mind whirled seeking the right words for an answer. I needed to enlist J.D. as an intermediate, but I couldn't say why. Hopeful of my choice of words, I told J.D. that President Kennedy had been shot and probably killed; that I had been near the scene and that the suspect had escaped. Also that I had traced him to a Beckley Avenue address and believed he was either there or might come there soon. I further explained that I needed to get back to the scene and would appreciate his taking the stake-out and watching for Oswald. While we talked, the dispatcher again called "78," but J.D. failed to hear his radio and missed the call. It was 1:03 p.m. I closed with the suggestion, "If you find him, he's all yours; I owe you for past favors. And don't forget," I emphasized, "he killed the President; don't take any chances. If he so much as blinks an eye, drop him. In fact, if you get a chance to, drop him. Maybe I can explain it later."

J.D. thanked me for the tip and said he would handle it. I thought for an instant just how convenient it would be if J.D. spotted Oswald, Oswald resisted, and J D. wasted him. Case closed.

It didn't happen that way.

J.D. pulled up in traffic in front of Oswald's residence on Beckley and stopped briefly. I stopped a block away to watch. He circled back through the driveway of the service station on the opposite corner and looked back in time to see Oswald leaving his apartment. As he watched, Oswald walked to the bus stop on the corner directly across the street from J.D.'s position. It was then 1:05 p.m. Oswald saw J.D., appeared to become alarmed; he turned and walked hurriedly away in the opposite direction, south on Beckley. J.D. waited awhile, watching Oswald's reaction. Being a seasoned officer, he didn't rush things. Giving Oswald a slight lead, J.D. pulled out and followed him southbound on Beckley Avenue.

Hastily walking a few blocks while watching over his shoulder, Oswald was satisfied that the officer in car #10 was following him. He could guess why. Probably concerned that he was behaving too suspiciously, Oswald changed directions, turning east on Tenth Street, walking along with rapid strides. After allowing him to turn, J.D. turned, too. I watched them from about a block behind, considering whether I should assist J.D. or leave. I chose to leave and looked for a place to turn around. We were out of the heavier traffic on Beckley, and I was satisfied that Oswald had "made" him. J.D. picked up his microphone probably to inform the dispatcher that he was preparing to stop a suspect. They were approaching the 300 block of Tenth Street, and he would either ask the dispatcher to send him an additional officer to assist, or busy as it was, he might have "checked out" with his subject. This time it was the dispatcher who was busy, and he missed J.D.'s call. It was 1:12 p.m. Oswald stopped and turned, then appeared ready to reverse his route, but he turned east and resumed his original course at a much slower pace. J.D. followed Oswald at a slower speed. I guess he considered the radio was too busy for him to check out; maybe he was considering what I had said. It would seem that by then, experience told J.D. that his quarry seemed ready to run. Not wishing to give Oswald any further chance to "rabbit," J.D. apparently decided to stop him. They had reached the 400 block of East Tenth Street.

Easing to the curb, J.D. called through his open right window something like, "Hey, fella, hold up a second. I'd like to talk to you."

Oswald stopped momentarily on the sidewalk, and then he walked across the parkway to the curb next to car #10, leaning down to look at J.D. through the right front window of the car while J.D. spoke. Then Oswald said something, and J.D. replied.

J.D. engaged in a brief exchange probably calculated to distract Oswald, to get his thought process confused. Then, hoping to catch him by surprise, J.D. likely asked, "You're Lee Oswald, aren't you?"

At that point I completed my U-turn and drove away. If I had stayed J.D. would have left things to my initiative. God only knows how many times I've regretted the decision to leave. My description of the events that followed are drawn from witnesses' accounts.

J.D. reached back with his left hand and opened the door, turned to his left, stepped out of his car, walking toward its left front. Maybe he remembered my warning. I would like to think he did. J.D. started to reach for his service revolver. In his highly keyed-up state, Oswald didn't miss the inflection. He must have assumed J.D. knew more than he had indicated, and he felt trapped with no place to run.

While in his apartment, Oswald had picked up his pistol, and it was now stuck under his belt, covered by his windbreaker jacket. *They're going to get me—this guy must be one of them*, he must have thought. Without further hesitation, Oswald reached under his jacket. With the skill of a desperate and determined person, he thrust his pistol forward, and at point-blank range, he fired and fired again and again and yet again in J.D.'s face. J.D. was dead before he fell. It was 1:14 p.m.

Oswald stood frozen in place for several seconds in a bewildered appraisal of his act. He was fully aware of what he had done, yet he still observed in disbelief. He had no idea how many shots he had fired, and he was unaware of a lady on the corner who had watched him kill Tippit. He was oblivious to the traffic coming toward him on Tenth; apparently, he hadn't even noticed the cab driver eating lunch in his taxi while parked on Patton, the side street adjacent to Tenth Street. He hadn't seen him, although he had walked past him at a distance of less than ten feet. He turned back toward Patton Street, pausing a moment to reload his revolver and carelessly cast aside his spent cartridge cases. As he passed, the taxi driver overheard Oswald mutter something about that "damn cop," or that "dumb cop." Oswald continued south on Patton Street, gun in hand. His temporary hysteria blinded him to the men observing him from the used car lot on the corner at Patton and Jefferson Boulevard.

Slowly Oswald regained his wits. He knew he had to get away, but how? He had no means or money. Where could he go? Who could help him? He scarcely knew anyone—actually, no one whom he felt he could trust. He couldn't go to his wife or to his mother, those would be the first places checked. He didn't know how to reach Freddie. And he was probably in on it. What should he do? He hadn't planned for this. What could he do then, but run?

Apparently not wanting to confront anyone, he turned right into an alley and walked in a westerly direction. Reaching the rear of a service station, he apparently decided to alter his appearance, so he discarded his windbreaker. He continued walking west, reaching Jefferson Boulevard with no idea where he was going.

CHAPTER ELEVEN

THE TEXAS THEATER

I will never forget that next radio broadcast. I had only driven a couple of blocks from the Tenth Street location when I heard a civilian using an officer's transmitter to announce that an officer had been shot; he appeared dead; they were in the 400 block of Tenth Street, east of Patton. Oh, God, no! I rolled to the curb, stopped my car, leaned out the car door and threw up. It was 1:15 p.m.

My mind wouldn't function. Should I continue to the book depository? What could I do there? No, I might seem conspicuous. Should I return to Tenth Street? No, I couldn't face it. I couldn't just sit here. Easing away from the curb, I hoped that by driving, by simply doing something, I might be able to think. Reluctantly, I forced myself to monitor the progress of the shooting in Oak Cliff. A general description of the suspect was broadcast, confirming my first assumption. It was Oswald. It had to be. The dispatcher called "78," but there was no reply. The officer had to be Tippit! In less than two minutes!

The suspect was seen running west on Jefferson. Then he was reportedly seen entering the branch library some distance back east of Patton at Jefferson and Marsalis. No, that was the wrong person. Then, an officer found Oswald's windbreaker where it had been dropped behind the Texaco Station on Jefferson at Crawford, a block west of the shooting. He was probably still headed west. Then there were a few minutes during which time no new information was broadcast.

I was anxious for anything in our favor when I had an instant flash of hope. What if that miserable creature escaped. It didn't matter how or where; I didn't consider the rationality of my thoughts. I only thought of how wonderful it would be if Oswald simply disappeared from the face of the earth and never was heard from again. He wouldn't have to be killed; he wouldn't even have to stand trial. He would be filed on as President Kennedy's assassin and as Officer Tippit's murderer, and that would end it. There was enough circumstantial evidence pointing to Oswald and to no one else. It's embarrassing to think of that fantasy now.

My dream was short lived. Oswald had reportedly been seen entering the Texas Theater on Jefferson, several blocks west of the scene. *Oh, God, don't let it be him*, I thought.

I joined the host of officers who converged on the theater. Some covered the rear exit as others entered the front. The manager was located and questioned. He pointed to a figure sitting alone in the rear area of the center section. As officers approached from the front and rear, the house lights were turned on. Officer Nick McDonald reached Oswald first. As he grabbed for Oswald, he stood up, and struggling for his pistol, yelled, "Well, it's all over now!" Nick grabbed the pistol by the cylinder and struck Oswald in the face. Other officers joined in the scuffle and secured Oswald. As they handcuffed Oswald and walked him to an awaiting police car, I hurried to my own vehicle and prepared to leave. Then I heard, "We have the suspect in custody and are en route to the station; the one that shot the officer. We've recovered the gun and are en route to the Homicide Office." It was 1:53 p.m.

That just about blows it, I thought. *What a mess.* Things would go so uncommonly well, then, they would suddenly collapse. There would be a ray of hope followed by another collapse, followed by another break. Now, things looked worse than ever. How many miracles could we expect? *I guess we've had it,* was my final thought as I felt a growing weight descend on me. I was nauseous, and I had never felt so depressed.

At 12:31 p.m. or so, the President had been shot and Oswald had been set up as the patsy— the fall guy. By 1:52 p.m., in less than an hour and a half, our careful plan had become a nightmare. Then I felt a sudden wave of humor. It occurred to me that all this in a book wouldn't sell a single copy. It was too unbelievable; it was more than a fairytale, it was one royal, king-sized screw up.

Then I realized that I had gotten so involved in my immediate actions I had given no thought to the anxiety that the other members of the group must have been feeling, nor had I given any further thought to John.

Composing myself, I looked for a phone. *I've got to contact the others; they've been waiting for me.* Maybe they've picked up something on the news broadcast that I don't know. Tony and Charlie were in a "safe house," Joe was with the Secret Service detail and he had an assignment at Parkland Hospital. The Old Man had not said where he would be all this time and nobody knew for sure. We doubted that he would be in town. I parked near a public parking lot and used the neighboring pay telephone to call Charlie and Tony.

CHAPTER TWELVE

THE COVER-UP

On that horrible day, Joe had a particularly difficult assignment. In his coat pocket, he carried three spent bullets that had been fired through Oswald's rifle. It was his task to get with the doctors at Parkland Hospital and to learn as quickly as possible the nature of the President's wounds. He was to observe the medical procedures and make critical determinations. Since John had used his own rifle to assassinate the President, it was absolutely necessary that the ballistics evidence not indicate the change in weapons. It must appear that Oswald's rifle, the one so carefully planted at the scene with the three spent shell casings, was the one and only death weapon, and not by suggestion but by proof. Joe was to substitute bullets to substantiate the proof; bullets that had been fired through Oswald's Mannlicher-Corcano rifle.

In observing the President the best that he could, he saw that there was a neck wound and massive head trauma. It seemed obvious that the bullet that caused the head wound would not still be contained; fragments of lead, maybe, but not the entire bullet. Assuming that the bullet had been lost in free flight after causing the lethal wound, he mentally scratched one bullet to be accounted for in his tally. The neck wound was another problem. And there was still a greater problem that had not been considered in our planning. Governor Connally had been wounded as well. We hadn't considered that possibility. Joe formulated a quick hypothesis that, if correct, would simplify his problem but only to a small degree. He assumed that one of the three shots had hit the governor and the other two, the President. He couldn't have guessed that John's first shot had missed. He was a pro; pros don't miss! However, the first of the bullets fired at the President was lost somewhere in the world. The neck would showed an exit injury that suggested the possibility that the spent bullet might still be lodged in the limousine. It remained for him to make further discreet inquiry into Governor Connally's wounds. He did not know that the governor had, in fact, sustained a rather peculiar system of wounds.

Later, the consequences of the shots, the number of shots, the timing, and the results would cause a great deal of conjecture, confusion, argument and frustration. The reason for all that is obvious when you know what really happened. Nobody has hit on the truth. It's a mess because *we* messed it up. We didn't know for sure what happened, and we still aren't certain. However, we had to use a good weapon for the "hit," and then swap it for Oswald's. To make that switch, we had to switch the recovered bullets, too. Not knowing what happened for sure, we could only guess. The end result caused the controversies over "the single bullet" and "the pristine bullet." Maybe Joe's dilemma and his solution will at least explain why these questions have no answers.

After checking with the doctors treating the governor, Joe learned that, from all indications, Connally had been struck by one, two, or perhaps even three bullets. He had been struck in the back, the bullet exiting at a point below his chest. In addition, he had a wrist wound and a leg wound. The doctors were unable to determine at that time whether one or more bullets had actually hit the governor. Joe wondered whether one bullet could have pierced his body, then his wrist, lodging in the thigh. Then the doctors gave him a real quandary. They had found a few bullet fragments, as they would expect. But they found no whole bullets! Quick arithmetic satisfied him that the governor could not have been struck by all three bullets as one bullet had been lost after inflicting the President's head wound. He wondered, had the bullet that made the President's neck wound also wounded the governor? Had the governor also been hit by a separate bullet? If the neck-wound bullet had hit the governor as well, where was it? And where was the other bullet, the one that caused the leg wound? Worse, if one bullet had caused all of the governor's wounds, where was that bullet now? Clearly, Joe had too many wounds and too many variables. He had to account for three shots, and only three. He was annoyed that things had to be so complicated.

No wonder the Warren Commission had such a problem with this. We engineered it, and to this day we can't explain it clearly.

Joe needed to recheck the back seat of the limousine, and fast. His once-over earlier hadn't indicated these problems. He assumed the bullets would be in the victims, that the doctors would recover them, that he would "collect the evidence," and make the switch. He trusted that these doctors were not pathologists and wouldn't notice such things.

What if someone found John's bullet before Joe could? He probably wouldn't have been able to make the switch. He hurried toward the limousine while he tried to think of a contingency plan. He knew that John's bullets were cast of alloy molded from bullets recovered from Oswald's rifle. That had been done so an analysis of fragments would not show inconsistency in the evidence. Fragments from John's bullets would have given the same spectrographic reading as would lead samples from Oswald's rifle because they were the same. Joe decided that if someone beat him to the bullets, he would just have to try to run a bluff and confiscate them. If they wouldn't release them, he would have to borrow them for an examination and try a switch, hoping the finder hadn't already made his mark on them.

Joe found that his first glance had been sufficient. He found no bullets or bullet holes in the limousine. There was a break in the windshield, but he couldn't tell whether it had been caused by a recent bullet or was perhaps some earlier and unrelated damage. He wondered again whether someone had already searched the limousine and made a recovery. He wondered how he could find out without attracting notice.

He asked the nearest Dallas officers how long they had been there. They replied that they had come to the hospital with the motorcade; they had not left the scene. He decided to ask whether anyone had been "messing around" back there, indicating the rear seat of the limousine. The officers assured him that no one had; some kid had come up and taken a picture, but an agent had opened the camera, exposed the film, then shut the door. They apparently knew nothing else. Joe thanked them and asked them to remain there and protect the scene until a lab technician could make a proper inspection. They said they would.

Joe then turned back to the limousine, as confident as he could be that there had been no discovery, and his own inspection had produced nothing. He felt safe in discreetly depositing one bullet so it could be properly "discovered" into evidence later. He reached into his pocket and came out with a bullet and noticed that it was pretty well mutilated. What he almost failed to notice was that two officers had quietly walked up behind and beside him. They were doing their job too well; they almost caught him making the drop. Joe had no choice but to drop the bullet he had out onto the limousine floor before they could notice. Thanking them again, he went back to the emergency room.

Joe returned to the emergency room to assess the situation with regard to Governor Connally's wounds. His fortunes were no better than before; the governor had been taken upstairs for surgery. Certain that he could not wait indefinitely, Joe decided to proceed with his best and last information: no bullet was in the governor. There was no way for him to penetrate surgery; it was closed and sterile, and he had no logical reason to be there. The emergency cart that the governor had occupied in the emergency room was still there. Pausing just long enough to muster up courage and to see if any last second intuition might warn him to do otherwise, Joe casually nested one of his surrogate bullets in the tangled mess of soiled linens. He hoped that some diligent attendant would, in due time, spot it, and dutifully pass it on to the authorities. The two remaining bullets were less damaged. The one he deposited on the cart was the least damaged of the lot. In his situation he could see no options. He did it and left. He had no idea how his last few desperate minutes would blow people's minds for years to come.

Since things had not gone well, he considered an emergency plan. He had learned years earlier that further confusion could be an effective alternative for dealing with confusion. To introduce further confusion into the existing situation, he decided on a diversionary tactic, one which, especially if successful, would be beneficial to the group's position. He was aware of the professional reputations of the local forensic pathologists. It would be a real advantage to the group if he could arrange for the President's body to be returned immediately to Washington for autopsy. The move itself could account for confusion of facts and details if not for the actual loss of evidence. If the initial doctors' reports were at odds with later reports, so much the better. The fewer the hard facts, the easier it would be to explain discrepancies.

Joe made the suggestion to get out of Dallas out loud in the presence of other agents, but to no one in particular. Shortly thereafter the idea grew into a full-fledged argument. The agents became adamant: they were taking the President's body back to Washington right then. The local authorities protested that the body had to remain in Dallas; that was the law! At the same time, Joe commented in front of those agents guarding the Vice President that it wasn't safe to remain in Dallas. There was no way to assess the possibility of a plot or to estimate what might happen next. For good measure, he mentioned that the President's wife would not leave without her husband's remains but that the locals wanted to hold the body for a postmortem. Those considerations were passed on to Vice President Johnson, who was enraged that Mrs. Kennedy would be treated like that.

A short while later the President's body was placed in a borrowed casket that in turn was placed in a borrowed ambulance. The locals were left standing at the emergency entrance protesting the act as an agent headed the stolen ambulance toward the sanctuary of Air Force One, waiting on the hardstand at Love Field.

The Vice President was placed in the police chief's car and driven as inconspicuously as possible to join the assembly now forming inside Air Force One. U.S. District Judge Sarah T. Hughes arrived to perform the swearing-in ceremony. Soon after being sworn in, the new President of the United States ordered Air Force One back to Washington with the body of the slain President aboard. Joe had achieved his diversionary goal. The Parkland staff had been unable to fully perform their duties, their excellent forensic staff had been denied the chance to do their medical-legal, and confusion became the order of the day. *If the group's involvement couldn't get lost in that turmoil, we deserve to be caught,* he reasoned. Joe's impulsive idea to get the President's body away from the expert pathologist turned out to be a stroke of genius. He had created a mess!

After a quick look about the hospital, Joe was satisfied that he had done all he could there. With a justified feeling of pride masking his apprehension, he left Parkland en route to the safe house to meet the others.

CHAPTER THIRTEEN

THE AFTERMATH

I found the group eager for information.

Tony answered my phone call and demanded, "Man, where have you been? What's happening? We can't make a bit of sense out of what we've been hearing. What's—"

"Wait a minute!" I cried, "I've been up to my ears in it. If you'll just hold on I'll tell you what I can."

Then I described how John had apparently gotten his three shots off but that Oswald had for some reason split the scene. Figuring that he had no likely place to go but home, I told them of going there. And I told of meeting Tippit and asking him to watch for Oswald while I returned to the book depository, that Oswald had returned home but he left. I added, "Not knowing where he would go or what he would do, I followed J. D. as he followed Oswald but—"

Tony screamed, "You went where? You went to Beckley Avenue? For the love of God, man, why? That's his cover house! His wife didn't even know the address! How would you have explained knowing it?"

Embarrassed, I replied, "Oh, God, I didn't think about that. All I could think of was to find him and stop him. It never occurred to me that—"

"It's stupidity like that that's gonna get us caught!" Tony continued. "We can't be running around half-cocked." Then he added in a softer tone. "I'm sorry, Davey, I didn't mean to be smart, but that kind of carelessness could blow us out of the saddle. It could get us killed!"

I continued, explaining that things had gone wrong with Tippit as it was Oswald who did the shooting and Tippit who got killed. Then I told them how Oswald had been arrested in the theater and was now in the Dallas Police homicide office.

Charlie, on an extension phone, sounded dejected. "God only know what he's telling them. He just might be spilling his guts!"

"So what if he is," Tony countered. "Who'd believe him? Would his story make any sense?

What do you think? After all, Freddie is supposed to have him programmed."

"Who knows," I said. "Who knows anything now? Maybe I should try to get in up there. I thought about going before I stopped to call you guys. I wasn't sure. What do you guys think? Do you think I ought to risk it?"

"Maybe I should go," Charlie injected. "I've stayed pretty much out of the picture. They shouldn't be surprised to see someone from the Bureau there. They sure won't like it, but they'll probably expect it."

Tony returned to the conversation with another thought. "Do you suppose, "he mused, "that if we arranged for a good lawyer, one who knows the ropes and doesn't mind controversy so long as he gets paid—do you suppose Oswald would keep quiet and let some lawyer handle it?"

"I don't know, maybe," I offered. "On the other hand, would he know a good lawyer from a red-mouth? I don't think he's ever had any experience with lawyers. If we sent him the world's best, he might tell him to get lost."

Charlie interjected, "And he might smell a rat. God knows, we've been messing with his head long enough. He might not be as stupid as we had hoped. Anyway, it wouldn't surprise me if he was at least paranoid by now."

I agreed, as Tony continued, "Okay, let's try this. I'll get started on running the Old Man down. He'll probably get in touch with us himself pretty soon. Anyway, I'll get cracking on who the right lawyer would be, just in case. And of course there's one more possibility. It's better for us if he's dead." Switching the phone from one hand to the other and tilting his head he asked, "Is there some way we can manage that, Dave?"

The question provoked a long silence. Finally, I answered, "I guess anything is possible. Look at what's already happened."

Tony interrupted, "We've said too much on the phone. Why don't we do this? Charlie, you go downtown and see what's going on in homicide. Dave, you think about what we just talked about, who we could get, and how it could be done. I'll get on the lawyer deal, just in case. And I'll be thinking about someone for your deal, too, Dave. Then we can meet here at seven o'clock. Is that all right with the rest of you? Oh, yeah! If anybody hears anything about John, sound off immediately!"

We agreed with the plan, put down our telephones, and wished that we were just about anyone else, just about anywhere else on earth.

* * *

Within the hour, Charlie was in the homicide bureau. He had correctly anticipated the welcome he would receive; one agency doesn't appreciate another one cutting in on its cases. Captain Will Fritz was holed up in the small interrogation room with his suspect, Lee Oswald. He had very little to go on at first. That didn't discourage the veteran of forty-plus years service. Wearing his ever-present vest with his ever-present gold watch chain, the weathered, balding detective had passed up promotions to remain just where he chose to be, commander of homicide and robbery investigations. Detectives conducting the investigation had learned the name of a book depository employee who was missing, Lee Oswald, that he had left immediately after the assassination, and the address where his wife was living in Irving. It was a coincidence that he had learned that Oswald was in custody not ten feet away. One of Oswald's arresting officers had overheard Fritz as he was telling two of his detectives the suspect's name and address with instructions to go to the house in Irving and try to pick him up. The officer turned to Fritz and asked, "Captain, did you say 'Lee Oswald'?" Fritz acknowledged that he had. Both Fritz and the officer registered frank surprise as the officer pointed toward his prisoner saying, "There he is." The officer went on to explain that Oswald was in custody as the suspect in the murder of Officer Tippit.

Captain Fritz had handled well over a thousand murders, several in which officers were killed. But this was his first experience with the murder of a President. And for that to coincide with the murder of a police officer was almost too much for his small select detail of men. It was also impossible to hope that he would have the suspect for both murders in custody in just an hour and a half. His situation was unique. Dallas Police Department officers had "solved" both murders with the arrest of the suspect well before they had a chance to assemble the evidence or develop factual ideas of the cases before them. Fritz now had to fill in the gaps in both cases. He had both cases solved with only a sketchy concept of what had actually happened.

Charlie reported that he sat outside the interrogation room anxiously waiting for any details. What he did pick up on was encouraging. So far, the detectives had accepted Oswald's rifle as the murder weapon. He hoped that Joe had been able to plant the bullets so they would become evidence, but nothing had been said about them. And there had been no mention of John, who was presumably still secreted in his packing case hideaway on the sixth floor of the book depository. They seemed to be working on the assumption that the only suspect had escaped from the building and that it was Oswald.

News media from all over the world had already deluged the department with telephone calls, each expecting an exclusive report on what had happened. Now hundreds of reporters, from the print media, radio, and television descended, filling the halls and offices with flashbulb bursts, hot floodlights, bulky television equipment, and microphone-filled fists, the holder of each trying to get closest to anyone who might speak. It is doubtful that at any time in the history of man had a crime received such instant and incessant media coverage.

The commotion didn't make Captain Fritz's work any easier. With so many people around the world watching, he couldn't make the slightest mistake and expect it to go unnoticed. Never had a detective had so many expert supervisors. Nevertheless, Fritz pressed on, treating it as any murder should be treated. That was his nature—unexcitable. He was aware of who his suspect was, but he exhibited no undue impression. Outside his office was like a three-ring circus, and that annoyed him. He had rules for behavior. He had his system: first, you determine as much as possible about the incident and what facts are available; second, you learn what you can about the suspect; last, you try to bring the facts and circumstance together so the truth results. The steps are infinitely easier to describe than to conduct. Fritz was woefully short on facts. However, he was in no position to sit on his suspect for a day or two while the world waited. In other cases so short on initial facts, the suspect could have been allowed to cool his heels in jail for a day or two. There's nothing like it for sweating out a suspect's uncertainty, wondering what the cops have on you, what all's going on, wondering what you ought to do. It breaks a suspect's self-confidence and makes him much easier to deal with. But Fritz had to start with Oswald when all he really knew about him was his name, and he wasn't absolutely sure about that. The captain worked first at trying to develop rapport with Oswald. Clearly from what he could see, this guy wasn't the kind who was anxious to clean up his business, one who, with a little sympathy and opportunity would open up and talk. To the contrary, Fritz's first impression was, "This young man thinks he's pretty smart, and it seems like he wants publicity. He's arrogant and he's not going to admit to anything."

Although Oswald was in custody for both murders, only his connection with Tippit seemed open and shut. Fritz decided to stay away from the murder of the President and let Oswald think about it. For openers, Fritz would try to get Oswald talking about the death of J.D. Tippit. But Oswald said little or nothing, often answering questions with questions. He was cocky, even impertinent, not the behavior you would expect from an innocent person. Still, he insisted he had done nothing, that he was a patsy.

Fritz's strategy was sound, and it might have been exactly what ninety-nine out of a hundred homicide officers would have done given the same situation. But it didn't satisfy the news people. They were ringside at one of the top stories of the century. They were covering the story of a lifetime and they wouldn't be denied. "What did you ask him? What did he say?" But Fritz couldn't tell them much. Still, he had to tell them something. They wouldn't leave him alone if he didn't. Thinking cautiously, he tried to thread his way through a statement that would satisfy the press without compromising his case. Still they weren't satisfied. "Where are your notes? Let us hear your tapes!" But there were no notes or tapes. Perhaps those were natural enough questions, Fritz thought, but they're only showing their ignorance. None of them had ever conducted a criminal investigation, and they weren't familiar with Fritz's style. "There are no notes, no tapes?" they demanded in total disbelief. Of course not! If you start an interrogation with a notebook or recorder, you just stopped your investigation. Suspects are usually nervous, even spooky. It's hard enough to get them to start talking. No need to shut them up at the same time with a notebook or a recorder. Those news people should know that, Fritz thought. But they had to ask. After all, they're just making a living. But it didn't make his task any easier.

Fritz wasn't crazy about the Bureau having people there. Additional FBI as well as Secret Service agents came while Charlie was waiting outside the interrogation room. But Fritz took the time to give them a review of what he had so far. They weren't too sure he was leveling with them, but what would they have told him if their roles were reversed? It's all in a day's work; that's how it's done. It seems right. Maybe it is, maybe it isn't, but it's always been that way.

Charlie felt comfortable with his progress so far, and not wishing to stretch his luck, he decided to leave. He was anxious to get back to the safe house even though it was only half past five.

Tony's task had been easier. A quick telephone call to the Old Man's personal secretary resulted in a returned call from the Old Man in less than three minutes. The Old Man had monitored events as best he could through the media, but he was ready for firsthand contact with his own people. Tony briefed him on the progress that the media could not know.

"Things went pretty much as planned for the first few minutes, but since then it's gone down hill! Oswald flew the coop. He killed an officer. He has been arrested. Charlie is trying to get a line on what's happening in jail. Apparently John got out clean, or he's still in his nest since nothing has been said about him. We haven't heard from him. We're now confronted with a new course of action. We get Oswald the best lawyer for the situation and see what happens, or we get to him and take him out."

"Do both, "the Old Man said quietly.

"Uh, what did you say?"

The Old Man didn't answer directly, but his further remarks made his point perfectly clear. "Do you know where to get an attorney of the caliber you mentioned, Tony?"

"Yes sir, That is, not off hand, but I can—"

"Very well," the Old Man continued. "You get onto that, and you get onto the other matter as well."

"Do you mean—" Tony began.

"Let's not dwell on it, Tony. You line up an attorney to get help to him now. It probably won't have a lasting effect, but it might keep him calm, that is, quiet, until you can carry out the rest. We can't risk him doing something that might blow our cover."

Tony started to explain, "I can contact—"

The Old Man stopped him. "No, don't tell me what you propose doing, Tony. Just get it done. We're in too deep for quibbling over details. Spare no expense. Just get him the right attorney so that boy won't be spooked. And be sure of what you do next. In other words, Tony, don't drag your feet. Get the best: whoever you think. Just get it done. And keep in touch."

Tony hung up without further comment. The Old Man had concluded the conversation; there was nothing else to be said. Now, it was time for Tony to produce. It was getting late. He would like to have things underway in time for the evening meeting.

Tony decided to use another telephone, just in case, without the logical realization that if anyone was onto them it was too late by then. But he felt better changing phones, so he went to a neighborhood drugstore that he knew had a secluded phone booth. He would be out of the way and unnoticed.

He put in a call to the Company to ask for a few confidential telephone numbers and some names, and several non-related pieces of information so he wouldn't raise a suspicious pattern in case anyone was interested. His next call reached an attorney who had handled confidential situations for past Company enterprises. Tony was brief and to the point. He wanted that attorney to find the right man and to be the confidential intermediary. For five thousand cash, he would interview and arrange for Oswald's legal counsel. The chosen attorney wouldn't know who had retained him, only that he would be paid an agreed upon fee to fly to Dallas and get with Oswald. Not every attorney was qualified and certainly not every qualified attorney would accept a client under these conditions. Five thousand might seem like an exorbitant fee for a few hours' work, but Tony would make sure the fee would be earned, and he would be worth every cent. He would arrange for a telegram to confirm that the task was completed, naming the attorney in a coded manner, the wire to he held at the telegraph office. The mission hopefully would be concluded by 6:30 p.m. Central Standard Time. That would allow the group to learn of developments with regard to an attorney. He was unable to make contact with anyone regarding the other matter. He decided to discuss it with me because whoever did it would in all likelihood have to penetrate the city jail.

Tony had worried about finding a "hit man." I thought, "This isn't real. I'm a cop, a good one. That's all I know." I couldn't overcome a feeling of silliness and dirtiness. I felt that my behavior was being dictated from a cheap novel. But every time I turned the thought over in my mind, it came out the same way. It had to be done, and if Tony didn't score it would be up to me to do it. At my wit's end and running out of time, I knew of no other course but to seek some help. Checking my watch, I was upset with myself because I had spent almost an hour reaching that decision. I spent a like period deciding whom I might call.

One of my oldest confidants in the department was Jerry Cole. We had worked together shortly after World War II. While we had never been close personal friends, we had always enjoyed a sincere mutual respect. It was a mature relationship that didn't have to be massaged. It could be taken for granted without risk or compromise. After our brief period as partners we had gone our separate ways as detectives. While I had been singled out for the Organized Crime Task Force and had gone on to make lieutenant, Jerry was still a working detective with some sixteen, maybe seventeen years "made good" on his twenty. His last eight or so years had been in the close-knit Special Services Unit, a small group specializing in vice, drugs, corruption and intelligence. Jerry, a slim, nondescript loner who never married, never even seemed to have a private life, had been working subversives out of intelligence for most of his Special Services hitch. In addition Jerry had helped me when I was with the crime group, and he helped me when I was lining up membership in the POL. He was never an active member when it came to attending meetings, but he backed me all the way. He was just what I needed then. I would be lucky to find him in all that mess.

I was unable to reach the office by telephone since the lines were jammed. Not really wanting to, I went to the station, hoping to be unnoticed. Maybe if I had a busy, harried look everyone would presume I was directed by some element of the assassination. It was worth a try. I found Jerry in his squad room, busily working files and phones. The department had picked up on Oswald's communist connections and Jerry was attempting to learn exactly what kind of communist Oswald was. Unfortunately, the department had no record on Oswald. Jerry had gone as far as he could with the New Orleans police intelligence unit. Now he was waiting until they made a few contacts and updated their records. They promised to call him on his private line as soon as they had the information, but would call in two hours regardless of the outcome. His New Orleans counterparts had told him that Oswald, under an assumed name, had applied to the FPCO national headquarters in New York for permission to establish a cell in Dallas. I wondered how New Orleans knew that. That was supposed to have been a secret. I thought, *Holy—how much has leaked? So help me, they'll be coming after all of us any second now.*

I waited until Jerry completed his New York call. Yes, NYPD Intelligence would run down the information on that end and would call back, but it would probably be late that night or early tomorrow. Having reached a stopping place, Jerry turned his attention to me.

"How's my old buddy?" he said, extending his hand.

I asked him directly, "Can we get out of here for a while?"

Jerry was ready. "You've got it. I could use a break. I haven't had lunch yet and it's almost dinnertime. Let's split." Picking up his coat and hat, he started toward the exit.

I thought, *So far, so good.* In all this pandemonium he's actually being loose and friendly.

Ignoring Jerry's reference to food, I drove east from downtown to Exall Park. I have no idea what he might have said during the five-minute drive. My mind had its own agenda. Easing to the curb, I suggest we walk a little way. Jerry had sensed by then that there was a problem.

"Jerry, I don't really know where to start or how to approach this, but—" I said, struggling for the right words.

He tried to make it easy for me. "Dave, you know me. If something's stuck in your craw spit it out. You don't have to do no dance routines with me."

I started again, "Thanks, that helps, but— look Jerry, I've got to ask you something and I can't say why. You'll figure it out soon enough, but really it's best you don't—"

"Hey, man, quit going in circles!"

I started once more, "If I needed someone to do something, do you know of anybody we've got 'up tight'—really 'up tight'?"

Jerry blurted, "Do what? You just shot past me, Dave. Now back up and speak English. What are you trying to say?"

I tried to be more direct. "Jerry, I need to know whether we've got some dude up tight, real tight, really over a barrel. Someone who, if I put the heat on him, he'd hop as high as he's told to without asking questions."

Jerry looked puzzled, and asked, "What the Sam Hill are you getting at?"

"That's a question you shouldn't ask, Jerry. I can't answer. Really, you don't want to know. The less said the better. All I need to know is, is there somebody and what do we have on him that I can squeeze—squeeze real hard?"

Jerry shook his head in slow, deliberate, negative motions. "You've dumped me on my butt, old buddy. Now, if you'll just give me a minute to—"

I didn't wait. "I'm sorry, Jerry. I hate to hit you with this. I know you don't owe me anything. I'm taking advantage of you, and I know it. But I had to ask someone I can trust, someone I can talk to on the square. Someone who could understand the mess and—"

Then suddenly, Jerry exploded, "Son of a bitch! It's that Kennedy deal! My God, man, what are you into? What have you—?"

It was my turn to get scared. My knees weakened, and I felt like I had blown it. "Never mind—drop it—forget I said anything. Let's go."

"Go, hell! No," Jerry said. "You've started it. You can't stop it. I've got to know something. What the hell is it? And don't jack with me. This ain't a bit funny. You got me stuck out here. I didn't ask you. You got me involved, so level with me or we're going to the station, quick. I can't help you if I don't know what it is, and I'm sure as hell not going to sit here deaf, dumb, and blind. If you can't level with me—"

I tried again to avoid the subject. "You're right, Jerry, I wish I'd left you alone. All I've done is drag you into my hot water. Here it is. And don't ask me for names 'cause that's where I draw the line. You've got the right to know as much as you need to know, but not everything. There's a, well, a group—some people—anyway, the assassination was no coincidence. That guy, Oswald, he didn't do it. He was set-up, a patsy. He's got those Cuban communist connections, he bought the rifle, and they think he killed the President. He's the perfect suspect. No jury would believe him. Then it hit the fan. He got out of the building while our man was still in there. We needed to control him quick. Then, it seemed he would be better off dead; you know, resisting arrest. But that backfired. He killed Tippit. Then, they got him in that theater. It's all out of hand, now. It's best if we can take Oswald out. That's what I need now. Someone who can burn Oswald, and quick. Someone who won't trace it back to us. I guess that's it, Jerry."

Jerry looked at me like I was crazy. He was probably right. "*That's it?* That's *all* you've got to say? Man, you are *into it!* You are—son of a bitch!" He stopped short, still shaking his head in utter disbelief. "Get out, Dave, get out! Whatever it is, get out!"

I answered, "It's too late, Jerry. There's no time. I need your help now! I'm sorry Jerry, really sorry, but that's how it is. No way out. No time."

Neither of us spoke for a long while. I didn't want to push things.

It was Jerry who broke the silence. Then he spoke. "I think I know someone. Yes sir, I just might have us an answer. The right dude for it; and it's high time we strapped something solid on him. Jack Ruby! He's had a free ride long enough. You know Jack don't you?"

"Not too well. I haven't run into him for a few years, but I know of him."

"Well, it's time he paid for his keep. He's a sorry bastard, always has been. He sees himself as a big shot, a high roller. Always dropping names, trying to be 'Mr. Big.' Well, this could be his Oscar-winning roll!"

I started, "How could I be sure he— How could I count on him to—" but I got no further.

"He's been messing with girls and games for years out of those dives he calls clubs—'neon whorehouses' is more like it. Anyhow, he's grown up in recent years. We think he's started playing

JFK CONSPIRACY - THE MISSING FILE

the drug scene. There's nothing big that we can be sure of. We think he keeps a little available for the girls. I think he got caught 'holding' a little recently. If he did, nothing's been done about it yet. That miserable creep would die if he had to spend a day in jail. But he could be made to think he's looking at fifty for sure, if they decide to put it on him. And I understand he's in bad need of money, serious money. I understand he's been trying to raise some mega bucks from all over.

"The way I see it, we do some good old-fashioned horse trading—his deal for yours. He's been pulling deals for years, and he always comes out smelling like a rose. He drops us a worn-out or trouble-making hooker, blows the whistle on a crap game; you know, little deals to keep himself out of jail. He always gets more than he gives. I think it's high time we balanced the books. That fat little weirdo owes us and now it's time for him to pay. You know, the thought of that tickles the shit out of me. To think that—"

I interrupted, "Who's got the heat on him?"

"I don't know, but it doesn't make any difference," Jerry replied.

"Jer, we can't make deals on someone else's case. How could we—"

"Don't sweat it, Davey," Jerry assured me. "We wouldn't have to pay off on the dope deal. That guy Oswald sure as hell ain't going to make bond. He killed himself a President—and a cop. He won't be allowed to make bond. That dude will never see outside. That means the hit would have to be made while he's in jail so the hit man is a lead-pipe cinch to be caught. He'd have to stand trial for the murder, not the dope! And if his lawyer's got any smarts he'll go 'concurrent' on the dope. The D.A. will agree to it for sure: it's another conviction—a two-for-one!"

I struggled to organize my response. "If he's sure to get caught, how do you get him to—"

"I don't see any problem, really," Jerry offered.

"You've got me confused now. Murder's a worse rap than dope. Why do you suppose he'd take one over the other?"

Jerry grinned, warming to the scenario. "He's a dealer, Dave. He has to have an angle. Nothing's ever straight with him. He's got to have a deal. What we have to do is make him an 'offer' he can't refuse.

"He's always wanted a super nightspot, *the* club in Dallas. And don't forget he thrives on recognition. You know, he'd become well-known, even famous—world famous! 'The man who killed the man who killed the President.' It's a natural for that egoistical bastard.

"All we've got to do is persuade him he'll get less for killing Oswald than he will for the dope; remind him the dope case goes away, and he gets 'fame and fortune' in its place. It's a bonus."

I was flabbergasted. "The idea even sounds good to me. Five years in Huntsville, parole, and Easy Street the rest of the way. Matter of fact, I don't think he deserves the deal. It would make him a living legend; he could get rich off of it."

"Speaking of money, "Jerry remembered, "Is there any money you could show to sweeten the pot, just in case?"

"Probably, "I replied, not wanting to seem too eager.

"If he gets tacky, then, we can offer a little sugar to sweeten the deal," Jerry sneered.

"When can we see him?" I asked. I looked at my watch and decided to move. We didn't have time to reconsider.

"Now, I guess," Jerry ventured. "He should be at the Carousel. It's about time for him to be there. It's a quarter to six."

I thought over my schedule. I would be late for the seven o'clock meeting, but it couldn't be helped. I would have to telephone them and explain. They would understand. I hadn't intended to, but impulsively I asked Jerry a last question. "You want to go see him with me?"

I was more than pleased with his answer. "I wouldn't miss it!"

CHAPTER FOURTEEN

CLEANING UP

It was months later that Tony learned of John's ordeal in the book depository after the assassination. John had checked the luminous dial on his watch. It was after eight, and the darkness added to his sense of confinement. He had wondered whether he could move. Then the thought occurred to him: do some exercises. He could barely move in his packing box hideout, but he could move slightly, enough to stimulate circulation. He had listened cautiously for any signs of life. He wondered whether the police had left officers to guard the crime scene, and when he might risk leaving. He wondered whether he could risk moving to do his exercises. He decided he wouldn't take the chance. Not yet. He limited his efforts to gripping and releasing his fingers, and to pressing his toes up and down against the insides of his shoes. He alternately stressed, then released his body. It seemed to help. Whether it did any real good, it made him feel less like a captive.

He said his original plan had been to remain late into the night, then slip from his nest and exit the building leaving nothing that would show he had been there. By nine o'clock, he was again submitting to physical as well as mental pain. His efforts at exercising wouldn't relieve the tension. Straining his ears against the surroundings, he again had sought any sound suggestive of human presence. Occasionally, he heard the creak and groan of the old building as if it were protesting its own existence. And there were the ever present, ever prowling rats. Oh, how he hated rats. He said he was terrified at the thought that one of them, smelling remnants of his cheese snack, would enter his tiny quarters. That thought frightened him more than the deed that brought him there. Dwelling on this helped him decide to abandon his position early.

He said he slowly and quietly started to ease the front box forward, careful not to disturb the smaller boxes that he had stacked on top of his lair. The new movement brought agony and pleasure to his body. Extending the box far enough to permit his exit, he paused to rest in his new position while he mustered the courage for his next move. He mustn't become anxious, he remembered that's how mistakes are made. *Take your time; think things out. What do I have with me?*

First, my surgeon's gloves. Mustn't leave fingerprints. Had he touched anything that needed wiping off? No, the only time he didn't have his gloves on was when he was inside the boxes. He'd take care of that later. His empty shells, all three of them, he put in the valise with his disassembled rifle. He opened the valise to be sure. They were there. He decided to put the wrapper from his food package there too while it was open. He kept his bottle out; he would empty it, then drop it in a storm sewer once he was far enough away from there. He wished he had more light. The windows of the sixth floor were well above the streetlights that, although bright, reflected downward toward the streets below. What light there was came from reflections off the County Records Building on the southeast corner of Elm and Houston. Next, he made certain he left nothing behind. He set aside the smaller boxes he had used in hiding, took the two larger ones in which he had hidden, opened the taped flaps, and collapsed them into their original condition. Returning to the stack of flattened boxes from which he had borrowed them, he raised the top half dozen or so and inserted the first one. A few boxes deeper in the pile, he deposited the other. Pleased with his progress thus far and with the quietness of his movements even in the dark shadows, he had felt his confidence and courage returning. That, too, pleased him. He was a pro with several "campaigns" to his credit. He didn't like uncertainty.

Retrieving his valise, he surveyed the field one last cautious time. He was tempted to take a look out the window. He hadn't taken much time earlier, just bare seconds. Satisfied with his conduct, he started toward the stairway when a sudden realization froze him in his tracks. Looking back to where he had arranged his hideaway, the small boxes were in disarray with a conspicuous void where his nest had been. No, wait a minute, he thought. What if some dumb detective got nosey and studied the crime scene pictures? What if he noticed a difference in how the boxes were stacked? If nothing were to be suspected, things had to appear as nearly as possible as they had during the day. Quickly, he looked around, found a couple of boxes off to one side which were similar in size to his, placed them where his had been, and then he replaced the smaller boxes. They could just wonder what the hell happened to the other two. Surely no one would figure that out. Then he felt certain he was ready to leave.

He made his way down the stairs, sure that the squeaking steps could be heard blocks away. In two minutes that seemed an eternity, he was on the second floor. Fire exit lights, which at first had been tiny red dots, appeared to be floodlights as he exited the stairwell. He went to a window toward the west end of the building, and checked it to be certain it was not wired to an alarm. From his valise, he took a roll of nylon cord, sought a water heater pipe servicing the radiator beneath the window and looped the rope around the pipe and worked it until both ends were in his hands. Next, he looked out the window. There were still people standing around down there, hundreds of people looking and milling about the scene. *What ghouls,* he thought with not a scintilla of irony. *Why aren't those gruesome creeps home in bed?* Anger surged through his body as he made his way to the other windows to see whether another one might afford him a safer exit. He could have saved his time. Even the rear windows were subject to the periodic view of people arriving and departing. "You morbid bastards! Go the hell home!"

The hasty exit he had anticipated had become more of a wake. He was determined that it wouldn't be his. He sat down to wait out the spectators. Fear had accompanied each trip to a window. He was becoming paranoid; they were certainly looking back at him. *Why don't they all go home?* Time dragged into hours. There were still maybe a hundred or more there at midnight. His frustration fueled his anger, and began to weigh on his judgment. He hadn't bargained for this. Several times he was about to burst out through the front door, never mind the consequences. At two in the morning, thirty or forty of the curious were still hanging on. It was encouraging that new arrivals were less frequent. Maybe soon!

At four that morning, he had become weak from hunger. There were snacks in the machines near the stairs, but he had no change. By then he was ready to smash the glass and eat. *No, that might arouse suspicion in some nosey detective. Better not,* he thought, although his stomach roared its protests. Half an hour later he knew it was time for a decision. Obviously, there would be people there all night. Those gruesome, morbid— In his frustration, he still couldn't find words. *What time would it be daylight?* he asked himself. *Let's see this is November, late November. The sun comes up later than it has been.* He wondered whether it was cloudy; he hadn't checked for stars. It hadn't occurred to him before now. What about the moon? Had he seen it? He guessed that whatever the answers were he didn't have more than an hour before it would start getting light again, and in an hour and half it would be too light. Daylight would bring the crowds again. The later it became, the more conspicuous he would be. That's all he needed was for some cop, trying to stay awake, to stop him for a quick shakedown just to break the monotony, only to find out what he had in his valise. *Why do I keep thinking these thoughts?* he wondered. *They are depressing. They can get to you.* He realized he must decide now!

The hell with it. It's time to go. Taking one last look at the remaining onlookers, he chose to stay with the original window. He passed the end of his nylon line around a large steam heater pipe. Easing it up just enough to squirm through, he dropped the ends of his line to the ground behind the building, and fastened his valise to his belt. No one had noticed so far. It was his turn next. Feet first, he left his prison. Trying to melt himself against the building he wriggled his hips over the side, took a grip on his line and lowered his upper torso into the fresh outside air. Reaching back, he lowered the window so that it barely cleared his line. Then he relaxed his grip and quickly lowered himself to the sidewalk.

Before he moved further, he stood as casually as his frayed nerves would tolerate to see whether his descent had been noticed. A row of ornamental trees and shrubs had shielded him, casting deep shadows on that area. The spectators remaining were centered across the street near the plaza where the light was better. Inconspicuously, he tugged on one end of his line, pulling that end until the other end retreated through the slight opening left under the window. It slipped back around the pipe, then out again through the window opening, dropping to the ground at his feet. Quickly coiling the line he unfastened his valise, stuffed in his line, and walked calmly toward the corner. Crossing the street he walked directly toward the milling crowd. He didn't want to act guilty and attract attention. A couple of people had departed the scene moments before, walking south on Houston, so it seemed smart to fall in behind them and blend in with the surroundings. At Commerce Street he turned east.

A few blocks ahead, the bus station offered the prospect of much-needed food and a measure of safety. Walking near the curb, not wanting a passing cop to think he was trying to hide in the shadows of the buildings, he wished the bus station were closer. While waiting for a signal light to change to green he remembered his bottle. It seemed silly waiting there for a green light at 4:25 a.m. without a single car or living soul now in sight. Don't do anything to attract attention, he had repeated to himself. He had walked two blocks, but the bus station appeared to be no closer than when he first turned the corner. As he walked, he emptied his bottle. Some few feet after crossing the street he dropped his bottle into a storm sewer without changing his pace. He could barely hear its breaking.

With a profound feeling of relief he entered the bus station. Temptation urged him toward the all-night diner section but logic said to act naturally and to put the valise in a locker. That only took a few more seconds, and it relieved him of a burden. In an effort to appear unhurried he decided to visit the restroom, although he had no real need. However, a splash of cold water on his face was invigorating. A few minutes later, he took a stool at the food counter, checked the menu, then ordered their best dinner, chicken fried steak, fried potatoes, a combination salad, and could he have a cup of coffee now? When the waitress turned away to fill his order he looked up for the first time. He thought his heart would stop. Immediately across the counter from his stool sat two police officers nursing their cups of coffee. Positive he had guilt etched deeply into his face, momentarily he wondered whether he should leave. *Be calm,* he thought. *The larger one is looking straight at me. Don't look away. Smile, not big, just politely. Say something, something in passing. Don't start a conversation.* "You boys had quite a workout today. I don't envy you. Sure sounds terrible." Then he accepted his coffee and acted as though the conversation was over. He had hoped that they would accept him at face value then forget him. From their behavior, he felt they regarded him just that way. They never uttered a word. Cops hate for people to butt in when they are eating or drinking coffee. They have only a short break and prefer a little rest rather than a dose of the same old well-intentioned baloney.

Feeling a bit more at ease he started his meal. As he was about to remind himself how hungry he was, and how good it tasted, he noticed that the officers, finished with their coffee, continued to sit there. Did they know or suspect something? They were watching him. They were playing cat-and-mouse with him. Why didn't they go? *Get out of here. Go arrest somebody.* He was halfway through his meal but with no realization that he had eaten, much less what it was. Then a sergeant arrived and motioned to the officers. They offered him a cup of coffee, but he declined. He told them to come with him, he had something for them to do. Dropping a tip on the counter they got up, turned and left.

John couldn't finish his meal. It was too difficult to swallow. He had to leave also. He counted out enough money to cover the tab and tip, dropped the money on the counter, and walked away.

He looked at the departure schedule and saw that the next bus out would be departing in eight minutes for Laredo via Waco, Austin, and San Antonio. If he could just make it onto that bus and that bus got out on the road—

"Waco, please," he said, handing the clerk a twenty-dollar bill. He took his change and his ticket, retrieved his valise from the locker, walked to lane four and boarded the bus. He still had an almost irresistible urge to run. He took a seat near the rear of the bus, put his valise under his seat, fastening it to his leg next to the wall, hit the "recline" button and eased back. He looked at his watch: 5:20 a.m. He could hold his eyes open no longer. If they caught him, they caught him. He shut his eyes and let go. He never felt the bus pull out of the driveway.

CHAPTER FIFTEEN

THE RUBY SET-UP

Tony and Charlie arrived first for the seven o'clock meeting. The Old Man would not be there. I telephoned them at a quarter past six. I was anxious to know that Tony and I hadn't both moved on the same deal. "I think I have a mark."

"Great!" Tony exploded with untypical delight. "I didn't score so you run with what you've got. I'll drop it on my part, Dave. Keep in touch though. Okay?" Then Tony briefed Charlie on what I had said, and on his own efforts to line up an attorney. It was hours before they would hear from me again.

Tony's 6:30 p.m. call to the telegraph office was fruitless. Charlie had been anxious to report on his progress, too. He spoke more to audit what he had learned and to organize the data in his mind into some order rather than to inform Tony. His presentation was brief, for all he had done was listen in on Will Fritz's activities. He had confirmed that Oswald was the prime suspect in both murders, they had his alias, both guns, and the mail order ads used in their purchase. They also had found a quantity of communist literature and propaganda. He explained that those things had been found at Marina's home in Irving. They hadn't searched Oswald's apartment on Beckley at that time. Maybe they had by now. Charlie added parenthetically that he would have to check back to see what they had found there, especially whether they found any reference to "Freddie."

"Oh, yes!" he remembered. "A lady who witnessed the killing of that officer, uh, Tippit, identified Oswald in a line-up. Also, they found a bus transfer slip in his pocket timed for him to have left the book warehouse, just about the time of the shooting of the President."

"That could be bad," said Tony. "I hope it isn't timed too early. If Oswald got that transfer before the shooting, or too close for him to have been in the building, he's got an airtight alibi! Do you know whether—"

Charlie continued, "The bus driver is coming down this evening to see if he can 'make' Oswald and give Homicide an affidavit. I understood Oswald or someone similar got on his bus just a few minutes *after* the shooting. If it holds up, it looks like Oswald split immediately after the shooting, was stopped by that officer in the lunchroom, and then hit the street, boarded the bus, got a transfer and got off."

Tony was puzzled, "Got off? Then how did he get out there in Oak Cliff to his house and to where he killed that officer? You realize this puts us on a helluva tight time schedule, don't you? If anyone can knock a hole in the timing, it takes our patsy smooth out of the picture where the President's concerned! We've got to keep an eye on that! Oswald's actions have got to fit the timetable. Watch that real close, Charlie."

"I understand he took a cab," Charlie explained. "He went to the Greyhound bus station and took a cab from there. I'm sure we're okay."

* * *

Tony decided it was time he called the telegraph office again. The operator excused herself for a minute or so, then returned to the line. "Yes, Mr. Davis, here's your message: 'Herb Finkler will purchase your property. Arrive tomorrow. Horace.' There's no forwarding or return address, sir. Will there be an answer?"

Tony thanked her, said there would be no answer, confirmed that it was a prepaid message, and concluded the transaction. He would not need a copy. Turning to Charlie, Tony managed one of the few smiles any of them had managed for quite a long time. Neither of them knew who "Finkler" was or what he could do. But, Tony, anxious for any good fortune, assured Charlie that if the Company attorney said he was right for the job, he was. Charlie was concerned with the uniqueness of the name. "The world isn't overrun with 'Finklers.' So what if that clerk reads tomorrow about a lawyer with that name coming in on Oswald's case, and she connects the telegram with Washington, and—"

"Cool it!" Tony interjected. "Let her. My God, man, there's a stack of messages in and out of that office all the time. She can't remember every one of them. I'll bet they never give those things a second thought. And if anybody did get nosey, the names we used are phony. It won't trace out in any way, and the message was prepaid with cash. I doubt the lawyer will come out of Washington, and the name is fictitious. It sure as hell isn't 'Finkler'! They never use correct names. Let 'em look, they won't turn up anything. I guess it could have been 'Smith' or something though."

* * *

Meanwhile, Jerry and I had reached Jack by telephone. Jerry told him to excuse himself, to explain that he had to go somewhere that he'd normally be apt to go, but then told him where to go so he could pick him up. "Go west on Commerce to Poydras and turn south. I don't want anyone following you, either. Keep walking until I pick you up. If you've got it, leave now."

"I'm on my way, Mr. Cole, just as soon as I tell my cashier something. I'll tell her I'm going back to the—"

"Never mind the details, Jack. Just get going," Jerry ordered.

"Yes, sir. I'll be there in a few minutes."

We parked my car among the few remaining cars on the parking lot behind a warehouse on Jackson Street and Poydras. From that point we could watch Jack, but he wouldn't notice us until we were ready for him. Checking my watch, I noted the call was ended at 6:40 p.m. Allowing five, better make it ten minutes, Jack should be here anytime from seven at the earliest to five after seven at the latest. If it didn't happen that way we could leave clean.

Jack didn't disappoint us. His dark suit and slouchy fedora and his unmistakable form and gait made him easily recognized from the instant he turned off Commerce. Watching him walk down Poydras Street, we were satisfied he had done as Jerry had told him. He was alone and on time. In fact, he had made good time for such a chubby guy. It was two minutes past seven. Satisfied with events, I started my car and eased it out of the lot. Jack was so engrossed with whatever he was thinking that he didn't notice us until we stopped next to him. Jerry reached back and opened the right rear door without speaking. Jack got the message and entered. I pulled away almost without stopping, driving to a nearby railroad siding off Wood Street. Jack said hello on entering, but nothing else was said until after we had parked, lighted cigarettes and waited a moment for additional psychological impact to take effect on Jack.

Jerry began with a stern assertion, "You don't have to talk to us, Jack. You know that, don't you? You're in a bind already and that's what we want to talk to you about. You want a lawyer?"

Jack answered. "No, sir. You guys are okay. I mean what the hell. I can talk with you guys. It'll be okay. Won't it? Uh, what is it you want? Why do you—" That was as far as he got.

"Can the crap, Jack. Clear and simple, we're going to talk to you and you're going to listen. If you start any lawyer shit, we stop right there and you're history."

"We can do what a lawyer can't," I assured him. "You call it. Do *we talk* or do *you walk?*"

That startled Ruby, "Aw, wait a minute, fellas," he whined. "I'm clean. I mean, you guys don't mean to file—you aren't going to try—my lawyer said—"

"Horse shit, Jack!" Jerry yelled. "That's what your talking. Pure, stinking piles of horse shit. Now get this straight! I'm not going to plow the same ground twice. No crap from you. We're talking, you're listening. It's that simple. You got it? Are you ready to uncork your ears and pay strict attention?"

"What the—" Jack stuttered. "You ain't giving me no choice. What else can I do? I mean, when you said you wanted to talk I thought you meant—"

"Don't think," I said. "Thinking gets dumb butts like you in trouble."

Jerry picked up the lead, "Jack, we know you're about to fall on narcotics—"

"Aw, no! You ain' t—"

"Hush your face, Jack!" Jerry ordered. "Now, as I was saying, you're going to fall. You've bullied yourself out of too much already. I'm telling you, you're facing fifty years hard time, Jack. Fifty you'll have to serve all by yourself, one day at a time. Considering your age and condition, that adds up to *life*. It ain't my case but I'll make it mine, my own special interest. You do realize that, don't you, Jack? Do you hear what I'm saying?"

Jack's face contorted and became flush. Beads of sweat popped out. "Yeah, yeah, I—"

Jerry continued. "You believe me, too, don't you? You realize I'll do exactly what I say I'll do, don't you, Jack? You sure as hell better!"

Then, I added, "If you got any doubts, Jack, you better spit 'em out now. You've screwed around for years, getting away with nine kinds of shit, throwing us some kind of cheap crap in return for your sorry ass. Well, that's over. It's all over! It's payday, Jack. It's time for you to pay, for a change. And no more feeding us peanuts in exchange for your sorry ass! No more deals."

Jerry agreed, "That's it, Jack. No more deals— unless we make 'em!"

"If you want to bail yourself out on this one, it's going to be on *our terms!*" I declared. "You take *our* deal or you take *fifty*. There's no other deal coming."

Jack was past being scared. Now he showed a mixture of terror and anger. "You're trying to screw me!" he hollered.

Jerry corrected him, "No, Jack, not at all! We're stopping the screwing. We're stopping *your screwing!*"

"That's right, Jack," I added, "no more screwing. It's time you do a little work. Your sorry ass is either going to work or go down for the next fifty years. That's *life,* for you!"

"And you ain't got fifty years left in you, Jack!" Jerry said. "You ain't got twenty!"

I continued to press the issue. "And when you get down to Huntsville some of those dudes you fingered will get you for sure! They haven't forgotten you."

Jerry added, "And if it will help, we'll remind them! You got the picture, Jack?"

Jack was trembling now, "You're trying to kill me. No other way to call it. You're trying to kill me. Why are you coming down on me like this? Hey, man, I never did you nothing—I never hurt you. This stuff doesn't figure!" He shook his head in utter disbelief. He was the kind of person who would sweat in the snow. Sitting there in the fifty-degree night air he had soaked through his suit coat; his handkerchief was soppy from continuously wiping his flushed, plump face.

We felt we had made our point. We didn't want to push him into a desperate revolt like a cornered rat. This kind of act required strategy, psychology, and practice, but the key ingredient was timing. You watch your "mark," you read his reactions, you have to know what he's feeling and thinking. When the time is right, you stop. The next move is his.

Near collapsing, Jack started to talk. "I'm listening. What is it you guys want. Is this a shakedown? Is it money? You know I don't have any money. If I had any money do you think that I would—"

I said, "Money? Money? I ought to stomp your—"

Jerry interrupted. "No money, Jack. Money can't buy us. You know that, and it won't buy you out of your rap. Besides, we know you don't have any money. You need it and you can't get it. How could you save yourself and pay a lawyer? It's deal with us or *fall!* I won't tell you that again."

Jack, his chest heaving, was now almost crying! "What is it then? What kind of deal's bringing you guys down on me this heavy? You ain't the D.A.! You can't make deals like that. You can't—"

"Shut up, Jack!" Jerry shouted. "If you don't shut up about what we can and can't do we walk! We walk, and you fall! Our deal's got nothing to do with the D.A. It don't touch him one bit. Not one little bit. It's ours. All ours! And we *can* do it. We *will* do it. You wanna find out? You wanna try me? Son of a bitch! I've had it with you! You ain't got enough sense to—"

Jack blurted, "I'm sorry, Mr. Cole. I didn't mean nothing. But I'm scared! You scared the shit out of me! I don't know what I'm saying! I don't what's happening? And how do you know about my money? I mean—"

"Here it is," Jerry said, slowly and deliberately, "You need a favor; we need a favor. You do us a favor; we do you a favor. It's that simple!"

Jack mustered half a smile and said, "Why didn't you say so? Gee, guys. Why the muscle? You know me! I'll do anything I can for you boys! You ought to know that! You only gotta ask."

Jerry decided the time was right to bore in. "It isn't all that easy, Jack. In fact, it's a little bit tough, but you can do it."

"That is, you can if you really want to. You only gotta *believe!*" I added. "If you would rather do a *favor* than do *fifty!*"

Then Jerry hit home, "You see, Jack, we need someone dead. You follow me, Jack?"

Jack's usually flush complexion turned white, his face registering the expected disbelief. "You guys want me to find you a hit-man? My God, I don't know any—"

Then Jerry lowered the boom. "No, Jack. Not *find* us one. We want *you!* We don't want you on the outside where you could hold it over us. We want your sweet little ass inside! Right in the middle of it! Up tight so you gotta keep your mouth shut or burn! You're it, Jack. You're our man."

"No! No! Wait a minute! No, not me! That's not my bag! I never—" Jack was frantic.

Jerry kept the squeeze on. "Stuff it! You've beaten the living shit out of hundreds of your customers over the years. Somebody gets you riled up, and you'd beat it out of him. You'd do it for no reason. Who knows how many—"

"Little nobodies!" Jack claimed. "I never took on anyone with class. Only creeps! Hey, boys, really, I'm a coward! I'm a smart ass, a show-off, a coward. It was all for show. Really, I'm not tough. I'm a chicken! All my 'mob-talk,' it's just that. It's 'talk'!"

"Then it's time for you to grow up, Jack," I said. "You've been wanting to be 'big-league' so it's time to go with the big boys!"

Jerry came back with, "It really isn't such a big, bad deal. It sounds worse than it is, and really, it's your kind of deal. It fits right in with your style."

I added, "Matter of fact, Jack, you could come out with both feet on the ground, and smelling like a rose, just like you always do!"

Jerry continued, "You could even become a hero. A legend in your own lifetime; famous, even world-famous!"

Then it was my turn again. "And you could become rich! Filthy rich. Buy yourself the biggest, gaudiest night club in the world, and stand there at the door and let your fan club pour in begging you to take their money!"

Jack tried to regain his composure. Shaking his head, he said, "There ain't no Santa and there ain't no deals like that. No, I can't do it. No way!"

Jerry struck back with, "Ain't no way you can take a fall, either. And there ain't no way you can handle fifty years. With this deal, you get five to ten years, maybe twenty years at the most. You could be out in five, maybe less. At your age, with good behavior there's no question."

"You'd have the best lawyer," I promised. "Anyone you want. No questions asked. And it won't cost you a cent. You do what you're told to do and you're covered. You're covered 'til you get paroled and get started again."

Jack was now as confused as he was nervous. "I don't know. What can you tell me—I mean, can you tell me what the score is? Ain't I got a right to know something before I—"

Now Jerry was ready to drive it home. "We don't vote on this, Jack. You do it or you don't. You try to blow the whistle on us and— Well, don't even think about it. You try to cause us a little trouble and you won't draw another breath."

Jack jumped and shook his head, "Hey, I don't fink, Mr. Cole. I know I ain't much, but I ain't that!"

"Let's put it all on the table then, quick and sweet." Jerry said. "You take it or you leave it.

Nothing else said, right? You know what happened to the President? Well, the punk who did it is in jail. He's an arrogant traitor, a communist, he killed the President, he killed Officer Tippit and he nearly killed the governor. The communists will get him a civil liberty lawyer and they'll find that somebody didn't dot an 'I' or cross a 'T' and the creep will walk. Now where will that leave us? It ain't right to risk it. That guy needs to be *dead!* The way *we* see it, once he gets transferred to the county jail, he's out of reach. Right now, he's still in the police station. So it's now or never. There's a crowd of people all over the place. It's a mad house. In all that confusion, someone could shove a pistol in his ribs, and it's all over. In the confusion you might even get away. But there's a greater likelihood you'll be caught. Just drop the gun immediately so you don't get hurt. We guarantee you the best lawyer money can buy. He will probably go with temporary insanity. You loved the President and feel for his family, you hate the arrogant, communist bastard who did it; in a sudden, insane instant you shot him."

Now in a sobering state of shock, Jack said, "I knew you were trying to screw me! Oh, man, is this ever a screwing! Why me? Why put this on me? So I'm a no good bastard. But why me?"

"Because we've got you where we need you, Jack," Jerry reasoned. "It's just that simple. The way we see it you can't say no. Man, it's tailor-made! You need us, and we need you! If you don't get some serious money real quick, you'll be dead anyhow. So what's the difference? At least we're giving you a fighting chance."

"Man I've gotta think! I've gotta think about this! You've hung it on me too heavy! I've gotta—"

I got up in his face, poking my finger into his chest. "You've gotta *do it!*"

Jerry continued, "There's no time for playing around, Jack. This is the crime of the century, the killing of the President. The whole world's watching every move. As soon as they get the paperwork done, they'll file on him and transfer him to the county jail, then we've lost him. It's got to come off quick."

Limp with dread, soaking wet and sobbing, Jack said, "And you want me to do the second biggest murder of the century, just like that, and never give it a thought! Hey man—"

We could see Jack was weakening. Now it was time to sweeten the ante. I promised him, "Jack, nobody has a right to expect something for nothing. I can't give you the exact details but it'll be worth the risk, more than worth it. There'll be some money besides your defense attorney, and paying off your debts, that should help you loads! We'll find you some money. You'll have some friends. You won't have to want for anything. While you're in custody it won't be so bad. You'll be cared for. You'll be where nobody can get to you, good food, good treatment. You know," Jerry played on Jack's tremendous ego, "people will be after your life story, your biography. And they'll probably want to make a movie! Man, did you ever think you'd be so rich and famous, a movie star?"

We knew we had him when he asked, "When would it have to be?"

I quickly answered, "Tonight!" I didn't want to give Jack time to think on his own. If we let due process take its course, the whole deal could fold with no time for an alternative.

"There's no other way, Jack. It has to be quick!"

Jerry put the cap on the deal, warning softly, "And if you crawfish, if you say one word, you're dead, Jack! You're a dead man! I assure you. That's a promise. You're dead!"

CHAPTER SIXTEEN

THE TRY FOR OSWALD

As I waited on the veranda, I summarized what had followed. Jerry and I completed our instructions to Jack. He was to have his revolver with him; he often carried large sums of money to the bank. It was a two-inch barrel .38 revolver that wouldn't show up in his baggy suit. In all the confusion he wouldn't attract attention. He had been in and out of the police station over the years, and he had a knack for remembering names. We instructed him to linger around the third floor until the opportunity arose, perform, drop his pistol, and surrender.

After letting Jack out of the car near his club, we discussed our next move. What if he chickens out? Well, we couldn't risk leaving him alive. Somewhat simultaneously, we agreed: we would wait near the elevator in the basement; if Jack failed to carry out his end of the bargain, we would quietly ask him for his gun. If he refused, we would demand it, but not too loudly as we didn't want to attract undue attention. As soon as he brought it into view, we would yell, "Watch out!" to attract bystander attention to an armed man. We agreed that we would each draw our sidearm and drop him. What else could we do?

I had suggested that Jerry drop out. It wasn't his action, and I shouldn't have dragged him into it in the first place.

Jerry assured me, "It's all in twenty! It's not the first time I've taken a chance, and it probably won't be the last. And really, the world would be the better if there weren't so many worthless assholes around."

From my car parked across the street from the Commerce Street entrance to the station we waited for Jack's 7:45 p.m. appointment. We watched him arrive a few minutes early, and speak to the officer assigned to guard the door. We hadn't expected that. What if he wouldn't let Jack in? We didn't need to worry. We don't know what he said but he got in without apparent delay. He must have dropped a name. We hoped he didn't drop ours. We felt a bit reassured that he did work his way in; he could have given us an alibi that he tried but was denied entry. The fact that he got in on his ingenuity was encouraging. It suggested either his resolution or his resignation. At any rate, he was inside.

Jack didn't go straight to the third floor. Either out of caution or reluctance he lingered in the basement before going upstairs. He spoke with a few officers and a couple of newsmen. Spotting some abandoned scratch paper he folded it as if it were a note pad like the news people carried. Perhaps people would assume he was just another of the dozens of reporters around the station. It must have seemed to him to be safer than just standing around.

Reaching the homicide office with a group of reporters, Jack tried to blend into the scenery. Oswald wasn't there when Jack arrived, but rumor had it that he was to be brought in soon. That accounted for the sudden return rush of reporters who had gone elsewhere throughout the building. With a chronic shortage of telephones and a growing problem of hotel rooms, reporters from all over the world were flocking into the police station.

Oswald was brought to the homicide office, entered, and was interviewed for a brief period. Then he was escorted to the third-floor prisoner elevator and delivered to the basement assembly room. There, he was placed in another show-up, then returned to jail. There had been no real chance for Jack to perform. He heard that there would be a news conference some two hours later. Not wishing to press his luck and welcoming a brief reprieve, he returned to the basement. Unable to handle his assignment and afraid to leave, Jack hung around talking to reporters, talking on the telephone with a radio station, and he spoke briefly with the District Attorney, Henry Wade. Having put off the inevitable, Jack decided to leave. He had again talked briefly with the officer guarding the Harwood Street entrance and mentioned that he was considering leaving for a while, that he thought he'd go pick up some snacks for the officers who couldn't get away. He felt certain that this officer would let him in later.

As Jack walked away, east on Commerce Street, Jerry caught up with him. He had missed connections in the basement. Jack explained he hadn't had a safe enough opportunity; there would be a press conference in about two hours, so he would return for another crack at it. Then he continued on his way. I stood near, half expecting to go through with our alternate plan. But since Jerry showed no displeasure, I felt more at ease. Jerry filled me in as we walked back to my car. I wondered, "Do you suppose we should have let him walk?"

Jerry shrugged, "Who knows? Our idea about the basement fell flat. If we'd done anything out here on the street we might never have been able to explain it."

"You're right," I agreed. "I'm too edgy. I gotta make a phone call, Jerry. You wanna wait here 'til I get back?"

"Why don't I run by my office for a minute?" he said. "I might have some answers to my calls—some of them, anyway. We'll both come back here when we're through. Shouldn't take more than fifteen minutes, half an hour at the most. Then we ought to think about eating. I can't remember ever being this hungry."

We walked across the street and went to our separate offices.

* * *

Jerry's business was quick. New Orleans Intelligence had called. Lee Oswald had been in New Orleans in the summer of 1963, working out of a shop and had been involved with the FPCO handing out literature on street corners and agitating for the cause. He had been arrested there in August. Through the summer he had a nondescript job while living with family members, and he was interviewed on a radio station about his FPCO activities. Oswald had obtained a visa for Mexico, completed his trip and in October, moved back to Dallas. They had nothing else on him since then. Jerry transcribed the notes into a quick memo, dropped it off in homicide and returned to my car. It was a little past eight-thirty.

* * *

I found the group still waiting and anxious for my call.

"Where are you?" Tony demanded. "Where have you been? What's going on?"

"There's no way I can tell you, Tony. I'm not even sure I remember. Anyway I can't go into it now. I called to let you know that we've got things going. Nothing has happened, yet but it looks good—as good as we can expect for now. The next hour or so is going to be dead time. We'll just have to wait it out. In the meantime, we're going to—"

"We!" Tony exclaimed, jumping to his feet and glaring into the faces of his companion. "Who the hell are 'we'? Are you with someone? Good God man, have you—?"

"Cool it, Tony!" I interrupted. "No sweat. Yes, I've been with somebody. He knows what I gotta do and that's all. He doesn't know why, and he doesn't know with whom. But I couldn't have done it without him."

Still feeling near rage, Tony continued. "How can you say that for sure? Is he a cop?"

I tried to answer. "Of course. Who else could—"

"How do you know he isn't setting you up? What makes you think that if he gets scared or feels he's in over his head he won't pull the plug? If he knows *anything* it's too much. He's bound to know you're not working alone in this. What have you told him? What does he know?"

"Will you hold on a minute! I can't say much. I'm tired, I'm hungry, and I'm scared. And I'm in no mood for your lip. I know what you're thinking but you're wrong. I've trusted you. We've all had to trust each other. But you aren't the only ones who can be trusted. You've got to trust me. I'd trust this guy with my life. In fact, I am, and he's already in too deep to trap me, and he's in too deep for backing out. Like I said, I'm sure of him. He's with me, and I couldn't do it without him. I can guess how you guys must feel. I'd feel the same way, and it wasn't an easy decision. But you've got to trust me. I don't know when I can get back to you. Like I said, the next hour will be dead time. Nothing can be done. I'll be in touch soon as I can."

I was glad that call was over and upset at the ruffled feelings as I returned to my car. While I made my way there, I thought how pleased they would be with the results, if it came off all right. That realization stimulated me and made me more determined than ever. I decided I wouldn't say anything to Jerry about Tony's outburst. He had enough on his mind already. When I reached Jerry in the car, I was almost smiling. Saying nothing, I took my seat behind the steering wheel, inserted my key, started the motor and pulled away from the curb. Stopping for the signal light at Central Expressway, I turned to Jerry. "Where to, buddy? We ought to feed our faces while we've got the time."

"Sounds like a good idea," Jerry replied. Since no suggestion was made regarding where to go, I continued in an easterly direction. In a few minutes we were at Brownie's. It was a natural thing to do; they never close; the food is good, and it was the unofficial East Dallas Precinct for police officers. No one would notice or remember our having been there.

* * *

Returning to our post across from the police station shortly before 10:00 p.m., we started our vigil.

"Think he'll show?" I wondered. Actually, I was only making conversation.

"Sure," Jerry answered. "He'll make it. Like I said, he's a dealer. He can't pass up a deal. He certainly doesn't want to spend a long stretch in the pen. And he can't pass up the chance to get out of the trouble he is in. And he won't pass up the chance to be rich and famous. His ego would bust wide open if he tried. He'll be here, and I'm pretty sure of it now. I'm betting he'll do it."

I wasn't convinced. "I wish I could share your confidence," I said. "What kind of money do you figure this is worth, ten thousand, twenty-five?"

Jerry asked the obvious question. "Who do you have on the string, Davey? No, wait, I'm not prying. I was just thinking out loud. But you've promised the best lawyer, you've promised to help out while he's in the pen, you've promised to help him when he gets out, and you're talking about some extra yardage for his debts as well. That adds up to a bundle—the kind of bundle you sure ain't got. You probably never even saw that kind of money outside of a bank!"

I started to wonder. Had Tony been right? Was Jerry starting to—? No, I refused to give it any further thought. Like I told Tony, it couldn't be done without Jerry. I had to have Jerry's help up front. Once I opened the door, I had to invite him in—all the way in.

I finally answered, "If anything leaks or blows up, you'll probably find out soon enough. But as it is, and I'm sure you understand, it's best if you don't know anything else. It isn't that I don't trust you. I'm here, ain't I? You know me and I know you. Let's leave it there. If anything happens, maybe you can walk away."

"Not as long as Jack's on the ground," Jerry corrected. "That slob would blow the whistle for sure. You know he can't keep his mouth shut. Nobody really believes any of his bullshit, but if it would burn a cop, the media would give him headlines. Like you said, we're in for the whole ride, win or lose. It's best I don't know; I really don't want to know. It was just the cop in me. Always gotta ask questions. It's just a habit. Let's let it ride."

Suddenly I felt much better.

* * *

At ten o'clock we recognized Jack's unmistakable form trundling down the sidewalk with a medium-sized sack cradled in his arm.

"What's he got?" I gasped.

After a moment's curious reflection, Jerry said, "Ain't no way of knowing. Maybe we, or one of us, should follow him in. We ought to have some idea of what he's up to."

Without waiting for my reply, Jerry opened his door, stepped out and started across Commerce Street on a route that would leave him about fifty feet or so behind Jack. They continued in this fashion to the Harwood Street entrance. Jack descended the steps to the basement door while Jerry waited above checking on Jack's progress.

"It's me, Jack Ruby, I'm back," he said to the officer guarding the door. "You been able to eat yet? I brought some sandwiches for you boys."

"I ate a while ago. I'm okay," the officer answered. "You might try the guys on the information desk. They've been busier than a long-tail cat in a room full of rockers. They're probably starving."

"Good, I'll do that," Jack eagerly replied, opening the door with his free hand. Entering the basement, he looked back over his shoulder and walked on saying, "I'll see you later, and I want you to come by my place. Bring your wife, your girlfriend. You'll be my guest, okay?"

Jerry waited a few seconds, finishing his cigarette. Tossing it, he followed Jack inside. He watched from around the corner near the I.D. office while Jack offered a few of his sandwiches around. Then Jack went to the elevator and pushed the "up" button. Assuming he would go to the third floor, Jerry stepped across the hallway to the narrow flight of stairs leading to the first floor. Then he continued to a landing between the second and third floors. He waited there, certain that Jack would alight from the elevator shortly.

Jack stepped off on the third floor and walked toward the homicide office. He entered, but didn't stay long. As Jerry left his perch and started down the hall for a closer look, Jack came out and started toward him. That gave Jerry a flushed feeling. *I hope he's got more sense than to stop or even speak,* he thought.

Jack walked straight past Jerry. *Thank God he had some brains,* Jerry thought. Jack went to the elevator and mashed "down." Jerry realized that no one was watching him so he reversed his course. Turning right toward the elevator, he saw that Jack was alone in the elevator lobby.

"What's the deal?" Jerry asked quietly without stopping as he angled off to his right toward the men's room.

Without looking at Jerry, Jack answered, "The news conference will be in the assembly room at twelve o'clock. I must have got the time wrong before. I'm going to stay away 'til then. I don't like hanging around." Jerry disappeared into the restroom.

After a few seconds, Jerry heard the elevator doors open, then close. He exited the restroom, skipped over to the stairs and scurried to the basement. He cut back to his right past the jail office entrance and into the basement parking area. Turning right again, he hurried up the vehicle exit ramp to Commerce Street, crossed the street, and returned to me, waiting in my car.

"We still got some waiting to do, buddy."

Shaking my head in objection, I complained, "Oh no! What is it now?"

"Looks like midnight. That's when they're supposed to hold the news conference in the show-up room. Jack said he must have got the time wrong before."

"Do you still feel like we can trust him?" I blurted. "Is he trying to 'crawfish' on us? And what are we suppose to do in the meantime?"

Jerry tried humor, "Why not run over to Jack's joint for a free beer!"

I made no reply. I shook my head slowly, indicating "no," but he managed to crack a bit of a smile. Jerry's levity had a refreshing effect. I realized that I had been up and going since five that morning. Not only had the hours seemed longer than usual, the pace and the mental strain were far more than I had ever known, more that I would have believed I could endure, had anybody asked me. Then I remembered Jerry had problems, too, so I asked, "How are you feeling, Jerry?"

"Lousy! How are you making it?"

"Better than I had expected, but I'm tired. In fact—"

Jerry interrupted me, "Why don't you lay your head back and catch forty winks before you fall out. You ain't that young, you know. I'll be the good-eye and you get some rest. I didn't come in 'til noon."

I couldn't resist the offer; I didn't even reply. I scooted my body a bit deeper into my seat, laid my head back, shut my eyes and collapsed. I was unaware of life until Jerry nudged me saying, "There he goes. He's going back into the building."

"What time is it?" I blurted, bolting upright in my seat. "What time is it? Did I go to sleep? What's happening?"

I woke up so fast that my entire body remained numb, and my mind was no better. Frightened that I might have screwed up in dozing off, my system started pumping adrenaline in its race to catch up.

Jerry calmed me down. "Easy boy! Cool down before you blow a fuse! Everything's fine. Jack just showed up and went downstairs."

I looked at my watch. A quarter 'til twelve. He was cutting it close—too close, "Think we ought to go over there?"

Jerry wasn't sure. "Think somebody might wonder why we were there so late? We've been off duty for quite a while. But there have been a lot of people in and out. We might not be noticed. There's probably no duty rosters in this confusion. What do you think?"

I thought a moment, "If Jack does it and we were in there, we would have a tougher time explaining. On the other hand, if it happens, man the shit's gonna hit the fan. Nobody's going to know or remember a thing." Then I remembered, "What about photographers? All we need is some son of a bitch photographer taking our picture smack dab in the middle of where we ain't got a lick of business being."

Jerry agreed. "I think we've answered the questions. As much as I hate to say it, we've got to wait."

I sighed and settled back for the additional agony of sitting and waiting. Neither of us spoke for a while. We knew of nothing that needed to be said about this, and we were too physically and emotionally drained to waste our remaining energy on small talk.

At twelve o'clock, we felt our tension level rise in response to an unconscious signal. Each minute thereafter dragged by even slower than before. Each minute heightened our anxiety. Each sign of life, each movement near the entrance to the police station sent a wave of excitement pulsing through us. Then we saw him.

Jack walked out rather casually, too casually for an executioner. He stopped at the corner waiting for the signal light to change. Crossing the street, he stopped on the opposite corner and looked back at the intersection. Since he saw nobody in sight, he started east on Commerce again. As he neared my now familiar car he asked, "Should I stop?" We were too tired for further cat-and-mouse tactics. Reaching back, Jerry opened the curbside door and said, "Get in."

Jack stepped hurriedly into the car and took his seat. I started the motor and pulled into the traffic lane. At the corner, I turned right and drove south on Pearl Expressway.

"Well?" Jerry inquired.

"I didn't do it!" Jack shot back. "There were so many people, and it was so crowded I couldn't get within twenty or thirty feet. I didn't feel like I could do it from that far away. I kept waiting but I couldn't get any closer. All those reporters with their microphones and cameras, they kept pushing and shoving. I just couldn't get up to him. I couldn't get a clear line on him. And when it broke up, they took him out first. There was no way I could get to him then. They hustled him out and back to the jail. It was all real fast. They didn't keep him down there very long; just a few minutes. I'm sorry, really. I tried. I just couldn't—"

"Okay! Okay!" Jerry cut in. Then turning to me he asked, "What do you think?

"I don't know. I'm so wrung out and strung out I don't know which end's up. You got any ideas?"

Jerry thought for a moment. I pulled over into a loading zone at a shuttered produce market and stopped. Spreading my body as fully as I could, I responded. "I don't feel like driving around, that's for sure," I said wearily, "and I'm smooth out of ideas. If they've put him away for the night, that's it."

Jerry noted with resignation, "Fritz and his boys can't go on all night either. If they're going to be worth anything tomorrow they've got to get some rest, too."

"Let's drop Jack off at the club and go get some rest ourselves," I suggested. "We still have a lot to do and we won't be any good ourselves if we don't get back in shape. My brain actually hurts and my reasoning is all fuzzy."

"I ain't feeling anything, anymore," Jerry said.

"Then that's it." We drove west to Field Street, turned north toward Commerce and let Jack off. We had agreed to do nothing until I called them. They would stay free and near their phones so they could be reached. I knew that I needed to get back with the group. Surely by then they would know I hadn't pulled it off; still I dreaded confirming that to them. One of them might have some new information or a fresh idea. But for now, we were through. Dropping Jerry off at his car, I stopped by a payphone to place a call to the safe house, then decided not to. I went home to bed.

CHAPTER SEVENTEEN

The Third Try

I reached home shortly after one o'clock. I entered quietly hoping to get into bed without waking my wife and hoping to sleep at least until noon. I had just opened the door when the bedroom light flashed on, and I saw my wife slipping into her robe.

"Are you hungry?" she asked. "Have you had a chance to eat?"

"About nine, I guess. No, it was a little earlier. I don't want anything. Just a shower and a bed."

Mary went to the bedroom, got fresh underwear from my bureau and took it into our bathroom. I had started to undress as I walked through the house. While I showered, she turned back the covers. I entered the room, turned out the light and climbed into bed. She leaned over, kissed my cheek and wished me a good night. Her actions reminded me of the problems of being a cop's wife. It has to be the more difficult of two lives. Mine was more demanding in action but she always has that gnawing and constant uncertainty, while being always ready to give comfort. With the events of the day making worldwide headlines, she confined her knowledge to what she had learned from the news coverage. She wouldn't ask me, but, had I felt the need to talk, she would have listened.

I didn't make it to noon. At 9:00 a.m. Mary gave me a gentle shake and I bolted upright in bed. "What is it!" Then I realized where I was. "Oh, morning. What time is it?"

"It's the telephone," she said. "I hated to wake you but he said it's urgent. Would you like to have breakfast when you finish? It's nine."

"Uh, okay. That would be fine," I said, reaching for the bedside extension. It was Tony.

Before I could speak, he demanded, "Dave, is that you? You didn't make the connection, did you?"

"No," I replied, "it was too crowded. He couldn't get close enough. Then, they took Oswald back upstairs. Anything else happening?" I could feel Tony's angst.

"Can you get over here, quick? Seems the whole deal's going sour. The press is hollering 'conspiracy' all right, and they seem to accept Oswald as part of it, but some of them are trying to implicate the police, the government, everybody. Could they be onto something?" His voice was unusually strained.

"I don't know. I doubt it. What could they have? Maybe I'd better go down to the station and see what's going on before I see you guys. I feel like I've got a hangover from a two-week drunk!"

"I guess we're all bushed," Tony agreed. "Charlie's going by the local office and the Secret Service, the Old Man's still out of town. I haven't heard from Joe and I don't know anything about John. I guess he got out. There's been nothing on that. Haven't heard about Oswald's attorney either. Altogether, we don't know a damn thing!"

I tried to reassure him. "I'll get down there as soon as I eat; then I'll be right on out to see you guys. Maybe we can start drawing things together."

* * *

It was almost five o'clock before I arrived at the safe house. Charlie was already there. Tony got onto me, instantly. "What's all this 'police conspiracy?' Have they found something? What do they have? What's going on?"

"According to our local news people, it's all the imagination of the out-of-town news people," I answered. "They're selling sensationalism. You know, indict Dallas, indict the police, indict the government, indict the whole conservative philosophy. I'm positive they are only pushing sensational innuendo. They don't have anything. Actually, nobody really knows anything. And get this—Oswald turned our lawyer down! He asked for someone else, some guy from New York, but couldn't get him, at least, not yet. So far he's not being represented by a lawyer. But he's denying everything. He isn't saying anything! He's not even trying to save his own hide. He hasn't said a thing except that he hasn't killed anybody. Not the President, not Tippit. Nothing about Freddie. Nothing about his rifle. Nothing! He *is* claiming he's a patsy, but without details. He's being a real sarcastic smart-mouth."

Tony was astounded. "You're kidding! Oh, yes. Joe called. He's back in Washington. Said he made the drop but it's too early to know whether they'll go for the switch. Did you hear anything about the bullets?"

"By the way. The FBI has requisitioned all the evidence and is collecting it in Washington.

They're cutting the Dallas police smooth out of the picture! Some bullets were sent to the forensic lab for processing, but that's all. There are bullets from Tippit and from the President. I'm not sure which were which. It takes time to make the determinations."

Charlie entered the conversation, "The talk at the Bureau and the Secret Service sounds like they believe they have the fatal bullets, but I thought they were talking about only one actual bullet."

"There are several bullets or particles," I said. "The one from the President, from Connally, and from Tippit. I heard about 'bullets,' but wasn't always sure just which ones."

Tony resumed his previous position. "Well, Joe made the switch. Said the head shot was clean through; didn't leave a bullet, maybe scraps. Anyway, he said he almost got caught when he tried to drop one in the limo for the neck shot. It was clean through but he never found John's bullet in the floorboard or seat. And he left one on the hospital cart for Connally. That's the one they found, I guess."

"On a cart!" Charlie exclaimed. "On a cart? What in—"

Tony interrupted, "Wait a minute. The doctors couldn't find a bullet in Connally, only some scraps. But he's all shot up. He got it through the back and out the chest, through the arm or wrist, and in the leg. He got hit enough to have been the target. But they couldn't find a single bullet. Then when Joe got back to the emergency room they had already taken Connally up to surgery. He couldn't do anything up there. He remembered a doctor saying how bullets in a muscle, if they're not too deep, often work back out when the victim moves around. So he nestled the bullet in the mess on the governor's gurney, hoping that when they cleaned it up someone would find it and turn it in."

Charlie said, "I haven't heard of a bullet being found in the limousine. What if they turn up more lead than they need? Some from John's shots, some from Joe's drops. We could come up with too many! That will—"

"That will make some poor detective have kittens," I said. "He would probably assume more shots were fired or that there were more shooters than was originally believed. That area is an echo chamber. No telling what those three shots sounded like from various places. And all those bystanders running and ducking. Probably no two of them will report hearing the same thing. You know how unreliable witnesses can be."

As it turned out, the Warren Commission and just about everyone else had fits about that. How many shots and from where?

"Anyway," Tony suggested, "we better get that information to John so he can destroy his barrel in case they do find too many bullets and one of them is his. God, I wish we would hear from John. He couldn't still be in there. And nothing's been said about finding him or any suggestion of his even having been there. That surely would have made the news."

He reached for the telephone and called the telegraph office, explaining that his message was long overdue. "Just a minute, Mr. Dooley. Let me check again." Several minutes later the clerk returned to the line. "I'm terribly sorry, Mr. Dooley. That message had been misfiled. Shall I read it to you?"

"Yes, go ahead."

"It says, 'Earline arrived safely.' Will there be a reply?"

But Tony had already hung up. "He made it! Hot damn, he got out clean! Something finally went right for us! Man, that's great!"

We expressed our agreement.

"Now where were we?" Tony continued with renewed vigor.

"The bullets," Charlie reminded us. "We have to watch for the first word of too many bullets."

"John's no rookie," I said. "He'll pay attention to developments. He'll know what to do. Now, let's summarize what we have and call the Old Man."

* * *

I explained to the Old Man what we knew or reasonably suspected, and what we planned to do. He was glad to hear that progress was becoming more favorable. Then he admonished us to be both cautious and tenacious. Don't get careless and don't let up. After our talk with the Old Man we felt better. With renewed enthusiasm we discussed coming probabilities and our appropriate reactions. I opened with, "Let's put some things to trust as being so. If they prove otherwise we go with the difference. But we can't vacillate, we'd get too far behind. Let's assume that Joe's switch is accepted, that the bullets he dropped are accepted as the real thing, and that John's extra bullets don't show up. Let's assume Oswald's connection with the communists, especially the Cubans, is enough to convince them that Oswald did it because of what Kennedy tried to do to Castro—"

Tony interrupted. "Wait a minute. It isn't common knowledge that Kennedy put out a contract on Castro? The government isn't going to admit it just so they can put a motive on Oswald. Can you guys imagine the public's reaction if they knew the Company's operations included the elimination of unfavorable foreign politicians, and especially some heads of government? That would be a big enough 'bang' to destroy the Company. Every demagogue in Washington now and for years to come would be anti-CIA. That's all they would need—the chance to suggest that it isn't nice to go around killing people. Let me put it this way. There are some things that have to be done if our concept of civilization is to survive. God knows I don't have to tell you guys that. It isn't nice, but 'nice' won't do the job sometimes. The Company does what *has* to be done. There's no one else to do it. Our enemies do it, they've always done it, and they are not going to stop. That kind of work is never nice. There are things you don't know about; things you'll never know about and I can't tell you. But believe me, they'll never admit to a contract on Castro. You can forget that angle as a motive."

"What about the Bay of Pigs?" Charlie offered. "Wouldn't the President's knowledge alone, even without his support, be enough to make Castro's people want revenge? There's no secret about that!"

Tony agreed. "If Castro is offered up and the media takes the bait, yes. I think it will head off suspicion."

"Okay then," I said. "For the sake of our present effort, let's assume that Oswald is accepted as the assassin. Let's assume that if he says anything else they won't believe him, and that it can't be traced back to Freddie or anyone else, that suspicion all stays on Oswald. In other words, they buy the whole conspiracy as being his deal alone. Let's assume that the rifle and the trip to Mexico helps to add up to Oswald. Now, where are we, and what's the worst that can happen?"

Charlie groped for the answer. "I don't like the idea of Oswald still being in jail. So what if he hasn't talked yet? He's not the kind who'll take the rap and keep quiet. Even if things can't be traced back to the group, I'd feel better if he was out of it. As long as he's alive, he's a threat. He isn't too strong, and he can't be too sharp or Freddie couldn't have managed him so easily. I don't want anybody even be thinking about us, much less be looking for us."

"I agree with that," Tony said.

"I still feel pretty good about what's happened so far," I said. "I think we can take him out. We just need a clean chance. So far, we haven't had it."

Tony continued, "Then it looks like the next act on our program is that. When and how? What do we know or need to find out to make this happen? What's next down at the police department? If we knew what was going on, maybe we could see an opportunity, or make one."

I got up to leave, saying, "I guess I'd better get back down there and run up my antenna."

CHAPTER EIGHTEEN

PLANS FOR TRANSFER

At the station that Saturday morning, I learned that Oswald had been filed on for both murders, Kennedy and Tippit. That meant he would be taken from the city jail to the county jail as soon as Fritz's people had all they could get from him. So far, they had nothing. Once Oswald was transferred, the group would stand virtually no chance of getting to him. If we were going to do it, it had to be done before he was transferred.

Discussions were already being held on how to make the transfer. As there had been anonymous telephoned death threats made against Oswald, his security had to be considered. Even though threats are not so uncommon, this guy had killed the President and an officer. Accordingly, the world press forces would be closely watching every move. While the threats were most likely from typical crackpots, they couldn't be ignored. This was especially true since some of the media had made suggestions of a conspiracy, and more especially since some suggested the police department was at least negligent if not a party to a conspiracy.

There were some strong feelings to send him by some undercover method. Normally, the county transfer wagon would come to the city jail each morning and pick up the prisoners who had been filed on. To try to get him then was considered too risky; there would be a heavy guard present. Several plans had been suggested and discussed but nothing was decided. And there was a new and unexpected problem. The news people, learning that he would be transferred, demanded to be let in on the deal so they could cover the event. Captain Fritz denied them the transfer information; this was a criminal investigation, not a three-ring circus. The news people turned to the city fathers for help. They insisted on their being allowed to cover the transfer.

The best tactical plan from a security point of view involved whisking Oswald away in a police officer's uniform. Dressed as a cop and mixed in with a group of policemen leaving the building, it would appear that they were routine patrol officers returning to their cars to resume their assignments. That, done in the dead of night, seemed to be the safest and least conspicuous method.

Since Dallas was being severely criticized in the world press for the death of the President, even accused of complicity, the city fathers were anxious to cooperate with the press in any reasonable way. The media wanted to make a show of the transfer, so the powers reasoned the transfer should be set for a time and place, and the media be allowed to cover it. They assured the media people that the switch would not take place without plenty of advance notice. The most probable time would be Sunday morning, before noon.

I also learned that the bus driver and some others had picked Oswald out of line-ups, and the driver confirmed that Oswald boarded his bus after the shooting and that he had been given a transfer. Also, the FBI had traced the rifle to Oswald. A paraffin test showed Oswald had fired a gun, and the lab boys had found his palm print on the wrapping paper that had contained the "curtain rods."

Returning to the safe house, I reported that to the group and said that I would get with my contact and arrange for him to be ready to perform his end of our deal when they started the transfer. Perhaps since the media wanted to make a production of it, there should be enough confusion to cover the hit.

That judgment almost caused the plan to fail. During Saturday night, Captain Fritz, with the cooperation of the night patrol captain, Cecil Talbert, was very close to disregarding the city fathers' promise to the media by transferring Oswald without delay. At one point I was but a whisper away from losing Oswald to the county jail and probably losing him permanently. But, our misfortune gave way to a break. When the captains decided to make the transfer they attempted to notify the chief, but they were unable to reach him. Without anyone's knowledge, the chief had told his wife, Bea, to hold all calls other than from the City Manager. The captains seriously considered making the transfer on their own but eventually decided against it.

* * *

After telling the group of my intentions, I telephoned Jack Ruby and arranged for him to follow the same route from his club to meet me as he had on Friday night. Setting the time for the meeting, I left to keep the appointment. I drove west on Main to Lamar Street, turned south to Commerce Street, then east on Commerce. Rather than go back to the parking lot, I stopped near Poydras Street and waited. At the designated time, I saw Jack approaching from the direction of his club. When he turned the corner and I determined he was not being followed, I started my car and followed him, calling for him to get in. He looked back, crossed the street and joined me.

"Where's Mr. Cole?" he asked.

"Never mind," I replied.

I drove for a few minutes in silence mentally reviewing the instructions I would give to Ruby. Returning to the same railroad siding off Young Street, I lit a cigarette and turned to Jack. "Listen carefully, Jack. This has got to be right. There won't be another chance. Fail this time and it's Huntsville. No more chances, no more deals, no more nothing, you understand?" Not waiting for an answer, I pressed on. "You stay home where I can reach you first thing in the morning. As soon as I get the word on the time, I'll call you. You've got to be ready to move, get it? You've got to move, move fast, and do it right. That's it! They will transfer Oswald to the county jail sometime tomorrow, Sunday morning, a little before noon. I don't expect anything else to develop tonight. But you stay ready just in case I call. Now I don't know exactly how they plan to do it but it will probably happen in the basement parking area of the police station. It's too risky to do it on the street. They're talking about setting it up so the reporters and TV people can cover it. You've been passing as a reporter. Maybe nobody will mess with you. We'll see about that. Anyway, that's how I expect it to go; I'll know for sure later. You just be ready and be where I can reach you. And when I do call, you move, okay?"

Jack nodded his understanding without speaking. He wanted to say "no" but he couldn't. Without saying so, to me or to Jerry. I think, the idea, as frightening and dangerous as it was, had started to appeal to him. Sure, he didn't want to pull any hard time in the pen, but a couple of years beats fifty. But I think he was beginning to dwell on the notion of fame and fortune. I believe he had already started to visualize himself as a wealthy hero with customers anxious to shake his hand and spend their money in his club. And what a club it would be. Big as his ego. Man, what a deal!

I respected his silence, started my car and returned near the club and let Jack out with the parting reminder, "Stay home where I can get you and be ready. This is the last chance!"

Jack shook his head in the affirmative and got out, standing there as I drove away. I turned east on Commerce and stopped at the police station.

It was almost dark, and I remembered I hadn't eaten since breakfast. I returned to Brownie's, ate, telephoned the group, and then went back to the station.

The word around the hall was that the transfer had been set for noon Sunday, in the basement. Reporters would be given passes; no one else would be permitted in the parking area for an hour or so before the transfer and until it was over. After the basement had been closed, officers would conduct a thorough search to ensure that there was no unauthorized person and no contraband present. Authorized news people would be admitted after their I.D. had been checked. Oswald would be brought out, loaded into a car and driven away. That just about queers it, I thought. If reporters had to present passes for their entry, how could I get a pass for Jack without tipping my hand? Jack would have to slip into a closed and guarded enclosure. I felt tempted to walk away, but I was in too deep to quit then.

The underground parking area in the basement was busy that evening. With the usual traffic for Saturday night I figured no one would notice me. It would be a good time to scout around. There had to be a way to make it. Working my way through the entire basement parking area and the adjoining rooms several times, my depression grew. I couldn't find an assured opening. Next there was the engine room right off the parking space and the sub-basement below. These were dead ends. Maybe there was a way to hide Jack there so he could come out at the right time. But what if they searched the engine room too? Surely they would. No, the engine room wouldn't do. Could I hide him in the trunk of a—no, they would search the cars. The elevators might—no, they would turn them off when the offices upstairs in the Municipal Building are closed like they will be Sunday.

It looked like the only possible opening that would be accessible to the outside was the stairway that came down to the basement in a remote corner behind the elevators. Even though it served as a fire escape, its remoteness rendered it almost useless and often overlooked. I walked over, opened the door and walked up to the first floor of the Municipal Building. Looking around, I saw nothing inviting. To the west, the floor-to-ceiling security gate separating the municipal building from the police building was closed and locked; to the north and south were the locked doors to Main Street and to Commerce; and to the east was the freight elevator. *Wait,* I thought. *There's a door out to the back, behind the elevator.* It went out to the trash service area behind the building. I checked it.

The door to the service entrance, while locked, had been so beaten and banged on during the years of pushing freight in and garbage out that it was easily opened. Checking it, I found that I could open it and insert a piece of match stem as a wedge to keep it unlocked if necessary. I judged this was probably my best bet. For an interim plan, I visualized having Jack come to the back door, the latch wedged so it could be opened just before the appointed time. Jack would let himself into the hall, then go through the fire escape door, go down to the basement landing and wait behind the shut door. Just before the time, I would have tape over the lock so it could be pushed open a few seconds after I tapped on the door to signal Jack, seconds before Oswald was brought into the basement. It would be close, but it could work!

I worried about someone remembering seeing me over by the door and beginning to wonder whether I had let in the interloper who shot Oswald. I decided, okay, tell Jack to insist that he walked down the Main Street driveway entrance to the basement. It would be guarded, but if he swore he walked in that way it would simply become a swearing match, if anybody cared.

That was the best I could do that night so I decided to get home at an earlier hour. I had remained so busy the past two days that I was beyond feeling fatigue. But I still had one more task. I couldn't call Jack from home; Mary couldn't be involved! So I had to find a pay telephone. That booth at the convenience store at Live Oak and Skillman looked suitable so I stopped and placed my call. It went something like this.

"Jack, you know who this is?" I asked.

"Okay. Yeah, I do."

"Then listen carefully. The time is noon. Got it?"

"Yeah, noon,"

"All right, you be fully ready at least half an hour before. Be there by 11:30 a.m., and no later. You know where the alley comes in off Pearl Expressway, behind the Western Union Building for service to the Municipal Building?"

"I can find it."

"Okay, you pull into the alley. It's a 'no parking' area so you won't have to look for a place to park. Wait in your car until you see me at the back door of the Municipal Building. Are you still with me?"

"Yeah, I'll pull into the alley a little before 11:30 and watch for you to come to the door."

"Right. After you see me, wait fifteen minutes. Then you come in that door. Inside, you go through the door on your left, then go down the hall, go twenty feet and through the door on your right. That puts you in the elevator lobby of the Municipal Building. You'll be on the first floor. Got that so far?"

"Okay—"

"Next, you enter the center corridor and turn right toward Main Street. The second door, the one past the mail box, has a fire exit light. That door leads downstairs to the basement. You go down to the next door, but that door will be shut. You stop there. Just before he's brought out, I'll tap on the door. Two raps, then two more. You wait fifteen seconds so I can join the officers by the jail entrance. Then you push the door open real easy, remove the tape from the latch and walk up to the crowd. That should be about the instant they bring him out. Everybody will be pushing and shoving, trying to get a look.

They won't pay you any mind. You shove up with the rest and it's all over. You follow that?"

"I understand, but what if—?"

"No time for 'what ifs.' It's then or never. If anything goes wrong, you're on your own. You figure out something. And don't forget to remove the tape from the door latch, roll it up and toss it. And drop your gun, real quick. Don't resist! And don't try to figure out anything else. If you blow it, don't try to save yourself by trying to burn me. If you do, you're dead. Otherwise, you're covered: lawyer, money, the works. You play it right, and you're all right. Queer it and— you know the rest. Jack, you've always wanted to be a big shot. This is it: your one big chance. Don't blow it!"

"Don't worry. I've got enough trouble already. I sure don't need any more."

"You've got the picture, Jack. Now here's one more detail. Anybody wants to know how you got in the building, you say you walked in down the Main Street driveway ramp when the officer guarding it wasn't looking. You stick with that story no matter what. You just happened to be downtown, you saw the commotion, you walked in. You saw Oswald; your mind went blank; you don't know from nothing! Nothing, you hear that?"

"Yes. I, that is, should I—"

"Nothing, Jack! You walked in, saw that no good communist S.O.B. and your mind went blank. The lawyer will take it from there. Don't say another word until he gets to you. You just tell them what lawyer you want. I'll see that you get him, okay?"

"I guess so."

"Guess nothing! What is there to guess about? Either you understand or you don't. Now which is it?"

"I've got it. It's just that I'm nervous as—I'll be okay. I've written it down."

"No, Jack! No writing!" I hissed. "As soon as you get it, burn it! Writing it down is evidence that could kill you. That would prove premeditated murder. Burn it!"

Hoping I had reached Jack with logic, had been clear in my instructions, and that he wouldn't forget, I signed off and left for home and bed. But I didn't get much sleep.

CHAPTER NINETEEN

RUBY THE ASSASSIN

November the twenty-fourth was fresh and sunny. A few billowing, white clouds spaced themselves across the pale blue sky. It looked more like early spring than a day in mid-autumn. It was a calm, quiet, peaceful Sunday morning. There was nothing to suggest what would happen in just a few hours.

I slept until half past six. I needed more rest but I couldn't risk the self-indulgence, so I shaved and dressed as Mary prepared breakfast. For the first time in three days, I even took the time for a glance at the morning newspaper. There was no mention of the impending transfer. Accelerating my leisurely pace I hurried through the last of my meal, grabbed my coat and hat, said good-bye to Mary, and prepared to leave for the station. Ordinarily, I was off-duty on Saturdays and Sundays. This week I had been gone all day Saturday and now I was going to work an hour earlier than I would have on a regular workday. I read that one of my former partners, back when we were patrolmen, had died. His funeral was at noon. I would like to have paid my respects but that was out of the question. Mary wondered what was happening, but she wouldn't ask me. I appreciated that in her, but it didn't ease my feelings of guilt.

* * *

The plans for the transfer were still set for the basement garage. Joining a few associates for a cup of coffee, I heard how my plans had almost been scuttled during the night by the captains when they nearly transferred Oswald on their own. I felt an uncontrollable tingle throughout my body. I was afraid the shock might have shown in my face so I quickly picked up my cup and simulated a long, slow sip. I couldn't afford to cause my fellow officers to wonder why something that was none of my business should cause me such an emotional reaction. Feeling my composure return, I lowered my cup. They hadn't noticed. *But,* I thought, *if I can't handle it better than this, I'd better stay away from people; I'm getting too edgy.* God, I wished it was over. Making my excuse before the rest were finished, I explained that I needed to return to the office, that I had some catching up to do.

In my office I telephoned Jack. My hands started to tremble as I dialed; the tension was mounting but I also felt a twinge of elation since one way or the other it would all be over very soon. My blood pressure probably reached close to three-hundred points.

"Jack, It's me. Are you ready?"

"I guess so. As ready as I'll ever be. I just got up," he replied slowly and soberly. Ordinarily, Jack spoke in a much faster, high-pitched voice. I had wondered if the change reflected resoluteness, or what. Had he taken something?

"It's a little past nine, now," I said. "You start getting ready; you can't be late. No flat tires, no dead batteries, no changes in plans, no distractions. Do you understand?"

"Yes, everything's all right. I'll be there, don't worry. I'll be there," he grumbled.

I paused momentarily while searching my mind for any missing details. Was there anything unclear, anything left out? I couldn't think of anything, but I couldn't believe it was finally reaching an end. I couldn't forget how the previous plans had failed. Jack had failed in the hall outside of the homicide office, and he had failed at the news conference in the basement assembly room. *This is it. It has to be. It has to work now.* There was nothing else I could say or do, so I said, "Okay." Then I ran through his instructions one last time. He confirmed his acknowledgment so I ended with, "I'll see you later. I won't call back. You're on your own from right now. And don't speak to me or Jerry; you don't know us."

"Don't worry," was his only reply.

Later, Jack would tell me he thought he would ease his nervousness by reading the morning newspaper. It was almost ten when he realized that he had fingered his way through most of the paper but had no idea of what he had read. A bit peeved with himself, he tossed the remaining sections aside and went into the kitchen. He routinely started to prepare breakfast before he realized he wasn't hungry. He returned to the living room turned on the TV and sat down to wait.

His waiting was interrupted at 10:19 a.m. by the telephone. He said he answered because he thought it might have been me. Who else would call? But I said I wouldn't call again.

He said he answered the call, and it went something like this.

"Hello," and the long distance operator confirmed a collect call.

"That you, Jack?" a female voice asked. "This is Karla."

Jack answered, "Oh yeah, Karla. How are you? What's going on?"

She sighed, "Jack, I hate to bother you, but I've got a problem. You always said that if I ever needed anything—"

"Well, what's wrong, Karla? I gave you some money last night."

"I need a little help, Jack. I need about a hundred dollars for about a week or so."

"A hundred bucks! Karla, I don't have that kind of cash on me; just a few bucks. You know I leave the receipts in the safe. I couldn't use that money anyway, and the bank's closed; it's Sunday."

But she said, "How much could I borrow, Jack? Could I get twenty-five? I'm sorry, but I really do need some help."

"I could let you have twenty-five if that would help. Where are you?"

"I'm in Fort Worth, and twenty-five will help a lot; I'll pay you back just as soon as I can."

"I've got a couple of things to do. I'll run by the telegraph office and wire you the money. It will probably be ready for you to pick it up sometime after twelve or twelve-thirty, I'd guess."

Karla said, "Thanks," and hung up.

He checked his schedule mentally. It was almost ten-thirty. If he left now he could go by the telegraph office. He remembered that it was on the corner of Main and Pearl Expressway, just east of the Municipal Building, *right where I'm going*, he remembered. No problem. He finished dressing, picked up his revolver, opened it, looked at it, closed it, then checked himself in the mirror. He studied what he saw. He then looked back at his two-inch barrel .38 revolver. I wonder what he thought about what he saw; Jack Ruby, a chubby loser, but not for long? As strange as it seemed to him, he was beginning to feel the part. He thought, *By God, I'll show them!*

Jack said goodbye to his roommate, George Senator, left his apartment, taking his dachshund, Sheba, with him, and walked to his car in the apartment parking lot.

It was a little past 10:30 a.m. His route to town took him along Thornton Freeway into the downtown area, a course he had followed uncounted times. Following the freeway to northbound Stemmons Freeway, he exited at the Triple Underpass. Turning right onto Main Street, he said he glanced at the assassination site off to his left. It was crowded with bystanders. That bothered him. He watched momentarily, then continued east on Main through Dealey Plaza and toward the telegraph office, a route choice that would take him past the police station at Main and Harwood. Since he was to park in the alley that serviced both the Municipal Building and the telegraph office, he planned to turn right off Main at Pearl Expressway, then right into the alley and park. Then he would go to the telegraph office and wire the money, then return and wait for my signal at the door.

As he passed the police station, he noticed through the Main Street driveway entrance a large crowd gathering in the basement. He slowed down and responded to a sudden thought. It was just a little past eleven. If he parked in the alley now, he would have almost a thirty-minute wait. Someone might get suspicions. Impulsively, he cut left into a public parking lot, sat there a minute, locked his car, leaving Sheba, his dog, inside, and walked across the street to the Western Union telegraph office. He told me he brought his dog both out of fondness and to suggest he had no intentions other than to return home after he sent the money order. I mentally complemented his clever reasoning. That could be considered an indication of no pre-meditation on his part. He entered the lobby, and at the counter he gave the clerk the twenty-five dollars and a couple of dollars for the service charge. He inquired as to how soon it would be available in Fort Worth. The clerk replied that it should be en route in ten to fifteen minutes. Jack noted the time as he turned to leave. It was 11:17 by Western Union time.

Jack's method of getting into the basement caused the Warren Commission and myriad others a lot of argument over the years. I'm sorry that my idea for Jack to claim he had come down the Main Street ramp caused some embarrassment for the officer on duty there; he's a good man. But I understand that he won a civil case that proved he wasn't negligent. I hope we're even.

* * *

At eleven-fifteen I was feeling apprehensive so I decided I should go up to homicide and check the schedule, just to be sure. On the third floor, I stopped in the men's room as I might not have the time later. Besides, my anxiety was giving me a problem. When I entered the homicide office it seemed strangely quiet and empty; I thought it should have been much busier. Walking up to the desk officer, I asked, "Have they all gone up to the jail? It's only eleven-twenty."

"Naw, they're on their way down. They were going to move him at ten but the guy from the

Postal Inspector's Office came to interview him, and that made them run a little late."

I turned without speaking. A little late, I thought. What was going on? I tried to exit calmly, but I could hardly restrain myself. Late? They had said noon! Why hadn't I checked again? Maybe I should have risked staying upstairs all morning instead of going to my office. I ran to the elevators and hit the down button repeatedly. Then I turned around and rushed to the stairs. I would never make it in time!

Since Jack figured that he had almost fifteen minutes to spare, he thought it would be a good idea to check the alley to be sure there was room for him to park before he moved his car. He walked to the rear of the building. There, just as I had described it, was the service entrance to the Municipal Building. He stood there surveying the area, deciding where he should park to be sure of seeing my signal.

He considered that he had finished with time to spare and had nothing better to do than to stand there waiting. But that seemed too risky. Temptation suggested that he walk up to the door for a closer look. No one was in sight. They were all probably in the basement waiting. Impulsively, he tested the door. It was not locked. Pushing it open, he entered but stopped to look at the lock. A piece of match was stuck in the lock holding it open. He wondered; had I already been there? He felt a wave of panic. Was his watch wrong? Had he missed me? No, he had checked the time in the telegraph office. Had he misunderstood me? What should he do? After a brief pause, he said he felt he should take a closer look. Following my earlier instructions, he made his way to the fire escape stairway and down one flight to the basement. He paused again, then shoved the door easily. It opened. He looked across the parking area some sixty-five or seventy feet to the double door entrance into the jail office hallway. All he could see for certain were the backs of newsmen and rows of cameras. Across the driveway were several detectives and few uniformed officers. He said everyone's attention was fixed on the doors. He searched his head for directions. He didn't see me anywhere and couldn't risk talking to me if he had. He tried to think about what he should do. He reasoned that since he was inside, and where he was suppose to be, there was no sense in going back out. But what if it took too long for them to bring him out? It was eleven-thirty. *I can't wait here until noon. I might be spotted.* But nobody was paying any attention to anything but those doors. Then he saw that they were backing a car down the ramp. There's no other choice.

I have to stay. He was sure they were about to bring him out. *Oh, my God! They are bringing him out. There he is. Oh, God! It's him! It's Oswald!*

Jack's right hand was in his pocket as he rushed up to the rear of the crowd. Reporters were chattering into their microphones. Bright flood lights suddenly flared, and a hundred flashbulbs popped. For an instant, he couldn't see. There was just a million little bright violet stars whirling about in his vision. He was possessed by an electric frenzy. *There he is! There's that damn communist, that no good*— Ruby stepped suddenly forward and thrust his revolver toward the prisoner. At point blank range, he fired. In an instant Jack Leon Ruby had registered his name indelibly on the pages of history.

* * *

Later, Jack told me that his movements seemed mechanical. It was as if he had been programmed. He said he couldn't have stopped if he'd tried. And that once he started, the idea of stopping had never occurred to him.

* * *

I had just reached the basement door behind the prisoner escort when I heard the shot and witnessed the commotion. It had been surprisingly quiet, a rather insignificant sound in view of its historic consequence. *What the hell! Who? Was it someone else? This is crazy, all screwed up.*

Then I saw some officers bring the assailant to his feet. It *was* Jack! He *did* it! I don't know how he did it, but he *did* it! I was confused. For a second the whole deal appeared to have blown up in my face, but that lousy little slob did it on his own! He *did* it! He's *pulled it off!* All by himself! Lee Oswald was stretched out on the basement floor, mortally wounded. He died without uttering a word.

CHAPTER TWENTY

AT THE SAFE HOUSE

Tony and Charlie had awakened early that morning at the safe house. They had read the papers and nibbled at breakfast, anything to help pass the time. They were concerned that I had not telephoned them. They worried whether that meant something was wrong. Maybe it meant everything was all right. But I hadn't said I would call. They hoped it meant I was busy and nothing else. Tony said it went like this:

"Why don't you turn on the TV, Charlie. Let's see if anything is on the news." All other programing had been halted out of respect for President Kennedy.

"It's still an hour until the transfer. You want to sit and watch it that long?"

"You got a better idea?"

Charlie didn't reply. He walked over to the set, turned the knob and waited for it to warm up and quit flopping so he could find and tune in on some news. He hoped that at least one of the stations would be carrying the ongoing story. It was ten minutes past eleven, and a news report was showing.

Sitting down, they started with fresh cups of coffee and picked up on the activity at the police station. The newscaster was saying Oswald would be brought out any moment!

"What the hell! Did you hear that? Did he say 'any moment'? It isn't twelve o'clock! That's forty-five minutes too early!" Charlie exclaimed.

"Hold it. That's what he said. Maybe he meant something else. Listen," Tony barked.

The TV camera was transmitting from the police department basement, and was focused on the jail office doors opening from the basement garage. There were several officers in plain clothes and in uniform, clustered about the entrance to the jail office, and facing the doors expectantly.

"What the hell!" Charlie demanded again. "What's going on? Do you suppose Dave screwed up on the time? Do you suppose—"

"How would I know!" Tony yelled at the interruption. "He's been dogging the action by himself. God knows it hasn't been easy, and he has to be exhausted. Maybe he missed something."

"Maybe he's there. Maybe he's on top of things. God, I hope so. If this blows up—" Charlie didn't finish.

"Well, all we can do is watch. You don't see Dave in the crowd, do you? I haven't."

"No, not yet. Do you suppose Dave would—"

"Would be late?" Tony offered.

"No! Do you suppose, uh, suppose—I was thinking, would take care of it himself if it blows up? If that guy of his doesn't connect, do you suppose Dave would do it *himself*?"

"Oh, God, I hope not!" Tony replied.

"That would take Oswald out," Charlie reasoned.

"He's too close to us. That's why it wasn't in the plans, even as a last ditch option," Tony explained

"He wouldn't fink!" Charlie said.

"That's not it, Charlie. The authorities wouldn't believe he was in it by himself. They would look at everybody he's seen or even talked to for the last ten years! They would look for the rest of us. They'd check everybody he ever said hello to. It's too risky. I'd rather leave Oswald in place. At least they would have far less chance of reaching us through him than they would through Dave."

"Look! No! It's *him*. They're bringing *him* out! It's *Oswald!*" Charlie was on his feet, leaning eagerly toward the set. They watched in stunned silence, until that silence exploded.

"Oh, my God," Charlie gasped, in shock despite himself.

"I don't believe it!" Tony said.

They watched this figure surge forward from the crowd of reporters. They saw him raise a pistol. They witnessed Jack Ruby as he assassinated Lee Oswald. Right there in front of their eyes, on live TV. They watched it all. In just bare seconds, Lee Oswald was *gone!*

"Who hit him?" Tony pleaded. "It wasn't Dave, was it?"

"That wasn't Dave, it was a little fat guy."

"You suppose it was his guy? Dave never said enough about him for me to know. Did you pick up on him?" Tony asked.

"No, I'm with you." Charlie answered. "If it isn't his man, who could it be?"

"I guess Dave picked up on the time change and got the word to his man in time. Anyway, things suddenly look better for us."

"Look! They've got him! Looks like a short, stocky guy. Watch for Oswald. See if you can tell how bad he's hit. Watch for Dave!" Charlie directed, peering deeply into the screen.

"Haven't seen him yet. Those detectives went down on him. I wish those people would shut up! I can't hear what the announcer's saying." Tony complained.

They stopped talking for a moment to try to see or hear anything that would answer their questions. The reporter was saying Oswald had been shot and that his assailant had been captured. A little later he reported an ambulance was waiting, that Oswald appeared dead, his left arm dangling lifelessly off the stretcher.

* * *

I stood aside happy that others would handle the shooting. I was limp with both anxiety and relief. Allowing the other detectives a few minutes' head start, I followed them. They had taken Jack upstairs. I certainly wanted to avoid a confrontation, but I needed to catch what word I could. Most of all, I wanted to run. I felt like throwing my hands up, my head back and running as far and as fast as I could. Upstairs Jack was giving an Academy Award performance. He gave his name, and reminded them who he was, but nothing else.

Not wanting to overstay my presence I decided to leave.

While I was en route from the station to the safe house, my mind raced over past events and considered those to come. I couldn't think of any loose ends. That bothered me. With all the confusion intruding on our plans we were bound to have missed something, but I couldn't put my finger on anything that seemed out of place. The next order of business was up to Jack. He would have to select a lawyer. Come to think of it, he hadn't mentioned one.

He would explain how he had seen the crowds on Friday and Saturday, and how he ambled unnoticed into the basement, and on seeing Oswald, how he blacked out. There could be no doubt that he had shot Oswald. That was open and shut. There were too many witnesses. It was broadcast worldwide. It was a question of culpability. To the extent Jack could enlist public sympathy, he was likely to be treated with leniency. But all that was in Jack's hands for the time being. If he played his cards right, we could all come out of this.

When I entered the safe house, I was greeted like a hero. Usually Tony and Charlie were waiting, ready to explode like time bombs—ready to explode if they weren't brought up to date instantly. Now, they met me at the door grinning widely with open arms and unaccustomed hugs.

"How did you do it!" Charlie demanded. "When we found out the time had been changed we almost—"

"I can't believe it," Tony chimed in. "I tell you, I can't believe it! It was—it was a miracle! That's what it was, a miracle!"

I was surprised. "You know what happened? Oh, you heard it on the news. Then you know that Oswald's dead."

"Heard it? Man, we watched it! Where were you?" Charlie asked through a wide grin.

"We sat right there on the sofa and watched the whole damn thing! A cotton picking ringside seat," Tony bragged.,

"I never saw such bedlam! It was wild," said Charlie. "Where were you? We never saw you."

I was startled now. "Oh, no! I never thought about those cameras. Come to think of it, those floodlights were on. I guess they were shooting. Don't ask me how he got in."

"You mean that fat guy? Is he your man?" Charlie fairly yelled. "It was him?"

"Yeah. He's the one, Jack Leon Ruby! I went upstairs to get a last minute confirmation of the time. Oswald wasn't supposed to leave there 'til eleven forty-five. When I got upstairs at eleven-twenty I found out they had already gone down. We must have passed on the elevators or when I was in the john. I got down there in the jail lobby, the hallway, in time to hear the shot. I hadn't even reached the doors. I couldn't believe my eyes when I saw them come up holding Ruby. It was just like something taken out of a movie script! I waited around for a couple of minutes. Didn't want to run into Jack, and I wanted to see if I could find out about Oswald's condition. When I found out he was good as dead, I went upstairs. Ruby's telling his name and who he is but that's all. Has the news said anything else?"

"Naw, that's all there is. They just keep talking about how unbelievable it is," Charlie answered. "Fantastic! That's what it is—Davey boy, you're great!"

"There has been some bad news of a sort," Tony corrected. "Some people have started expressing doubt that this is just a coincidence. They're already talking about some kind of link; something that would connect them both, Oswald and Ruby, with a plot, a conspiracy."

"Let 'em," Charlie huffed. "Oswald can't connect with us except through Freddie. They don't have any idea who Freddie is because Oswald didn't. Now he can't tell 'em, and we won't! Nobody else can. I wouldn't want to work this case! And there's no way to connect Jack Ruby with Oswald, is there? You never said so. Is there any chance?"

"I doubt it," I answered. "When I told him who he was to take care of he didn't say anything about knowing him. I didn't ask him specifically, but I think he would have let on if he had known him. Why wouldn't he?"

Afterwards, it amazed me how so many people were able to dream up nonexistent connections between them. The Warren Commission couldn't even do it, and they had leads.

"Anyway," I commented. "I guess it's time to call the Old Man and cut him in. Have either of you talked to him today?"

They hadn't but they agreed with me and they gave me the honors. As we expected, the Old Man had watched it on TV. Not the original broadcast. He started watching at about 11:45, expecting the transfer to take place at noon. He caught the information when it was being repeated. He was well pleased with our performance, and he would return to Dallas shortly. He left us with a parting suggestion: "Get in to see Jack in some safe way if at all possible; it's important to know firsthand what questions they are asking, what he has said, and how he is doing in the general sense."

Tony checked the role, "I can't. Charlie, you could, and Dave, you could, or maybe your connection?"

I chuckled, "You mean you're not afraid of him anymore?"

Tony grinned, "How could I be? Not only is he in over his head already, face it: He's 'good people' as well! He turned Jack Ruby for us! Not only named him, but he helped us turn him out. Don't know what we'd have done without him!"

Charlie added, "We probably owe a large measure of our overall success to him; we don't have any idea what we'd have done without him; and we don't even know who he is. We've never even seen him! We haven't, have we?"

I assured them, "He *is* 'good people,' and he probably will be glad to help us along the way. He's in a logical position to ask Jack some questions. You know, conduct an interrogation in jail without arousing anyone's curiosity. He works—never mind. I'll get with him and see. I'm sure he will. The best time is going to be tomorrow, sometime early. It's probably a madhouse down there right now, and it would be less likely that he would be noticed tomorrow. Jack's not going anywhere, not for quite a while. He won't be bondable."

We decided it was time to part company, each to go tend to his own business. We had been away long enough. Tony and Charlie left. I called Jerry, who said he would be happy to help.

I left for home, for some companionship, and some rest. Mary would be surprised. It was not quite three in the afternoon, instead of the morning. For a change, I would be home for dinner.

CHAPTER TWENTY-ONE

PREPARATIONS FOR THE TRIAL

Shortly after his arrest, two local lawyers appeared at the jail to interview Jack Ruby. Monitoring events from a distance, the group was unable to know whether Jack had chosen them or they had come seeking the opportunity to land a case that could be very profitable in recognition as well as fees. We decided to let matters ride for a while; best not to push things.

In the early stages, lawyer-client contacts are largely routine matters. The client must solicit the lawyer. It isn't ethical for lawyers to solicit business. The terms and conditions must come about in due form and be agreed upon before matters of guilt or innocence are considered. After all, guilt or innocence is of no great consequence at that stage. If the client seeks the lawyer and the lawyer accepts the case, the lawyer doesn't concern himself with moralizing about his client's conduct. His task, in the simplest of terms, is to ensure a fair trial and hopefully a successful defense. Guilt has nothing to do with it. The first lawyer dropped out, and Don Thomas remained

Meanwhile, Bill Alexander, the chief felony prosecutor for the district attorney, was in the middle of the case. He had entered the action within minutes after the assassination by reporting to the book depository from his office in the nearby County Court Building. And he had reported to the scene of Tippit's murder in Oak Cliff. Later, he was present when police searched Oswald's living quarters. Seldom had the district attorney's office been so immediately available to directly assist in the investigation of a crime it would subsequently prosecute.

I was smugly pleased to hear that the assumptions our group had hoped for were developing as planned. Detectives had found a quantity of communist literature in Oswald's quarters, and they had found the hiding place for his rifle when they had met his Russian wife, Marina, and had searched the Irving quarters where she lived. They had learned of Oswald's earlier defection and of his pro-Castro activities. It was logical to assume that he had assassinated the President. This was reinforced when he killed Tippit in an effort to perfect his escape. It was an added bonus when it was learned that

Oswald had attempted to kill General Walker. It tended to prove that Oswald was capable of planning and conducting a capital murder. Our belated complements to Freddie.

It is unbelievable the number of people who have tried to show Oswald didn't kill Tippit. How could it have been otherwise? Oswald's entire behavior supports his guilt. Everything was wholly inconsistent with an innocent person. This is especially true considering the urgency of his frantic behavior, and that it all happened in conjunction with the assassination of the President, in his presence. In other words, consider what had happened and then what he did.

Detectives and federal agents had been busy trying to find a link between Oswald and Ruby. That was the greatest point of stress for our situation. Jerry and I were the only contact between the group and Ruby. Jerry couldn't implicate the group, and I wouldn't. Theoretically, then, there was no link that could be discovered. Nevertheless, efforts to find such a link were watched with anxious caution. If Jack held together, so would the conspiracy. If not, would we be able to manage things?

A profile of Jack Ruby was forthcoming. Born into poverty on March 25, 1911, in Chicago, the product of an unsettled family, he had spent his life trying to "be somebody." He craved quality, class, and dignity, according to his perceptions. In his own perverted way, he made his life a quest for class. Nothing made him happier than recognition from people he considered to be important, people whom he felt had position and class. He even changed his Jewish name from Rubenstein to Ruby to avoid what he considered to be a social stigma.

Now, some new information was beginning to emerge. One police commander, for instance, remembered that Jack had once accused him of arresting him only as a means of harassment because the commander "knew" Ruby was a communist. It remained to be determined where the collection of information would lead, if it led anywhere. In such well-publicized crimes, informants appear from anywhere and everywhere, each with "absolutely indispensable" information. Some are motivated by publicity. Some are well-intentioned citizens, some are harboring grudges, and some are plain crazy. Then there are a few who have viable information. All the offerings had to be tested and qualified. This was the present state of affairs. Was Jack an undercover or covert communist agent? Was he a party to a plot? Did he know Oswald in the past? Had he engineered the whole thing, or was he acting on orders from higher up? Did he kill Oswald to silence him? Was he a hired hit man? Or was it a sudden impulse? There were a great many questions to be checked out, just as the Warren Commission did.

Lawyer Thomas advised Jack to say that he had killed Oswald impulsively as an act of compassion, that he wanted to spare the President's family the ordeal of returning to Dallas for a trial, that he saw Oswald's sneering face and felt that he was unworthy of any consideration and that he ought to be punished. Thomas felt that they could live with something on that order. If they could pick a reasonable jury, formulate some human appeal and stimulate public sympathy, Jack should receive a light sentence. Thomas considered the issue of insanity but Jack wouldn't hear of it. No! He wasn't crazy, and he wouldn't be branded as crazy! The defense of irresistible impulse wouldn't work either. That had been tried before and usually failed. Jack had received quite a volume of mail, largely favorable. He was the center of attention and pleased with the glory. So far, things were working out according to earlier speculation.

I had even confided to Jerry, "That miserable little S.O.B. is probably going to come out of this, do you realize that? He really is going to be famous and probably rich. At least, he'll be well off. He's going to do the short side of a five-year hitch and walk away smelling like a rose. And you *know* there will be a book deal, and probably a movie! Can you believe that?"

Then, an unexpected problem entered the picture. Melvin Belli, a flamboyant, notorious showman lawyer, known for his flashy dress style and courtroom tactics, arrived from San Francisco to head the defense team. It was uncertain just who had been instrumental in retaining his services but he was there and he took charge. Don Thomas remained, and Horace Hanna, a lawyer from the Piney Woods of Texas, was added as a third member of the defense team. Belli's appearance threw earlier speculations into confusion. His fame was largely based on tort cases: he dearly loved to tackle the big insurance lawyers and win generous sums for his injury claimants. While he had handled criminal cases, they were not his principal practice.

It wasn't long before the picture became clear. Belli's tremendous success in tort law was a product of his showmanship and his knowledge of medical issues. He knew his law, he knew how to conduct his case, and he could argue medical-legal questions with the best of doctors and lawyers. Perhaps Ruby felt he could be publicized best by this well-qualified and famous lawyer. Ruby felt kindly toward Don and the other local lawyers, but they just didn't seem to have the necessary class. Melvin Belli had class. He had contacts as well as know-how. He could certainly defend him as well as anyone else, and his fame would amplify Ruby's exposure. And he could not only handle the forthcoming trial, he could handle articles and the inevitable books and movie that would publicize Jack Ruby and his life as well. For a while, Ruby felt he had in Belli what he wanted and needed. For a while.

Belli would seek a change of venue. Dallas had shown its colors. How, he argued, could Jack Ruby get a fair trial in Dallas, the *capitol of hate*? There was no love lost over Oswald's death, neither was there any love for his killer. Since the assassination, Dallas had been sharply and frequently criticized in the national media. Belli believed that Dallasites would be anxious to convict and execute Ruby as a public offering; a living sacrifice; the city's apology for the death of the President.

The killing had occurred on live TV in full view of uncounted millions. TV and magazines had shown and preserved the event for those who had not seen the killing live. The coverage was worldwide, a permanent reminder for posterity.

In denying the request for a change of venue, Judge Joe Brown held that the range and extent of coverage likely precluded finding any jurisdiction in the state wherein twelve citizens eligible for jury duty had not seen the evidence of the crime, discussed it, and formed some sort of opinion. The issue, then, was not whether a pristine jury could be seated, but whether a jury could be selected that would guarantee Ruby a fair and impartial trial. Judge Brown was satisfied that the lawyers, exercising skill and diligence, could seat a jury in compliance with the law. The motion for change of venue was denied.

Belli really hadn't expected and perhaps hadn't really wanted the change of venue. It was clear to him that Brown wanted the trial. Denial of the motion served a purpose for Belli. He had his first cause for an appeal. Besides, a quiet trial in a remote court would sacrifice some of the spectacular and highly valuable notoriety that would come from a heated trial in Dallas. Such sensationalism was his forte. No, Belli was not just defending Ruby, he was getting ready to try the entire city. This was no more than the end of Act One.

Jack's romance with Melvin Belli was brief. He felt a measure of reserve toward this famous lawyer, but he did appreciate his reputation. Now, he was experiencing feelings of disenchantment. Henry Wade, the district attorney, had taken personal charge of the prosecution. But that didn't worry Jack either. He knew Wade and Alexander by their first names; they had been acquaintances, "friends," for years. They wouldn't hurt him. They had to prosecute him, that was their job. They were pros, and he wouldn't have it any other way. Belli couldn't understand Jack's attitude, and Jack couldn't explain it. But Belli was adamant. The buddy-buddy crap had to stop.

"My God," he insisted, "These people are the enemy. They are out to kill you, and you are eaten up with childish hero worship."

Belli's attitude upset Jack. Dallas was Jack's adopted home, it was *his* town. It had been good to him. He loved it. It had made him what he perceived himself to be today, and he was counting on Dallas for his future. The last thing he wanted to do was to make enemies, certainly not among the important people, in this city. But Belli wanted to involve Dallas in the trial; brand it as a city of hate. Jack objected, but it was a wasted effort. Belli was running the show according to *his* script. His plans didn't include any "Mister Nice Guy" acts. Their strained relationship peaked when Belli revealed his intended defense: insanity!

"No!" Jack raged. "I'm not crazy! What are you trying to do to me? I've got to live with these people! They're my friends—my business—my life! You're trying to kill me!"

In total exasperation, Belli retorted, "Me kill you? I'm trying to save you. I'm the only one who can. You've got problems! But if you'll trust me, we can make it. If anyone's going to kill you, it's you. The only thing you have to do is listen to me. Do what I tell you and keep your mouth shut. Every time you pop off you hurt yourself. If you expect me to save you, you have to listen to me. Do what I say, nothing else. You've got to trust me!"

Melvin Belli explained his strategy to his associates. "The M'Naughten Rule is not and never has been a rational test of sanity. I don't like it, I never have, and I won't use it. Listen carefully now: 'Psychomotor Epilepsy.' Does that mean anything to either of you?"

It didn't, and he knew it wouldn't.

Belli explained, "Psychomotor epilepsy deals with a theory of organic brain damage. It can result in a disturbance in the electrical rhythms from the central nervous system. This can cause convulsive acts; it can cloud consciousness; it's a form of amnesia lasting from moments to days. In such a mental state, the actor has no control, thus no legal responsibility or accountability for his behavior."

Horace Hanna was properly impressed. While he had never heard of psychomotor epilepsy and didn't really understand it, he was confident in Belli's judgment.

Don Thomas wasn't so quick to join in. "I share your feelings on the M'Naughten Rule; it leaves too much room for argument. Juries are too easily confused; they expect to see a raving lunatic. If the defendant sits quietly in court, it's too easy for them to presume he's sane."

"What do you suggest?" Hanna asked. "You don't favor some kind of irresistible impulse or something on that order, do you?"

"No, I don't favor any form of sanity issue. It's too hard to get around the law. M'Naughten's 'knowledge of right from wrong' test with an understanding of the consequences of an act is too broad. Many acts seem insane—that is, no 'sane' person would act this way or that— but everyone who acts *insanely* certainly isn't *insane*. We could lose our boy for sure," Thomas concluded.

"Not so with psychomotor epilepsy," Belli assured them. "It's new. We will amaze the jury, we'll overwhelm them! We'll introduce some unimpeachable medical experts to support our claim. That will catch these cornball hicks flatfooted. There's no way they can mount an attack against it because they don't know anything about it. Dallas needs to be educated, and I'm ready to teach them! What do you think?"

Hanna agreed. A brilliant new defense in such a widely publicized trial would make national, no, international legal history. Although it was inconsistent with his usual style, Hanna endorsed Belli's proposal.

"I hate to disagree," Thomas stated. "But I do! I must! I don't think you understand the people around here. This is a murder where the accused killed someone who the people don't really mind being killed. Some even feel like he needed killing. The press, the out-of-town press, are howling for Ruby's scalp, but they're the only ones, and they won't be on the jury. They don't have a dog in this fight! I believe our best bet is a simple, uncluttered trial. Play to the people. Our boy was emotionally upset, concerned for the President's family, annoyed by a sneering Oswald. He blacked out, no premeditation.

Then we put him on the stand to say he's sorry. That's all the people want: *I'm sorry!* I know these people. I know what kind of jurors they make. I know that's our best bet."

"Best bet? Best bet for what? Ten, maybe twenty years?" Belli demanded.

"No more than five, I'd guess," Don replied.

"Why sell him out for even five? What I'm proposing will walk him. *Not Guilty!* Now what's wrong with that?"

Don wasn't sold on the idea but Belli's dominant presence prevailed. With the issue grudgingly settled, they prepared for the next act, jury selection.

* * *

February 1964 ushered in the tedious, time consuming process of jury selection. The cold and dreary days were enlivened by the new business in Judge Brown's court room. Jury selection is an art and a science more than a legal procedure. Wade and Alexander, those two "hick lawyers," would be at Belli's mercy. Their overdue lesson in trial tactics was about to begin. Belli aimed his heavy artillery while the hick lawyers sat back and prepared to cut him to ribbons with their dull pocket knives.

Belli didn't want a jury of Dallasites. Those narrow-minded idiots wouldn't understand "psychomotor epilepsy." He preferred more sophisticated suburbanites from the fringe cities who could appreciate his defense. Wade and Alexander wondered whether Belli had given any thought to where these fringe city suburbanites came from. They were, for the most part, transplants who had prospered well enough to buy homes in the suburbs, but who fundamentally *were* Dallasites. If they were noticeably different, it was that they were even more conservative.

Belli watched the hick lawyers carefully. He could read the opposition like a book. He wouldn't waste his strikes needlessly; he would let the prosecutors work for him. Wade and Alexander weren't very careful. They telegraphed their positions conspicuously and regularly. Belli kept his antenna beamed in on their signals. Occasionally, the boys would unconsciously shake their heads displaying their disapproval of a potential juror. Belli reasoned that if the prosecutors were so unsatisfied with a prospect, that prospect could be suitable for the defense. Belli accepted some of these as jurors. Occasionally, the prosecution telegraphed incautious enthusiasm for a candidate. Belli promptly struck those. Occasionally, the hicks would pass along an undesirable candidate. Belli wouldn't fall for that; he'd use a challenge. The fencing match continued for days with Belli firing salvo after salvo at point blank range. Two weeks later it was over. Belli had taught those hayseeds a lesson in jury selection. He had selected an ideal jury—*for the prosecution!*

"That fella sure knows how to pick a jury," Alexander confessed.

"I couldn't have done better," Wade agreed. "If the prosecution ever had a capital case jury, this is it."

"We really can't take any credit, though," Alexander reminded him. "We had some real whiz-bang help from that snazzy lawyer. He really deserves all the credit."

The scene was set for the next act.

CHAPTER TWENTY-TWO

THE TRIAL OF JACK RUBY

The prosecution's case was not so expansive, as I remember. There was no question that Ruby had killed Oswald. Not only had he done it in the presence of the homicide division, he had done it on worldwide live television. He had been immediately subdued, disarmed, and arrested. The problem was to show the degree of the act. If he was wholly unaware of what he was doing, in other words insane, he was legally not responsible for his action and thus was innocent of a crime. There was no chance for a claim of accident, mistake, or justification. All that remained, other than the sanity issue, was to determine whether or not the act was premeditated. Where there is no premeditation, the law provides for a more lenient sentence for a lesser crime. Where the act is pre-planned and carried out, the penalty could include death in the electric chair. The state, of course, went for the whole score: capital murder. This was the usual process, to aim as high as possible. You can back off if necessary, but you can't increase the charge once it's lodged.

* * *

To show premeditation, Alexander produced witnesses who testified that Jack had made various comments Friday and Saturday that Oswald needed killing. While that alone might not prove premeditation, it could show a trend of thought that logically could evolve into the act of murder, especially if there were other supporting factors. Next, Alexander produced witnesses who testified to Jack's frequent acts of violence; that people who trespassed on his rules of conduct in his clubs suffered quick and often furious physical assault. Further testimony told of Jack's common practice of carrying a gun. In a further effort to develop premeditation the prosecution suggested that Jack had visited the police station on Friday carrying his gun, presumably for the purpose of killing Lee Oswald. Being unable to commit the act, he had returned Sunday and succeeded. The prosecution supported this allegation by showing that Jack, having no authority to be in the basement of the police station, had awakened early on Sunday morning, something he didn't usually do, armed himself with his revolver, and drove downtown. To complete the deed, he slipped into the basement for one intended purpose: murder. Case closed.

Wade and Alexander had carefully considered the possibility of a conspiracy. But evidence, however suggestive, was totally lacking. To have introduced testimony mentioning Ruby's possible role as part of a plot when no tangible evidence could be introduced would seem more like a witch-hunt and an effort to prejudice the charge with an irresponsible implication. It probably wouldn't be admitted into evidence anyway, and such a maneuver could backfire. However, if a clean trial could convict Jack Ruby of premeditated murder, there was no worse offense for which he could be convicted. No more exacting penalty could be imposed. Should later evidence link him to a conspiracy it would be a moot issue so far as trying and punishing Jack was concerned. He couldn't be executed twice, so why cloud the issue?

Thus far the hick lawyers had convinced Melvin Belli that his early assessments of them were correct. The yokels hadn't known the first thing about jury selection. And they were crude. They frequently referred to the judge as "Joe," and once or twice they even instructed the judge on a point of law. *What a way to run a court*, he thought. Yes, he was ready to educate these people; the whole rotten city. And with his unique defense, he would make legal history. What a book it would make! It wouldn't be Belli's first bestseller, but probably his best!

Wade and Alexander were satisfied that they had sized up Belli with equal skill. Alexander described it succinctly. "He might be a tall and well-feathered rooster where he comes from, but he ain't even a fuzzy little chick down here."

* * *

With the prosecution concluded, Belli was ready for the defense. He brought on for examination, his professional expert witnesses, psychiatric professionals with the necessary credentials and expertise to offer the testimony through which he would develop psychomotor epilepsy (PE).

Belli's opening questions and the answers introduced PE before he enlarged on details:

Belli: "What is behavior?"

Witness: "It is any manner of conduct or action engaged in by a living organism."

Belli: "In human organisms, what governs behavior?"

Witness: "The brain."

Belli: "How does the brain do this?"

Witness: "Through electrical impulses to the central nervous system."

Belli: "Ordinarily, then, in a functional human being, the brain transmits information and the central nervous system carries out the brain's orders."

Belli summarized. "That is a simple but accurate statement. Ordinarily, that's how people come to behave. Now without moralizing or qualifying behavior as good or bad, what would happen with regard to one's behavior patterns if the brain were damaged?"

Witness: "If the injury were severe enough it could cause absolute dysfunction. That is, all usual function could cease. The person could remain alive but, depending on the area of the brain and the extent of the injury, the person could become non-functioning. In effect, one could become a living vegetable. The person could require life-support equipment if he is to remain alive."

Belli: "That describes more massive damage. What about the more minute form of injury?"

Witness: "Perhapsnothing. Perhapssome minute damage would never be recognized in one's behavior. Not even by those who are in very close contact. Medical practitioners might not suspect the damage. On the other hand, there could be changes ranging from barely perceivable to highly conspicuous. There are a great many variables to consider."

Belli: "What about frequency?"

Witness: "Again, there are variables. Behavioral changes could range from intermittent to continuous in the event of severe injury and in the event of minute injury, perhaps never. Also, there might be episodes of dysfunction. The person might in many or most ways behave ordinarily. Then, on occasion, behave inappropriately or even in a berserk manner."

Belli: "Then is there no uniform standard of behavior for one having minute brain damage?"

Witness: "No. In fact, minute brain damage might not be suspected, and it might not readily show up in tests."

Belli: "How would one test for such brain damage?"

Witness: "An electroencephalogram, properly taken and expertly read could, on occasion, show evidence of even minute damage."

Belli: "Since behavioral change depends not only on the extent of damage but the location or the site of the damage as well, explain what is meant by 'location.'"

Witness: "Different portions of the brain regulate different human function; sight, speech, taste, movement, and so on. Thus, damage confined to a specific area would cause an effect in the function regulated by that area of the brain."

Belli pressed on: "Directing your attention to the temporal lobe, what behavior would be consistent with minute injury there?"

Witness: "He might experience episodes of abnormal behavior; behavior inconsistent with social norms, with 'norms' meaning behavior that the public has learned to expect from a person as a member of a society. Or one might act in a psychopathic manner ranging from anti-social to irrational, to aggressive outbursts."

Belli starts to close in: "What would cause these psychopathic outbursts?"

Witness: "Psychomotor activity—that is, muscular activity arising from conscious mental activity, one would experience some degree of dysfunction. In other words, physical activity would be to some degree disassociated from ordinary mental activity or mental regulation."

Belli: "Why?"

Witness: "Because of epileptic activity."

Belli: "What is meant by 'epilepsy' and 'epileptic activity?'"

Witness: "Epilepsy describes disorders in the flow of electronic rhythms of the central nervous system."

Belli: "How do these epileptic episodes occur?"

Witness: "They usually are observed as convulsive attacks wherein the actor has no control over behavior, nor is there knowledge of events during, or conscious recollection of events following such epileptic attack."

Belli feels he is tightening his noose: "What causes these attacks?"

Witness: "These attacks, that is to say, the origin of epileptic episodes are not fully understood. There is strong belief that events such as fatigue, stress, or excitement can promote an attack."

Belli: "Do epileptic attacks occur in a predictable manner such as every so often or with any regularity?"

Witness: "No. In fact, many people possess a latent potential for epilepsy but never experience an identifiable epileptic episode or seizure. There is much that isn't known about epilepsy, and it is a grossly misunderstood situation."

Belli: "Does the epileptic person have any forewarning of, or control over the seizure?"

Witness: "Probably not. They usually occur with no controllable warning. That is to say, they just happen. One can't avoid episodes by will. Neither can one will them away. They come, and they must run their course."

Belli: "If a person experienced some genetic problem or injury to the brain, then, that person, without warning or ability for self control, could suddenly and unexpectedly behave in a violent manner because of a problem between the brain and the conduct of the nervous system?"

Witness: "Yes."

Belli had made his point.

Wade and Alexander were certain that everybody who had a friend or relative who had unfortunately experienced epilepsy now hated Belli's guts. In his effort to create a sensational defense, Belli had alienated a great number of people and, no doubt, some of the jurors. Wade and Alexander could have rested their case then and probably have won a conviction. But it would have been Belli's conviction, not theirs. They would in effect be sentencing Ruby for Belli's conduct. However, they owed the state a trial so they proceeded with a brief cross-examination.

Alexander: "Was this Ruby's first episode of 'psychomotor' whatever it was?"

Witness: "This is unknown."

Alexander: "Could he have been that way all his life? Could he have been born with an injury or defect; and could he have gone all his life until now without showing any outward signs of his having any kind of problem?"

Witness: "Yes."

Alexander: "That is until now. Now that he needs some kind of an excuse—uh, explanation for—never mind. Let me phrase my question this way. You have no evidence to support the opinion that the defendant does, in fact, have this psycho-whatever, do you?"

Witness: "No."

Alexander: "Is there any evidence that can be offered that would connect this so-called condition, and the act with which the defendant is accused?"

Witness: "No."

Alexander: "You can't say, then, that this so-called condition actually resulted in the alleged act, or that the accused actually has it, can you?"

Witness: "No."

Alexander: "Thank you." Alexander concluded his cross examination.

Belli wasn't bothered by the prosecution's assault on his argument. That was to be expected. His next expert would help settle the prosecution's challenge.

In his examination, Belli asked his expert witness, "Did you conduct an electroencephalograph examination of the accused?"

The witness answered, "Yes."

Producing a yards-long strip of graph paper, Belli offered it to his witness. "Is this graph a recording of your examination?"

"Yes. That is my electroencephalogram."

"Would you explain the significance of this chart and your examination?" Belli asked.

"Electrodes were connected to the subject. Through these connections electronic waves, brain waves, were transmitted to the electroencephalograph. The machine translated its reading of the subject's brain waves into the tracings on the charting paper, this electroencephalogram."

"And what did you conclude from your examination?" Belli asked, his expression evidencing smug satisfaction.

"There's evidence of some damage in the temporal lobe."

Jack's reaction to his lawyer's defense was obvious. He hadn't liked the idea from the start. Now, he was seething. I was worried. What if Jack became so vexed he lost his composure? So far, he had conducted himself even better than we dared hope. He had become world famous. Most of his mail had expressed favor with his act. Jack didn't want that to change. He had killed a demon: he had become a celebrity.

At first, he had exalted in this strange new role. Although he had been blackmailed and induced into it, he had now assumed the nature of his role. He was headed for the top of the world.

Was he a communist? Was he an agent for organized crime? Was he a party to a conspiracy? No, no, no! He was Jack Leon Ruby, a simple Jew, a good American. He did what any red-blooded American would have—*should* have done!

Had he shamed the Jewish people? No! He had shown the world that a Jew had guts. So what if Jews are by their usual nature quiet and passive? That didn't mean they were gutless or cowardly! No! He had shown the world!

Had he shamed Dallas? No! It was his town! He loved it! It was the best place in the world! Outsiders blamed Dallas for the President's death. Dallas hadn't killed the President! That little smirking, sneering communist bastard Oswald, did it! And he, Jack Leon Ruby—he took care of him. That's how it was here. You took care of business. He didn't bring shame to Dallas: he had canceled her debt!

Now, that damn lawyer is trying to say I'm crazy! Well, I'm not crazy! I know what I did, and I know why I did it! That dumb son of a bitch! He's going to ruin everything. He's out to make Dallas hate me. He's already made my old pals, Wade and Alexander, mad at me; he's made the police mad at me. Dear God, what's he trying to do?

Melvin Belli offered further expert testimony regarding the reliability of the electroencephalograph and the meaning of its tracings. He was certain that with his astute examination the hick lawyers would show their lack of sophistication. Belli had offered the best of expert testimony, but all the hicks could do was make fun of it by asking foolish questions, proving their ineptness.

Alexander wanted to know whether outside interference such as fluorescent lights wouldn't affect the outcome of a reading. Belli's expert witness assured Alexander that the test had been administered a safe distance away from fluorescent lights. Then Alexander made some off-hand remark about ceilings and walls also having some kind of "hums" if one cared to listen.

Belli chalked all this up to cornball foolishness. So what if Alexander had found out about "fluorescent light effect." That didn't show much in the way of research. Humming walls? Really!

What Belli didn't know was that when the jury retired. its members moved quickly to the nearest walls, leaned over and fastened their ears, eager to listen in on Alexander's "hum." This, they had remembered. But what did they remember about Melvin Belli's exacting expert witnesses' testimony?

Summation and charges to the jury ended at 1:06 in the morning of March fourteenth, "a marathon more than a trial," Belli observed. Judge Brown was anxious to bring the trial to a conclusion so he kept the last session going until both sides had concluded their presentations and he had instructed the jury. The parties to the trial retired for the night, exhausted, but glad that much was over.

The next morning, the sequestered jury arose, ate breakfast, and assembled for their deliberation. Belli was up and about early. Dressing carefully, he ate a light breakfast and journeyed to the courthouse to test the air. But, to his enormous surprise, he was informed that the jury had reached its verdict.

He had realized that the first trial could end in a guilty verdict. Accordingly, he had already begun to prepare his careful groundwork for an appeal. He would get the next trial to be held out of Dallas and in a court rather than a circus, and he would enjoy the satisfaction of having had a superior court support his argument.

But, the jury had reached its verdict in just a couple of hours. A surprised Melvin Belli was excited. He was certain that meant they had ruled *not guilty* . He knew that they couldn't condemn a man to death after such an indifferently short period of deliberation. Hallelujah! He had won!

Returning to the court and radiating his pleasure, he took his position next to his client. He didn't even take the time to return to his hotel to change into his usual courtroom attire.

His exuberance was brief. The verdict, "Guilty," the penalty, "Death."

Melvin Belli raged at the jury, "My congratulations! You have struck a lasting blow for bigotry and injustice. The people of Dallas may be justly proud of you. You have served them well." To the media and anyone listening he added, "This trial and verdict is a disgrace to the American justice system. There is no justice here. This defendant has been railroaded by a kangaroo court!"

In departing the courtroom, he refused Judge Brown's extended hand. "No you have too much blood on your hand for my taste."

He then prepared to leave Dallas, stopping only to give spontaneous press releases to the hordes of reporters outside. There was still method to his madness. With rare perfection, he was playing his role leading into the next act: the appeal. Leaving his associates to work out the details, Melvin Belli left for a brief vacation.

CHAPTER TWENTY-THREE

REGROUPING AT THE LODGE

With the trial over, the Old Man called for the group to meet him at the lodge. It was cold for the middle of March. The trees had only started to bud so the atmosphere, while quiet, was depressing. Some sunshine would have been welcome but low, heavy, clouds persisted, effusing a constant mist.

The Old Man got straight to the point. "Lads, it is time for us to compare notes. We need to share what we know and what we expect so we might develop our strategy. Dave, how tight a hold do you have on Ruby? That situation could reverse on us since he was given the death penalty. What do you think?"

"I guess anything could go wrong if you consider that we don't have any guarantees. Actually, it doesn't seem too bad." Thinking back on what Jerry had told me, I continued, "My guy got with him immediately after the trial. He had fully expected Jack to jump on him. You follow the thought; how we let Jack down, how he got the death penalty after we told him five years? Well, it didn't happen. Jack was mad, but he was mad at Melvin Belli and mad because he felt like he was made to look like a fool. He's hollering for a polygraph so he can prove he isn't lying and he isn't loony. Can you believe that?"

"No! Absolutely, no! If he gets on the box he can blow it for all of us!" Tony exclaimed, and the rest joined in with their agreements.

"I don't think so," I said. "Not now, I think he's told himself his story so many times he's come to believe it. But even more important, I think the poor guy is flipping out. He's so unstable I'm not sure they could even get a good test. Even if they did test him, they would probably declare it to be invalid. I think he's become too unstable. Since he's been in jail and on trial, there's been a change in his personality. He's not the same. He has never said a word about us, or what we had talked about. He has said he wants a new lawyer, though. He's madder'n Cootie Brown at that Melvin Belli for trying to make him out to be crazy."

"I don't think we should take that situation too lightly," the Old Man said. "Whether he's unbalanced or not, a polygraph examination is too risky. He could make statements that could prove embarrassing. Statements that would have to be checked out. What if it started someone thinking; started someone to try to do a follow-up, and they got lucky? Even though there is no real connection with Mr. Ruby and the group, I would rather not risk an accident. That puts more on your shoulders, Dave."

"Yes sir," I agreed, "but I really don't feel too threatened. However, if we could stall or prevent a polygraph without being obvious, I would feel better."

"Stall, maybe, but not prevent," Charlie corrected. "If anybody made that an issue it might attract attention." The others agreed.

Sensing an opportune time, Tony rose and walked to the front of the group for the most prominent position to speak. "I've been watching the Warren Commission's activity as closely as possible, and have been able to do a little business with them," Tony offered. "Hopefully, I can stay close enough to keep in touch with their plans. So far, they don't have a firm game plan. They are still considering strategies, priorities, and politics. Can you imagine the immense job they have to do? They have to do a rundown on Oswald from the day he was born; trace his and his wife's activities, their friends, and their friends' friends, and so on. They have to do a number on the Secret Service security plans, and that's a bad scene because it involves some dirt about agents getting drunk in Forth Worth the night before the assassination. And they have to do a rundown on Ruby. There are rumors about some connection between Oswald and Ruby. Then there's Chicago. You get the picture? They'll be collecting reports all year before anybody sees daylight enough to start making any reasonable decisions and conclusions on directions to take on investigations."

"Have any of you heard the name 'Freddie' in any of this? Or on notes in Oswald's personal effects, anything?" the Old Man wanted to know.

We looked inquisitively at each other, and then assured him that Freddie had so far escaped all attention; it was as though he had never existed.

"Let me run things through and see if everything is covered. Interrupt me if you need to," the Old Man directed. "We assume that no one has any ideas with regard to the existence of our group; Freddie is the sole connection between the group and Oswald; Freddie's out of the picture now, and Oswald is dead. Tony, Freddie can reach you. Is this safe?"

"Yes sir," Tony replied. "He's worked for us before and wants to be able to work again. He won't go after the goose that lays his golden eggs. You paid him well, and really, he isn't that ambitious. With him, it's just the way he makes his living. And if he went sour, there are people who would take him out and he knows it. I guess what I'm trying to say is, he isn't the type to crawfish or get greedy, and he can't afford to start now."

"Very well," the Old Man said, "let's continue. But you stay on top of that, Tony. We might have to 'reach' Freddie before someone else does. I'm sure you understand my meaning. Charlie, what is the Bureau's position?"

"We have Oswald as an ex-Marine who defected to Russia, renounced his citizenship, married a Russian, and had a couple of kids, tried to become a citizen of the USSR, then he asked to return to the States. He lived a quiet life until he got active with the 'Fair Play for Cuba' business, he moved from Fort Worth to Dallas, went to New Orleans, applied for a visa to Mexico, and it seems he planned to go back to Russia by way of Cuba later that year, presumably fleeing from the assassination. A lot of pro-communist literature was in his room as well as a holster that goes with the pistol he used on Tippit.

The rifle and the pistol have been traced back to him, shows that he bought his guns under the alias, 'Hidel,' and the handwriting analysis confirmed it was actually Oswald. I don't know if this will deserve any attention, but the police department's paraffin test was positive on the hands but negative on the cheeks. This suggests he could have fired a pistol, but not necessarily a rifle. He really should have had some trace of nitrate on his right cheek if he had fired his rifle. Oh yeah, they found a camera and some photos."

"We haven't had all that success with paraffin testing in recent years; too many ways to get nitrate on yourself, and then again, he could have washed his face," I injected.

"Maybe no one will think to do a test comparison with that old rifle," Tony added. "God knows how bad it might spit. With everything they have to check, and as open-and-shut as this thing is, maybe it won't be considered necessary. Let's move on. What else do you have, Charlie?"

"I guess that's about it." Charlie added. "We have a known communist sympathizer and activist, of a sort, who bought the rifle under an alias, lived in an apartment under an alias and away from his Russian wife. He worked in the building from which the shots were fired, and we have the shell casings and the rifle, *his rifle.* There's been no mention of John. Oswald split immediately after the shooting, rushed to his apartment, got his pistol and started somewhere, was interrupted by Tippit, panicked, killed Tippit and ran. He got caught, resisted, made no statement, denied doing anything, claimed he was being made a patsy, and now he's dead. Oh, yeah, and nothing about our friend, Freddie."

"Someone has mentioned the fact that Oswald's route down Tenth Street would be a reasonable way to go if he were heading for Ruby's apartment. I don't like that," Tony said.

"Best we leave that alone," I suggested. "It isn't likely to go anywhere because Ruby was nowhere near the place at the time; he was probably still at the *Dallas Morning News* building downtown. If someone wants to connect them, let them do it on their own; I don't see how they can since they never knowingly met. If we move with this, it might attract attention."

"Agreed," the Old Man pronounced. "Now, if we may, please continue."

"I was through, sir," Charlie said. "We have a lot of research to do. You know, still doing backgrounds on just about everybody who ever knew or might have known Oswald, and especially whether there's any link with Ruby."

"Is all that necessary with Oswald dead? After all, there can be no trial," the Old Man mused.

"Yes sir. President Johnson's Warren Commission will have to cover all the bases, and tack down every loose end in this kind of investigation. It's even necessary to prove what you can't prove and what didn't happen. Their investigations and conclusions will be scrutinized and challenged for years to come. This will be history's most thoroughly investigated murder. Nothing will escape consideration. But it can't last too long. I understand President Johnson wants some quick results. Now that Ruby's trial is over, they'll pick up speed. They couldn't mess with Ruby before he had his trial, only trace his past and who he knows, things that wouldn't compromise the trial."

"Are there ways for us to have any influence on the progress of this investigation?" the Old Man said.

"Well, sir, it isn't that simple," Charlie responded. "It isn't an investigation; it involves a whole series of investigations. It involves more than one bureau. Tony, Joe, and myself are staying as close as possible within our respective spheres, to see what we can do. But, we can't be pushy. We'll just have to wait and see what develops. You know, fight brush fires."

"I see," the Old Man said. "Are we through with Oswald? Shall we move on to Ruby?"

I started off, "So far it's worked out okay. He's generally considered to be a self-styled pseudo big shot who saw a chance to score really big and did. A lot of people want to believe that he was either in cahoots with Oswald, or that he was someone else's hit-man to shut Oswald up."

"Now why would anyone think that?" Tony smiled.

"Yeah," I said. "Anyway, his story of compassion for the President's family and his blacking out when he saw Oswald was a good trick. It's too bad that slick lawyer came in and screwed it up. In my opinion, when that lawyer ran head-on into the DA with that psychomotor epilepsy deal and tried to get Ruby off as a crazy, he put him in the electric chair: the judge and jury had nothing to do with it."

"It sure seems that way," Charlie agreed. "I don't know all that much about local juries, but when that dude lawyer tried to hang the city, he put the noose on his own client's neck instead. That seemed stupid to me from the start. If I

291

had defended Ruby I would have thrown him on the mercy of the court. If the jury could have had the chance to tell Jack he was a naughty boy, and spanked his hands, they would have been satisfied. Nobody was really mad at him until his lawyer got into that sanity bullshit. Then he got everybody ticked off, even his fellow lawyers, I think."

"That gets me to the present," I put in. "The 'crazy' argument has left Ruby in a real snit. Thankfully, he isn't mad at us, at least not yet. He knows that 'crazy business' stands to queer his future chances. And what's worse, he's stuck in jail for the duration of the appeal. That could take a couple of years. Instead of being about ready to get out, he could just be starting a new trial. And he couldn't very well go back and start over with a 'compassion for the widow/ blackout' defense, not after all that psychomotor business.

"All this is weighing heavily on the poor guy. As I have said before, he's changing, going downhill. His personality definitely isn't the same. No spirit. He isn't rational, he's very inconsistent, and he's dead set on having a polygraph. I guess that wraps it. I expect him to stay pretty much as he is, at least for the time being. I don't know what else we can do."

"I still don't like that polygraph business," the Old Man said. "It is simply too risky. This Mr. Ruby is definitely a weak link. Are there any suggestions?"

The others shifted around, looking at one another for some clue to the other's feelings or intentions. What was he implying about Ruby? They then mumbled their agreement with the Old Man's concern, but offered no answers.

The Old Man surprised them with his response. "I agree." Maybe he hadn't implied that someone should take out Jack Ruby. Then maybe he had. They would never know, because he changed the subject of his conversation.

"What are the conspiracy theorists starting to say? Since there is a chance that some enterprising wizard might stumble onto something, even accidentally, even a wild guess, I feel that we should concern ourselves with what they are saying."

We looked at each other to see who would answer. Tony accepted the chore.

"There are already so many you can't keep up with them, and new ones pop up daily. There are people who swear that they have seen both Oswald and Tippit in Ruby's club. Ruby had a post office box just a few feet away from one Oswald had. That suggests the opportunity for a possible prior acquaintance.

"A Company man observing traffic in Mexico City took a picture that was said to be of 'Oswald' while he was at the Russian Embassy, but in fact it isn't Oswald and it isn't our guy, Freddie, either. But people are asking, who went to Mexico and why? That gives rise to either a second person or a stand-in. There are even some people who say it wasn't even Oswald who came back from Russia, but a Soviet agent. They suggest that the family is keeping quiet because the Russians still have the real Oswald as a hostage.

"Some people claim Ruby is a commie who has been a 'mole' for years, activated now as a hit-man. And a whole lot of shit has been circulated about Jack's supposed friendship with the Dallas Police Department. Some people felt like he was a real influential person there. They use his acquaintances inside the department to support theories that the police were in on a plot.

"Some people don't believe Oswald killed Tippit. And get this: some believe Tippit was a conspirator with the task of killing Oswald but Oswald beat him to it."

That comment gave me a start, but Tony talked on. "Then there's that AP photo that shows Oswald on the front steps of the book depository when the motorcade passed."

"I think there's pretty convincing argument that it was another guy, I think his name is 'Ladyman' or something like that." Charlie said.

"Well, was it Oswald or wasn't it?" the Old Man asked impatiently.

Charlie replied, "I'm afraid it was, or at least might have been. But we need him inside the building. The other guy was in several places during the motorcade; he's satisfied that it was him in the picture and that satisfies us. Even though others have contradicted this, who it is on the steps, the official view is that the guy himself is the best judge as to who it was. He says it's him and that's great for us because Oswald had to be on the sixth floor at that instant. We can be thankful that he and Oswald not only look alike, but were even dressed similarly that day."

Tony resumed his narrative, "As Charlie mentioned, nobody has said anything about John, but some people are of the opinion that someone else was in the book building or somewhere, shooting, mainly because they

JFK CONSPIRACY - THE MISSING FILE

feel that one person couldn't fire that fast, and certainly not that accurately. They feel that Oswald's gun couldn't be fired fast enough and that Oswald couldn't shoot that well. The theory is that Oswald was encountered on the second floor by that motorcycle officer too soon after the shooting to have been able to shoot, hide the rifle, run downstairs, get a Coke and calmly start drinking it. Also, someone said a man was seen running to a station wagon parked on Houston Street—that couldn't have been John; it took too long for him to contact us for him to have gotten out that soon. And there are those who reason that Oswald couldn't have left the building after 12:30 and made it to his place by 1:00 and still had time to run into Tippit by 1:15. And that's usually the reason that some people don't think Oswald killed Tippit."

"Can't people realize that everyone's watch could have had different times? It's not like they were all synchronized," Charlie groaned.

"At the same time," I said, "those people offer no suggestion as to why a guy who was always flat broke splurged for a taxi cab to rush home in the middle of the day, pick up a pistol, put on his jacket, then rush down on Jefferson, throw away his jacket, slip into a movie without paying, and fight like a tiger and try to shoot when one of the officers grabbed him. They've got to be crazy. And why did he leave his ring and most of his money at his wife's place unless he was figuring he wouldn't be coming back?"

"Not necessarily 'crazy,' Davey," the Old Man said. "We do hope, however, that they are not too efficient."

Tony spoke up again, "One theory which persists is that of a second gunman firing from the hill north of Elm Stet, the 'grassy knoll' as some call it. Dave, I think you mentioned a while back that the plaza forms an amphitheater and that there would be echoes. That seems to be what happened. People heard shots from every direction. The more they think about it and what others say, the more some people are gonna try to put a shooter on that hill."

"Wouldn't that frost you," Joe snickered, throwing his hands up in frustration. "What if there was someone up there killing the President? We do all this only to find it could have been left up to someone else with the same idea at the exact same time and location! Is there any chance that could have happened? What are the odds?"

"No way," I assured him. "Too many witnesses. And the more reliable witnesses heard three shots and that's it. A few actually saw the rifle barrel in the window. And there's those men on the fifth floor under Oswald's window who heard the three shell casings being ejected. Also, we had people on the overpass and people who ran up there on the knoll. No one saw anybody there before, during, or after, even though they were looking. Then, there were people right near there who didn't see or hear anyone shooting from behind the fence. No, I don't think it's at all possible. But—"

Tony continued, "We've had people who claim that Ruby was seen in Dealey Plaza, and at Parkland, people who claim past activities such as Ruby being involved in gun running to Cuba. You name it and somebody will swear to it. It goes on and on without end or reason."

"I suppose what we need to do is to let them look 'til their heart's content,' so long as they look in the wrong places and for the wrong things," the Old Man stated. "Let's not interfere with activity that supports conspiracy theorists so long as they are wrong. We want a certain suspicion, even confusion. We want them to connect this with the Cubans if they will. They can suspect others as well, the communists, the mob, labor interests, industrial interests, all of them. While they are busy elsewhere, they are amusing: when they look this way they must be reckoned with. We must be alert to such possibilities and determine how we might best manage events. Joe, how do you find things in Washington?"

Joe rose to his feet, fired up a cigarette, took a long meditative draw, then answered. "Well, sir, I guess it's about as good as we could hope for. The Warren Commission is still trying to get moving, but it will take a lot of time. With the Secret Service, as you know, the 'shit hit the fan' for a while. Our best argument has been budget, 'we do the best we can within our means.' That's a poor way to explain how we lost a President; not enough money to do our jobs."

"I'm particularly concerned with the autopsy," the Old Man interjected. "Your getting the President's remains out of Dallas was an exceedingly shrewd move, Joe. But what's holding up the details on the autopsy? Do they suspect the bullet switch? Is there a problem?"

"I don't think so. I think the holdup is due to sentiments and politics," Joe opined. "How do you reveal the messy details of the gory death of a President? Those people aren't really familiar with the criminal justice system and criminal pathology. And their futures depend on politics more than their performances. No one wants to do anything *indelicate.* They have the autopsy report but they don't know how to release it. I think they are afraid. I think that in addition to their fear of political disfavor, they are afraid they've botched it."

"I've heard the same," Charlie chimed in. "But I haven't heard that much. What have they done?"

"I'm not sure either," Joe continued. "But we sure could have a problem with our bullets. Instead of extra bullets, we seem to be short one. We're missing the bullet I dropped in the limo. I can only suppose someone grabbed a souvenir. They have the one I left on the gurney and some scraps. While things don't add up right, they take what they have as evidence. The idea seems to be that the first shot missed everything, completely, and the bullet wasn't found. The second hit the President in the neck or upper back, and then hit the governor. The third shot, the head shot, is gone, lost somewhere in the world. I think there's a problem with the bullet I planted on the gurney. They wonder why it wasn't messed up more. They seem inclined to follow a 'single gunman, single bullet' theory though; at least they hold that all the hits were from the rear. That's an absolute: all hits were from the rear. As I see it, the bullet question has caused as much a hassle as anything; that, and whether there were other shots and shooters, especially one shooting from the front."

"Remember the film the dress maker, Abraham Zapruder, took of the shooting? I wonder whether the autopsy report will take care of some of those 'grassy knoll' people who swear that the Zapruder film shows the head shot looking like a front hit?" Tony inquired.

"I can't say," I offered. "Like Joe just said, all hits were from the rear. However, a careful charting of the background and the blur in the film confirms that. The movie indicates that the President's limousine wasn't traveling at a steady speed. If anyone bothers to note, the limousine suddenly sped up just about the time the President went limp. That acceleration could have thrown his head back as much as a bullet. Even more likely, the back pressure of bullet gas as it passes through something like a head will actually push it back in the direction from which the shot was fired."

"Anyone with an ounce of brains should know that," Charlie snapped. "The magazine photos clearly show that the brain mass was blasted forward, into the wind, in the same direction the car was going, because that was the direction of force. It couldn't be any other way. God, how I wish these morons would stick to their knitting."

"Right! Anyway," Joe continued, "the other problem with this is the location of the back shot or neck shot; something about how it could hit so low in the back as they are saying, if it exited from the throat. That would indicate an upward projection of the bullet rather than downward, fired from the sixth floor. Also, since the front wound was first called an entry wound, it was referred to as a frontal shot. If it was from the front, then where did it exit? Out of the entry wound on the back? And if so, where's the bullet? It should have been buried in the upper part of the rear seat, but it wasn't there. If both were entry wounds, there should have been a bullet or two in the torso, but there was none! I think what they will say is, there's an entry wound on the back, but incorrectly located in some references, and that the bullet exited the front next to the knot in his tie. That accounts for one shot. The head shot is another matter, and it's presumed, based on the damage, to be a rear hit, and the fatal one. Then, there's the wounds to the governor."

"Let me respond to that," Charlie offered. "Some photo interpretations suggest that the first shot hit the President's neck. But, some people say the first shot hit the ground, a curb to the left and forward of the limousine. If that's accepted, we have one wasted bullet. There's one in the neck that also hit the governor with the bullet left on the gurney. Then there's the head shot that went off God knows where. That requires some real imagination. It is possible that the first shot hit the President in the neck, and hit the governor. However, our reconstruction suggest that tree branches could have thrown John off on his first shot and he missed. If that's the case it could explain the curb hit. But it doesn't really seem that way in pictures. Maybe the first shot hit something like a tree limb and split with part of the bullet hitting the curb. Far fetched but possible."

"Those were hand-cast bullets so the alloys would match. It wouldn't be the first time a homemade bullet separated," Tony added.

"Consider this." Charlie resumed, "We have a problem with arithmetic in terms of the number and order of hits, as well as the number of hits themselves. I understand that all the metal checks out with the specimen as we had planned, and ballistics checks with Oswald's rifle. But we have a bit too much lead. The whole bullet and the scraps they recovered add up to more than the originals should have for a single bullet, Joe. Your plants were a mite too large."

"No," Joe countered, "the problem was caused by whoever collected the bullet from the floor of the limousine and didn't turn it in. If we had that bullet too, they could take the position that the bullet they have—the pristine bullet—from the hospital gurney was from the neck shot, but it somehow got tangled up in the governor's clothes while he was on the floor. Then they could conclude that the messed-up bullet from the limousine hit the governor and then backed out of his leg due to muscle action while he was on the floor. If we had that bullet, it would clean things up nicely. But since we can't put it on the table, everybody acts like there couldn't have been another bullet. In fact, no one has even suggested such a simple answer, so far as I know. Instead, they would rather bust their brains trying to work out a solution based on just one bullet because that's all they've got."

The Old Man stopped the subject. "That is as it is. Let's waste no more time there. There are, no doubt, many questions which could be asked. More than they or we could ever hope to answer. Let us not borrow trouble. Let's concern ourselves with our position. I have heard you say that it is likely that Oswald will be regarded as the sole assassin, that Ruby will be regarded as the lone party to Oswald's death, and that Freddie and John are out of the picture, clean. Further, our next concerns are Ruby and his demand for a polygraph, Ruby's appeal, and how well Ruby holds up in custody. Then there is the Warren Commission's investigation. Is that a correct summation?"

We all voiced our agreement.

"All right then, let's not concern ourselves with these meddlesome spook hunters unless someone blunders in the wrong direction. Let's watch for them; otherwise, let's ignore them. Let them waste their energies barking at the moon. Frankly, we don't care what the official or public assumptions are, so long as they don't touch us. We accepted a terrible but necessary duty to our nation, and thus far we have been successful. For this we are thankful. Now, I charge you to be alert, be discreet, be perceptive, and above all inconspicuous. Dave, you see to it that Mr. Ruby is accommodated to the extent you can. He must feel as safe and protected as is possible under the circumstances. And if you can, keep him away from that polygraph."

Charles suggested, "Since Ruby is pressing the Warren Commission to get him to Washington for a polygraph exam, maybe I could do this. The director has a reliable relationship with President Johnson, and Johnson has a reliable relationship within the commission. What if the director persuades the President to persuade the commission—"

"That is a good idea, if you can manage to do so, Charles. Do what you can. Perhaps you can suggest that Mr. Ruby's deteriorating condition could make such test unreliable. That could provide us a plausible avoidance without appearing to seek it. Instead, we appear to seek it while amplifying the probability that Ruby will likely be an unfit subject for testing. Good idea! Meanwhile, the rest of you return to your assignments. Stay as near as possible to the commission. Be as involved as you can without being conspicuous. Should you encounter anything that would jeopardize our situation, do what you can to manage it. Stay in touch. Help each other. We are in as deep as possible, but we are too close to a complete success to get careless. With renewed resolve we will make it; I am certain of this. Take heart that you have each done your nation a great service, one for which you can never be recognized. Now, if we have no further business, I propose that we adjourn."

We decided we would not remain at the lodge. The weather had not improved, making it too dismal to stay.

CHAPTER TWENTY-FOUR

AFTER THE TRIAL

The months following the trial moved along more normally, but the rift that had erupted between the police and the FBI didn't improve. Since no federal crime had been committed, the jurisdiction for the crime rested solely with the State of Texas. However, Hoover had made it his personal case. He considered the Bureau to be the only agency capable of handling such an investigation. To a degree, he was correct. There were many ways the Bureau could assist the Dallas Police Department. However, the director was of no mind to help anyone. The rift started over a dispute of whether an agent had unwisely popped off about the Bureau knowing that Oswald was in Dallas and that he could be capable of an assault. The Bureau hadn't shared the information with the police department's intelligence unit. When that was revealed it was an embarrassment to Hoover. He ordered the agent to be exiled, the record to be destroyed and then denied all knowledge of the subject. The rift widened over matters concerning who should have what evidence and who should lead the investigation. The police had official jurisdiction, thus they had the responsibility to collect, classify, and preserve evidence for the court, to take statements, and to prepare their cases. No federal crime existed. Yet, the Bureau had made independent searches and seizures, but shared very little if any information with the Dallas police.

In Washington, Tony, Charlie and Joe met occasionally over a quiet meal to compare notes. The Warren Commission was making progress at an impressive rate. Their usual conversation dealt with how smoothly things were going. The Secret Service, suffering the most complete professional failure possible, the loss of a President, seemed most concerned with rationalizing their failure. The FBI was to evolve as the heroes of the whole affair. The Company wanted it concluded quickly because they detested any and all publicity. The new administration seemed most anxious to see the whole thing resolved promptly with no further problems. President Johnson was particularly anxious to know who or what group was behind the assassination, why it occurred, and was there likely to be any further activity. It seemed that all were doing their best to help the group achieve its objective.

The autopsy reports had been submitted. The military doctors concluded that the President had been hit from the rear in the lower, right of his neck with the bullet exiting the front of the neck. Further, that the bullet then passed through the governor's torso, then through his right wrist, then lodged in his right thigh before it fell out, that a second bullet hit the right rear of the President's head and exited the front, and that this was the fatal wound.

Governor Connally had reported hearing a single shot before he was hit. That would square with the old theory that you don't hear the one that gets you. After all, bullets usually travel faster than sound, and the trauma of such a hit would preclude his hearing the second and third shots. Some people questioned this, but the Zapruder film tended to confirm it. The film didn't record the governor's reaction until after the President had been wounded in his neck as evidenced when his arms reached up and his hands grasped at his throat in what was most likely an instant and involuntary physical reaction. The governor can be seen to turn to his right rear, then collapse.

Claims of a shooter on the grassy knoll had been checked, considered, and duly rejected.

Likewise, reports of previous associations between Oswald, Ruby, and Tippit had been checked and disproved or rejected. Reports of communist influence in the assassination were checked and rechecked. Undoubtedly, there was probable cause for suspicion, but no proof of any communist involvement was confirmed.

Claims of an imposter were considered but they led nowhere. Fingerprints and photographs of Oswald, before and after, were checked out without revealing any problem. There were description variations in height, both in printed records and in descriptions broadcast by the police. But those were common errors, and nothing with which to be concerned. An inch or so one way or the other, and a few pounds of estimated weight weren't that significant.

Questions of conspiracy frequently were leveled at officialdom. Some people even suggested President Johnson had engineered the assassination so he could become President. We wondered how Hoover handled *that* one! Others felt that the police had collaborated with the Dallas "establishment" in killing the President. Such broad suggestions were summarily rejected: too many people would have to have been involved. A conspiracy involving so many participants was considered to be impossible to assemble, impossible to coordinate, and impossible to manage afterwards. We appreciated that consideration.

The Chief Justice himself joined in an interview with Jack Ruby. Jack continued with his plea for a polygraph. In addition, he begged them to take him to Washington so he could tell them what had happened. The Chief Justice explained that they couldn't take him from Dallas County, but they did want to hear everything he wished to say. Jack only repeated the things he had previously said, and continued to insist on a polygraph. And contrary to what the Old Man had wished for, the Chief Justice promised that he would have his chance.

On July 18, 1964, an examiner and a doctor arrived from Washington to administer Ruby a polygraph examination. The equipment was set up in the sheriff's office and the test was scheduled to start that morning. Jack, anxious to get started, refused breakfast and was ready to go. Arthur Simmons, one of his Dallas lawyers, was not, however. He objected to Alexander being present and demanded that he and Sheriff Decker leave the examining room. The sheriff, refusing to leave his prisoner unguarded, assigned a trusted deputy before he and Alexander started to leave. Then the fight was on. Jack demanded that his old and trusted friend Alexander be allowed to remain. In a surprising switch, Jack insisted that his attorney, Simmons, leave.

After a morning's argument back and forth, the examination started. It was necessarily slow and tedious. First, there were the test questions and responses to enable the test administrator to set his instrument and evaluate Ruby as a subject. Next, there were several series of key questions, all of which had been carefully considered and prepared and then discussed. Then there were the disagreements between the lawyers. Alexander had a few questions he wanted added over Simmons' protest, and Simmons wanted some changes, too.

In due time, the actual questioning began. The questions must necessarily be brief so they can be clearly understood and not confusing. Also, they must be answerable with a "yes" or "no" response. They are asked slowly both for clarity and for the respondent to have reaction time. Sometimes, a response can prompt a change in a question or perhaps another question. Following a long series of questions and answers, the operator suggested a rest break. Jack didn't want to stop; he wanted to go straight through. Well past lunch, a break was again suggested but Jack still insisted on continuing. Later, nearer to time for the evening meal, Jack relented and took a break. He took a nap but still didn't eat. After a brief nap, he insisted on resuming the test. He was so eager for the test he frequently forgot that the questions required "yes-or-no" answers. He tried to carry on discussions and make explanations. A doctor periodically checked Jack to determine that he was physically fit to continue. During the ordeal Simmons telephoned Melvin Belli. His report on the proceedings put Belli in a rage. All he could think of to do was to fire Simmons right there. But the test continued over his apoplectic protest.

Jack wasn't mad at anybody now. He was having his long-denied chance. It was late in the evening before they concluded. But all the questions had been suitably covered. The operator had his completed list of questions with the appropriate notations added to the margin on the lengthy tape that recorded Jack's responses to the questions. Jack had nothing more to say.

The polygraph results were released later, but I had already picked up on the outcome. Jack had answered every question and had passed, which meant "no deception." Key questions were: Did you know Oswald previously? Did you know Tippit previously? Are you a communist? Did you alone kill Oswald? Did you enter the Main Street driveway? Did you plan to do it? Did you do it on a sudden impulse? Everything went as if our group had planned and conducted the test: Jack showed no deception in his answers to the questions. Belli felt it was nothing but further proof of Jack's mental incompetence. Maybe he was right.

I reported to the Old Man. "We can all breathe easier now, so far as the polygraph issue is concerned. And we can be thankful for their decision to use the polygraph. And think of how afraid we were for him to get on the box! All the poor sucker wanted to do was redeem himself. Mr. Belli had branded him an irresponsible crazy. Jack felt Dallas and Jews hated him. All he wanted was to let them and the world know that he had told the truth."

"How could it show that he told the truth when we know he lied? Is the polygraph that unreliable?" the Old Man sputtered.

"Well, yes and no," I answered. "What you must consider is that deception requires the subject to be *aware* of the deception; that is, to feel or believe that he is engaging in deception. I would say that Jack has repeated his story so many times, and has become so engrossed in his role, and has become so angry regarding how things have gone, that he *felt* no deception, therefore, he *registered* no deception. In other words, he beat the box!"

"Where does that leave us, Dave?"

"I'm not sure," I responded. "The results of the test won't be admitted into evidence; it's only a guide to the attorneys. I'm still worried about how Jack looks and acts. He kept urging Chief Justice Warren and Congressman Gerald Ford to notice how competent he was, but I think something is wrong, bad wrong."

"Is he otherwise well provided for?"

"I would say yes. Actually, we've done nothing for him. It seems like he didn't hire Belli in response to our promise of an attorney. I hear that Belli was promised a fee but that wasn't his objective. If he had gone for 'mercy' on a guilty plea and got Jack off for about five years, it would have all been over, but he wouldn't have been able to spring his psychomotor epilepsy defense. Since he did plead that defense, think of what he would have had in his hands if he had gotten Jack acquitted. It's hard to imagine the impact that verdict would have had on criminal justice jurisprudence, and likewise on his future reputation. And he might come out on top after all. There's still the matter of the appeal. As for creature comfort, the sheriff is taking good care of him. Jack doesn't like the public nature of his accommodations; they keep him in view with lights on, and he's under constant surveillance. That bugs him. He plays a lot of cards with the deputies and sleeps a lot. But we can't mess with the sheriff's business. Let me put it this way. Jack knows we promised to take care of him but I'm not sure that registers with him now. Even the results of the test didn't bounce him back like I thought it would. I don't know what he expected, but things didn't change. He is in a deepening depression, in my opinion. I think he's sick."

No miracles followed Jack's polygraph examination. He remained a top-security prisoner in the county jail. Having received the death penalty, he was ineligible for bond and had to wait out his appeal process while in confinement. Some observers described his conduct as more or less resigned while occasionally displaying temper tantrums. He was usually quiet and moody.

* * *

On September 27, 1964, the Warren Commission issued its findings on the Kennedy assassination in a publication generally referred to as the Warren Commission Report. The group was well pleased with the commission's findings. The report followed the group's plans as though we had orchestrated its development and preparation. The Old Man instructed his associates to familiarize themselves with the content of the report, and he scheduled a meeting at the lodge for the following month.

It was that meeting, November 30, that had brought me to the lodge now. I had enjoyed my quiet rest on the veranda while waiting for the others. The trip here and the wait gave me time to organize my mind and summarize things for this journal. It was difficult for me to accept the fact that my reflections during the last hours had covered several years and a wide series of events that my associates and I truly believed had changed history for the better, and had, at least for the present, saved the United States from social, political, and fiscal ruination. It was for that reason I decided to make a journal of my recollections. I know that this will put us in a place of infamy in our country's history. I wanted to try to explain things so history might not judge our actions too harshly. I hope my nation will understand and be forgiving. We believe that we did a horrible thing but only for the most noble purpose.

Would we do it again? If confronted with the same situation, I would pray that we or at least someone would find the courage and the resolve to respond.

* * *

Summer had prolonged its stay. The trees held their green although the evening air had an invitingly fresh nip, suggestive of the wintry days which would arrive within the next two or three weeks. Noticing now that it was getting dark at an earlier hour, I checked my watch. It was almost seven. The mosquitoes were gone for the season; the throaty songs of the lusty bullfrogs were entertaining, and it was time for the others to arrive.

CHAPTER TWENTY-FIVE

THE LAST MEETING

Joe Kervin arrived a little while later, driving a rented car.

"What's up with the coupe, Joe?" I asked. "Has the Secret Service gone mod or gone broke?"

"No, it's rented. And out of my own pocket, buddy-boy. You see, I'm not really here. I'm en route to L.A. I took a layover in Dallas to run out here." Joe explained. "I sure hope this meeting doesn't drag out. I've gotta get back to Love Field by 2:30 a.m. for a 3:00 a.m. flight to L.A. in time to check in tomorrow morning. The 3:00 a.m. flight will give metime to take a nap and freshen up. The 4:10 is the last one that will get me there in time, but just barely."

Tony Amatto arrived moments after that. As he approached Joe and me, he said he had thought to himself that we seemed to have aged ten years in the past months.

At the same time, I had leaned toward Joe and whispered, "My god, doesn't Tony look awful? He's aged ten years."

"Well, how old is he now? He must be pushing fifty," Joe replied. "Tony! How are you? You're looking great!"

"Hey, thanks old buddy! I know you're lying through your teeth, but I appreciate it! And how are you guys? You look great yourselves!" he declared, lying through *his* teeth.

As Charlie Evans approached and greetings were exchanged, I noticed that the Old Man's attendant had slipped quietly in through the rear door and had started a fire in the fireplace. "Let's go in," I suggested. "The Old Man's bound to be here in a few minutes, as soon as things are ready."

The others expressed their tacit agreements and moved toward the door. The attendant had finished opening the widows to add fresh air. While the fire was inviting it was too warm without adding the cool night air. As we settled down, the attendant was setting the table. Then as if on cue, he left and the Old Man appeared.

He was more pleasant than we had expected, almost jovial.

Joe nudged me and said, "I guess he's satisfied with what he's read. He looks rather pleased. Maybe this won't take so long."

"What was that?" the Old Man said.

"Uh, I was just commenting on how well you look, sir." Joe said, quickly. "We haven't seen you look so rested for a long time."

The mood was more sociable than it had been previously. The conversation flowed freely, and we were lighthearted and relaxed. The usual subject wasn't even mentioned: not at first. The summer heat passing, the first signs of autumn, and Detroit's new line of cars seemed to be topics that were more important. After we had finished the meal, we broke precedent again, lingering at the table over coffee refills. The Old Man had always considered such activity to be a waste of valuable time. Now, he even shared in our leisure, and appeared to be enjoying himself.

Joe finally broke up the social hour. Remembering his tight schedule he asked the Old Man, "Well, sir, how do you feel about the Warren Commission's report?"

"Let me ask you that same question. How do each of you regard their conclusions as they relate to our position? Joe, since you mentioned it, you start us off."

"I don't see where there's anything different to what we discussed last March. I think that what we discussed then is pretty much the same as they reported. They decided that Oswald was the sole assassin, that he did it for reasons he alone knew, and that Ruby killed Oswald the same way, by himself for reasons of his own."

"Those are conclusions, Joe," the Old Man admonished. "People can accept or reject conclusions as they will. I am more concerned with the strength of their facts, the evidence. How strong are the critics? Can the report withstand challenge?"

"So far, the report has been accepted by the media and the public," Joe said. "But it is too early to anticipate future or widespread acceptance."

"I'm concerned with who will challenge it and on what basis," the Old Man continued. "I want to know how well prepared the commission is to withstand attack. In effect, the commission is our insulation. I'm certain that a goodly number of so-called experts will come forward, some out of conviction, some for publicity and some for profit. They will look long and hard at every comma and period seeking out any fault, any point where they might drive a wedge of suspicion. What will they challenge? Why will they challenge that point, and perhaps most important, *how* will they challenge the point?"

"It's like a war. Know what your adversary plans to do and use that knowledge against him. When you know your adversary's plans, his strength becomes yours," Joe suggested. The Old Man's cherub-like smile indicated his agreement.

Tony started the next round of conversation. "I've always been a bit uneasy about those bullets. I don't see how any thinking person is going to buy what they call the 'single bullet theory.' It's too much, one bullet doing all that damage and not being messed up in the process! I believe that is a weak point. They're going to jump all over that. I wish Joe could have dropped a more believable—"

"Wait a minute! How was I to know?" Joe cried, his irritation obvious.

"Now, now, we don't need that," the Old Man shushed. "Each of you performed your best under the circumstances, and each of you did quite well—exceedingly well! We owe each other our comradeship and support, Joe, I don't think Tony was offering criticism—only wishful thinking."

"Yes sir, I know. It's just that I feel the same way. That's why it gets to me. God only knows how many times I've said the same thing to myself. I'm sorry, Tony. I didn't mean anything. Really, I'm angry with myself."

"Hey, drop it buddy. I know how it is. Not one of us is perfect. Just look at how big a hand 'Old Lady Luck' has played all along the way! What I was getting to is that 'single bullet' business. A great many people simply aren't going to buy it. Frankly, I don't see anything we can do about it. I'd like to find and fix whoever took that bullet from the floor of that limousine."

Charlie joined in. "We sure couldn't work a swap after they left the hospital. We'll just have to live with it, the 'single bullet' business. After all, it isn't impossible, only improbable—very improbable—but *possible!* Let the 'experts' howl their fool heads off. They can't prove a thing."

"They can generate a lot of suspicion, though." I reminded them. "Even though they can't prove or disprove anything, the point is, any opening for controversy can give strength to their arguments. Even though our bullet evidence withstands the attacks of the critics, it encourages them to keep hacking away at the whole investigation."

"And it could encourage others to join in," Tony added.

There was a pause in the action that the Old Man used as a strategic opportunity to speak.

"Your observations are well made, and I am afraid you are correct. As it has been pointed out, the matter cannot be proved or disproved, regardless of argument. True, the fact that there is an arguable point can generate further scrutiny into other points. As I see it, we have a matter subject to criticism that might well lead to further suspicion. That's regrettable, but it's a fact of life. As Charlie said, we can't change things now. I suggest that we pass this, at least for the time being, and hope that the subject fades from public interest. The critics can raise all the fine points they choose. If their arguments lead nowhere, the public will lose interest. What's next?"

"There's some talk about a second assassin," I said. "This usually refers to someone shooting from either the railroad overpass or the grassy knoll to the right and ahead of the motorcade."

"How in hell does stuff like that get started?" Joe demanded.

"Well, one of your boys helped, Joe!" Charlie stated. "At least, that's the way it seems. And that sure helps to suggest an 'inside' conspiracy."

"You mean because someone told an officer he was a Secret Service agent when we didn't have, or weren't supposed to have, anyone up there?"

"My God. How many times has some special deputy or such claimed to be someone else in hopes of being able to stay close to the action? So, he flipped out his Dick Tracy badge or some kind of identification to an excited cop. Now, that cop doesn't want to look foolish. He said somebody flashed Secret Service ID at him and he isn't going to change his story now! Would you? And maybe it was an agent. Maybe some agent in town on vacation picked the wrong time and the wrong place to watch the motorcade. After he badged the officer, he could have had second thoughts. After the shit hit the fan, he decided to keep quiet and split. There's no way of knowing what happened, but there are many plausible explanations!"

"What strength or support is there to the 'second assassin' idea, Dave?" the Old Man asked.

"Well, for one," I replied, "the chief said for officers to 'get up on the overpass and see what happened.' He simply made the only statement that seemed logical to him under the circumstances. He hadn't seen anything. It meant nothing."

"What about the motor jockey who jumped off his bike and ran up the hill?" Tony asked. "His action suggests something happened up there."

"No, sir," I answered. "The chief said for somebody to get up there, and people were running every which way. The jockey was only doing what he thought the chief wanted him to do. His actions were fully understandable, perfectly natural. You gotta realize it was like a bomb went off, a big bomb, an air raid. People were running, screaming, falling down. It was real crazy.

"Anyway, here's how it stacks up. Some people didn't hear anything, some heard one shot, others two and three and so on. In fact, to some it sounded like a machine gun! But most people—and they seem to be sound people— agree to having heard three shots. However, you must consider that nobody was expecting to hear any shots, and consider how fast it happened. And consider the echo effect down in that area; you know how Dealey Plaza drops down toward the triple underpass. And all those buildings on the west end of town tend to echo sound back at the crowd. It's a miracle that most people were able to recognize three distinct shots."

"Speaking of witnesses to the location and the number of shots, our Secret Service guys, people who are supposed to be alert for such things, were unsure of the direction and the number of shots. And that's what they're trained for, to observe and to expect anything, any time, and they missed it," Joe noted.

Tony couldn't resist another jab at the government, "Was that because of that drunken orgy in Fort Worth the night before?"

"No," Joe replied. "All that didn't help, but it wasn't like the rumors. The President's guys were off duty, and they didn't do anything like some people said. But they sure left themselves open for a storm of criticism. You know, those guys are kinda like Caesar's wife—they need to be above reproach. They put themselves and the service in a helluva spot. But nothing would have been said if the President hadn't been hit. That isn't the first time the boys went out for a breather. They are due some time off; they have a tough, demanding schedule."

"Hey, you don't have to sell us, Joey!" Tony consoled. "We understand."

"I'm concerned about the reference to the speed of the shots, that is, the time interval in which the shots were fired," the Old Man cut in. "We know that one person fired all three but why is there concern as to whether such firing was possible?"

"Well, sir," Charlie started, "first, the time frame was set by estimate taken from the Zapruder film. There is no recording of the sounds of the shots. By checking the camera's operating speed and by counting frames they estimated where the President's car was and how fast it was going. Nothing on the film proves when the first shot was actually fired. After it was fired, the limousine went behind a road sign. Before it went behind the sign, the President appeared to be all right but when you next could see him, he had grabbed his throat. Until then, you can't read any kind of alarm on anybody's face. One agent looked back over his right shoulder toward the book depository, but that's about it.

"Since you can't tell when the first shot was fired and the third shot is history, there's only an educated guess of about seven seconds or so for the three shot episode."

"I'm not sure I follow your point, Charlie," the Old Man puzzled.

"Well, sir, if you fix an estimated time for the first shot and count 1/18th of a second, the speed of the shutter on the Zapruder camera, to the third or last shot, you have some seven to eight seconds. Where people make their mistake is they divide the estimated time by three to time the shots, or some 2½ seconds per shot. That's *all wrong!* The first shot is a freebie, it *starts the clock!* You then have seven or so seconds for *the last two shots!* That's more than enough time."

"I follow you now, Charlie," the Old Man interrupted. "That's what I wanted to know. Thank you. Uh, please continue."

"I guess that's about it. If the critics accept the timing estimated from the movie and accept that a well-trained man, familiar with the weapon, could have fired it in the accepted time interval, we're in good shape."

"Speaking of 'well-trained' what about Oswald's qualifications?" Joe asked.

"Remember Freddie tried to take care of that by having him practice some," Tony returned.

"It would have been better if he had been a good Marine and fired 'expert,' but I guess we can't expect everything to fall into place. The power of suggestion can have a profound effect sometimes, maybe now. Maybe people will assume that since Oswald was a Marine, and since he had practiced with his rifle, he must have been a crack shot. I understand that he did qualify as a sharpshooter in the Marines."

"And there's that picture your people found, Dave," the Old Man remembered. "It clearly showed Oswald with his rifle as well as his pistol, and a communist publication. Doesn't that suggest that he had a feeling for his weapon that was at least a trifle above the ordinary?"

"It could," Joe entered, "but Oswald always denied that it was an honest photo. He alleged that someone superimposed his head on another's body. Could that be, Dave?"

"No way!" I almost yelled. I felt strongly about this. "They found the photo too soon after the shooting for that to happen. Besides his wife acknowledged it was him, and that she took the picture behind a house we didn't even know about until after we confronted him with it. His story doesn't add up."

"Speaking of the CIA, did you guys—?" Charlie asked, raising his eyebrows toward Tony.

Tony answered with a smile.

"Davey, I can follow your explanation so far, perhaps because I'm aware of what happened," the Old Man said. "But permit me to raise another point. That railroad man who was watching from the overpass told a different story. While the others described the number of shots they believed they had heard, and attempted to judge as best they could, the direction from which the sounds came, the railroad man described a 'puff of smoke' that he said came from under the trees on the grassy knoll at the time of a shot. Now, Davey, it's one thing to describe intangibles such as sound and direction, but what about a tangible such as that smoke? Doesn't that suggest a gun being fired?"

"I wish every issue could be explained as easily as that one, sir," I grinned. "Unless someone fired a big flintlock, one of those old Kentucky long-toms, there would be no such 'puff of smoke.' While I can't say *what* he saw, that is, whether he did or didn't see something, I know very well it wasn't from a weapon's discharge.

"That railroad man is confused. He has changed his story relating to how many shots he heard. He is up to six shots now, and he is confused about the order as well as the loudness of the shots he heard. I think it was the second shot, that came with the 'puff of smoke,' and he recalls that it wasn't as loud as the others. Like it came from a smaller weapon, a pistol, and the smaller the weapon, the less likely there would be any smoke. Certainly it would not be so much smoke that you could describe it as a 'puff'; and just how big is a puff? Does it mean larger than a wisp but smaller than a cloud? Really! Under certain weather conditions, you might get a wisp of smoke; a very faint and very brief vapor, but it wouldn't last as a 'puff' that floats on the air for a while.

"Besides that, why didn't others see the smoke? And why only he saw smoke; one out of the hundreds? That amateur photographer, Abe Zapruder, and the city man who takes care of the park grounds in Dealey Plaza, they were standing right there. They didn't hear what the railroad man heard from a greater distance, and they didn't see the smoke. Oh yes! He mentioned a big gun and a smaller gun. What did they have up there? A shooting gallery? I can only conclude that the guy remembered something from some other time or place. I can't say now whether he's making an honest mistake or whether, after telling a story for the truth, he now finds himself in the limelight and wouldn't change his story if hell froze over. As it is, he's become a part of history," I concluded.

"Neither do any of the pictures I've seen, still photographs and movies," said Charlie. "None of them show any 'puff of smoke' coming from up there."

"Another important point," Tony offered, "is that several people saw the rifle fire from the book warehouse window, but no one saw any smoke. Why not? If one shot from the knoll gave off a cloud of smoke under the conditions in Dealey Plaza, how do you explain three quick shots and not a hint of smoke at the window? And no one saw a shooter out in the open, at ground level, but they did see one shooting from inside a building, six floors up!"

"You're right, Joe, and I fully agree with you, Dave," Charlie said. "You don't get all that smoke with today's weapons. That guy's story won't hold up; it can't."

Then the Old Man shifted his posture, and the topic. "There is another point which has aroused my interest. Freddie said that Oswald attempted to assassinate that general, Walker. I don't recall any reference to that in our plans and discussions, and if I had heard of such plans

I would have prohibited that! It would have been far too risky. Could have placed the entire project in jeopardy."

"I guess that was something Freddie worked up by himself, sir," Tony offered. "I agree with your judgment, entirely. A mistake or a little bad luck could have been fatal to our whole operation. However, it was an understandable thing for Freddie to have done. When you are trying to set someone up you need a hook to hold him, something from which he can't shake free. But even more so, you have to consider this: Oswald wasn't a killer, he had never killed, so far as we know. So to give a hint of credibility to him in a killer's role, it was useful to have him at least try for a kill. After taking a shot at the general with his rifle, he demonstrated a capacity to kill. If he had balked, we would have us a big problem. Oswald passed the test: he fired! And if ballistics confirmed that the same rifle was used on the general as well as the President and that rifle belonged to Oswald, you see what that would look like? After Oswald fired at the general, Freddie owned him."

"Do you mean you really believe Oswald and Freddie shot at the general?" I asked.

"I think, yes." Tony replied. "The report suggests that at least a couple of people were there, and there was a car. Oswald didn't have a car. He didn't even have a driver's license. In fact, I don't know whether he could even drive a car. I suppose Freddie took care of that little detail, I never asked. He's very thorough. Anyway, if Oswald got that far, he probably fired the shot. But Freddie would have told me if Oswald got that far and chickened out. I'm certain that Oswald fired the shot."

"Maybe that's why he, or whoever it was, went by that car dealers and took a test ride," Charlie suggested. "It adds up. It would look like Oswald could drive a car. And whoever it was who went by there made sure the episode didn't go unnoticed. Supposedly, he gave the name Oswald, and mentioned that he was about to come into some money and then drove the demo like crazy."

"I understand that salesman identified Oswald's picture and said it actually was Oswald who made the test ride. How do you account for this discrepancy?" the Old Man questioned.

"The power of suggestion, sir," Charlie replied. "An identification from a single photo is, for the most part, worthless because of the power of suggestibility. No matter who paid the actual visit to the dealership, the name 'Oswald' on the slip, and his name plastered all over the news, when the dealer was shown a single photo, there's a great possibility that he, that almost anybody, would tie the two things together and say it was him."

"That's entirely possible," I agreed. Joe and Tony added their concurrence.

"Very well, lads, but while we're on the subject of people and identities, what about the information that Mr. Ruby knew Officer Tippit?" the Old Man asked.

"Oh, that's easy," I said. "While Tippit isn't all that common a name, J.D. wasn't the only one we had on the department. At the time, we had a 'Tippit' in patrol, in traffic, and in vice: three of them. Ruby knew the Tippit who worked in vice. He didn't know J.D. It was a natural mistake."

"How is it that Mr. Ruby seemed to know so many officers, Dave?" the Old Man asked.

"Pardon my Irish, sir, but that's a bunch of bullshit! It's something Ruby likes to claim, and the news people like to give him the credit; it makes for interesting copy. They *think* it makes interesting copy. But it simply isn't true. In fact, officers tried to avoid him. He was a pain in the ass. But he claimed to know them and the media bought into it.

"You have to consider that Ruby has been around for several years, and has always been in a business that involves contact with the police. He's had puke joints down on South Ervay and up on Oak Lawn as well as the Carousel, and he was usually his own bouncer. He had to protect his liquor license. That means that whenever there was trouble, he would call for the uniformed officers. So that's how he met a bunch of officers. Then there was the heat from vice and liquor officers who checked his joints on a regular basis. And remember, Jack is an ambitious egotist who never forgets a name, especially if he thinks he can drop it around town to his advantage. Also, he went out of his way to meet people he considered to be important or in official positions, and that includes the police. Over the years, he met quite a few, but only the rookies took him up on his invitations to bring their dates to his club because it gave them a chance to be a 'big shot.' They usually didn't go back again. It wasn't that good a deal, taking your lady to a puke joint! Besides, knowing who he was didn't make him a pal."

"While we're on Tippit, how is it some people doubt that he was killed by Oswald? Is that notion still receiving consideration?" the Old Man continued his quiz.

I answered. "That has to be one of the dumbest arguments of all."

"It shows the ultimate range of stupidity of which some critics are capable!" Charlie added.

I continued, "Add it up, sir, and there's no way that anybody with an ounce of brains could reach any other conclusion. Oswald killed Tippit! Just add it up. A guy who's poor as a church mouse and needs to be working but walks off the job, boards a bus that isn't going anywhere, jumps off and runs to the bus station and takes a taxi cab because he's in such a hurry—why? To get home. Then he gives an incorrect address, he gets out and runs the rest of the way home. He rushes into his apartment to change jackets and pick up his pistol. He's in a hurry because he is anxious to catch the one o'clock double feature at the Texas Theater! In his hurry, he forgot the best route to the movie and goes south on Beckley instead of just going out Zang Boulevard. Maybe he had to go that way because he wanted to throw his jacket away behind that Texaco station at Jefferson and Crawford, a block from where Tippit was killed. We can't guess how he got his pistol to 'the other guy,' but he did. Then he got it back in time to slip into the theater several blocks to the west. Then, when the cops approached him, he did the most natural thing in the world; he pulled his pistol and tried to shoot them. He hollered something like, 'Well, this is it!' and the fight was on. Sounds absolutely normal—to idiots. To reasonable people, it's bullshit."

"It makes perfect sense to us because we're familiar with it," Charlie said. "But people who don't want Oswald to be Tippit's killer will dwell on any possible discrepancy in an effort to avoid truth and create doubt. And there are places where you can raise some argument. There's the time element. Some people feel that Oswald didn't have enough time to be where we know him to have been and to have done what we know him to have done. For instance, that waitress who saw the killing from the corner. She said she waited several minutes before she ran to Tippit. That suggests he was shot at maybe 1:10 rather than 1:15. That means Oswald couldn't have walked the distance from his apartment in the 1000 block of North Beckley to Tenth and Patton in so short a time."

"Couldn't that waitress just be mistaken about how long she waited before she ran to help Tippit, Charlie?" the Old Man asked.

"Absolutely! No doubt about it!" he answered. "It's common for people under stress to make wild exaggerations. I mean, they are sincere, they believe it, that's how they remember things.

Only thing is, they can often be wrong and by wide margins. The chain of events and the acts of others prove her to be wrong. That civilian got to Tippit's radio only moments after Oswald ran from the scene. The radio time is history. It's locked in by a neutral timing system.

"Then there are people who saw Oswald running from the scene, and the discarded jacket, and his slipping into the theater and the rest. Those things fall into the right time line. No, Oswald did it and no sane person can doubt that."

"Okay. What about ballistics, Charlie? Tony said. "I understand the lab boys couldn't be conclusive."

"That's right." Charlie responded. "Oswald bought an old surplus Smith & Wesson revolver made for export, I believe to England. It was designed for a particular kind of ammunition. Instead, he had a mixed bunch of regular .38 caliber cartridges, and that's just what Tippit was shot with, a mixed bunch of junk. Wouldn't it be wild coincidence for two look-alike, dress-alike characters to be carrying the same kinds of uncommon, off-beat weapons with the same kinds of wrong bullets at the same time and in the same neighborhood?"

"Couldn't the laboratory people be a bit more concise, Charlie?" the Old Man wanted to know.

"No sir," he responded. "But that isn't all that bad. You see, the mere fact that the wrong size bullets failed to render clear land and groove marks on the bullets that killed Tippit is, in itself, a kind of signature. Oswald's pistol, fired with the same wrong ammunition gave the same smudged or indistinct bullet marks. Oh yeah, the firing pin marks on the primer caps; they matched!"

"I see. Uh, thank you, Charlie. Please continue," the Old Man directed.

There was a brief hush over the group. No one knew just which point should receive attention next. Joe took a quick furtive look at his watch, but the Old Man caught it. "Are you tiring, Joe?"

"Uh, no sir, I was just checking the time. I'm on a pretty close schedule. I have to get to L.A. before morning," was the halting answer. He noted the time as 9:10, and did a little quick arithmetic: an hour, no, an hour and half to Love Field, turn in the car, half an hour for check-in. "I'll have to leave here by midnight to make the 2:30 flight or by 1:30 to 2:00 a.m. to make the

4:10. I figure I've got four hours to make the early flight and six hours for the late. No, sweat," but *he was* sweating.

Picking up the slack in the conversation, the Old Man inquired at large, "What about these deals our Mr. Ruby has been involved in besides the nightclub business?"

Tony responded, "The main story, the one I suppose you're referring to is the one about gun running . . ."

"Yes, that and shall I say, gangster connections with the uh . . . the mob and Havana . . ." the Old Man offered.

"Okay, the core of that story came from a former Ruby employee who was separated from her, I guess you could say, "soldier of fortune" husband. She came to Dallas 'down and out,' and went to work for Ruby. In due time her husband returned, and she moved on. One night, as she tells it, she was with some people where her husband was working. There were some people there who, she said, were planning to run some guns to Cuba. She swore that Ruby came in, went into the back room where the others were, with another guy, and after a while, left without speaking to the people in the front of the place. She didn't speak to him. She concluded from what she saw and heard, I suppose, that Ruby was a party to the deal. Presumably, he was a bagman—uh, he was bringing money. But there's no proof, and I can't see any thinking person buying that tale."

"Well, what about the guns he was supposed to have bought in Dallas and sent to Cuba?" the Old Man continued. "Wasn't he supposed to be acting for some mob man or something? Does Mr. Ruby have, shall I say, organized crime connections?"

"I guess the answer to that question is an ambiguous yes and no," Tony replied. "He came from the poor section of Old Chicago. As a young man, he did minor jobs for some Chicago gangsters, small stuff—no hits or anything like that. Anyhow, he did meet a few others like himself who are still around. So he's not without contacts of a sort. However, from all indications, he is not a fellow traveler. He's not the 'family's man' in Dallas. Never has been. Never could be. Mainly because he talks too much. We're pretty sure he doesn't even have recognized status. Remember, too, he's a name dropper. I guess that's as good a way as any to put it. He made a trip to Havana that no one knows much about. But later, he was supposed to have ordered some guns from a Dallas dealer at the request of a minor figure with a shady past. The dealer denied all reference to the deal and showed that there was no reference to the transaction in his records.

"On the other hand, would you as a licensed dealer admit to a deal and keep a record of something that could put you out of business? No! You would deny it, and so would I. And so does he. So it's a dead issue now, *if* there ever was a gun deal."

While Tony had the floor, Charlie tossed him another puzzle. "Tony, I'm still confused about the Mexico City deal. Your guys watching the embassy took a photo of Oswald, only it wasn't Oswald. Who was it?"

"Yes, I meant to ask that same question, Tony," the Old Man said. "The fact that it definitely wasn't Oswald certainly raises the question of conspiracy. It does a little more than merely suggest that someone else was involved in this business."

Tony explained, "Freddie needed to build an escape plan for Oswald so it would weave a more convincing web of suspicion around him and his behavior. After all, if you really wanted it to look like he killed the President, it had to look like killing a President wasn't the end of his plans. You don't just kill a President, then go home and ask the little lady, 'What's for dinner?' You need to disappear!

"Freddie got Oswald to go to New Orleans in April of '63, and got him visible in the Cuban deal. That got him out of Dallas and away from possible discovery. Then, he had him get his passport. You don't need a passport to go to Mexico, so that made it look like he, Lee, was planning to go somewhere else. Remember, it had been announced a month earlier that the President would be here in the fall, so apparently Freddie was setting it up to appear that Oswald was making early plans to take care of his business and get out of town, even out of the country."

I had a question. "Excuse me, Tony, but why was it necessary to go to New Orleans? Why didn't he stay in Dallas?"

"First, he shot at Walker. It would have been a disaster for us if he had stayed here and the police had some way or another connected him with that, and he had been picked up. Next, if he had become active in this area, in something like the Cuban deal, the local feds might have kept a closer watch on him, especially with the President due in town. What if they had him under close surveillance, or worse, stopped him on a routine security check when he was going into the warehouse that morning with his rifle? It's happened before. Getting Oswald out of town was a good idea on Freddie's part. It put him at a safe distance from the general, as well as the federal agents, and he was furthering his pro-Castro identity with that FPC activity."

"That Freddie is one shrewd dude!" I smiled. The others mumbled their concurrence.

"Okay, back to Mexico," Tony said. "If he had applied for a Russian visa locally, it might have been picked up on too soon, and that could have queered the deal. The trip to New Orleans and Mexico were good ideas, and it had to be obvious that he made his trip so it would be remembered and reported to the police or somebody, after the assassination.

"Also, it was logical that anyone who was planning to kill the President would also plan to split the scene afterwards. It's reasonable he would get out of the country as quickly, and quietly as he could. Freddie needed to have it appear that Oswald, on his own, slipped off to Mexico, got a visa, then went home to Dallas to do the deed. If Freddie hadn't made Oswald's trip conspicuous, it might not have gotten out unless someone leaked it. And that could have raised more suspicion. So look at what Freddie did: he had Oswald travel by bus via Houston to Laredo, sitting on a bus, using his own name, and talking more freely than was usual for him. Then, when he reached Mexico City, he evaporated.

"In his place, a no-name face turned up as Oswald."

"Was that our Freddie?" the Old Man asked, while registering a dawning disbelief.

"Oh, no! No, sir. He would never make such a mistake!" Tony insisted.

"Then who—where did he get someone else to—" I blustered.

"A drifter, someone who needed money, someone in jail or with some kind of problem, somebody who couldn't talk. Drop a little money and tell him what to do. You don't meet him where he can see you, and you don't pay him until it's done. When you use a low-life who's got his own problems, he won't be anxious to go public later; if he does, then you hope no one will believe him."

Freddie was good at this, I thought. *He should have been writing pulp fiction.*

"But the photo would confirm it wasn't Oswald, wouldn't it?" the Old Man wanted to know.

"That was an unfortunate bit of Company efficiency," Tony allowed. "They happened to be giving cover to the embassy at the wrong time. They weren't scheduled to be working there that day. We'll just have to ride this one out and hope for the best. So far, whoever he is, he's kept his trap shut."

"How could Freddie get Oswald to go along with something like that, Tony?" I queried. "Why would Oswald up and go to Mexico City for no real purpose, at least so far as we know? What could Freddie have told him that would get him to string along?"

"Something about what Freddie had to do, and that Oswald might have to help," Tony said. "Anyway, he left a trail that any good investigator could pick up and follow. The end result is, Oswald could be regarded as a man with sufficient dedication to a cause that he tried to kill a right-wing general, left his family and went to New Orleans to work for the cause, learned of the President's visit to Dallas, made up his mind what to do, got a passport, went to Mexico to arrange to go to Cuba or Russia, then returned to Dallas on October third so he could start getting ready to kill the President. The only problem was he had no earthly idea what he was doing!

Only Freddie knew just how the parts would fit together in a few weeks.

"And consider how it looks that Oswald continued to show his dedication. When he came back, he didn't set up housekeeping with his family, he took an apartment under an assumed name. You see, there was scarcely an appearance of an innocent act in anything Oswald did."

This rambling narrative cast a hush over the group. The Old Man brought out some notes and examined them while the others helped themselves to another round of coffee.

The Old Man allowed us a few minutes rest, and then renewed the agenda. "Joe or Charlie, maybe you can tell me something about the claims of a frontal shot. I know we've touched on that before but it still comes up. Now that people have seen the ghastly photographs, it does appear that the President's head snapped back about the time he was hit and that doctor at Parkland reported he had been shot from the—or should I correctly say, a frontal shot?"

"Let me try to put that business to rest," Joe offered. "I saw the wounds, and I can assure you there was no frontal hit. We *know* that! The head shot, the only head shot, was from the rear. There's no way anyone can make it be any other way! It'*s talk!* It's only *conjecture!* Let the conspiracy speculators say anything they want to as long as they are *wrong!* We get worried only if they start getting *right!* My God, you guys haven't forgotten, have you? It *was* a conspiracy, *our* conspiracy!"

Surprised, we looked at each other, even the Old Man. Joe was right! Entirely right! We had labored over the arguments and details so intensely that we had lost focus. Joe set us back on track. This reality sobered us up real quick.

Joe continued. "For the record, let's be clear about the President's wounds. I just covered the head wound. Now, for the neck wounds: the autopsy described the entry wound to the right rear of the base of the neck as being lower than it actually was. Clearly what happened was this: putting his hands up repeatedly, waving to people during the motorcade, caused his shirt and coat to ride up on his back about four inches. For that reason alone, the holes in the shirt and coat match each other but they do *not* match the actual position of the back wound. Move the shirt and coat holes up about four inches and you've got a match. If the rear entry wound was as low as mistakenly indicated by the coat and shirt, the shot would have been fired through the rear of the seat, which it wasn't.

"I can see how that doctor called the neck wound an entry wound. But remember, the President's shirt and tie were snugly fastened. The bullet exited at the knot of his tie. The tight binding minimized the explosive nature of an ordinary exit wound. It was a small, clean hole rather than the usually larger exit wound one might expect. Another problem was the one of mass confusion. How often does a doctor get a dead or dying President dropped in his lap? It was mass confusion, everybody pushing and crowding. I don't think that doctors ever had time to really check the President's neck wounds. They had that massive head wound to deal with if there was any chance to save his life. And that was their task: to save his life, not to collect evidence. I'd say that while they were trying to cope with their problem, they simply overlooked the small hole in his back, and that was a perfectly understandable oversight. Then, when the President was pronounced dead, there was no need for an extensive exam. The pathologist's postmortem would do that. Before things got organized there was that business about getting the body out of Dallas. We all know the rest.

"We must stay focused on *facts!* Don't waste energy on crap. Remember, we must make the main thing the main thing!"

"But what about the head snapping back? Could there have been a head shot from the front? Is there any chance—?" The Old man was doubling back on his earlier questions. Evidently he was still submitting to the same fault as the others. He was focusing interest on the silly arguments of the conspiracy theorists.

"No chance," Charlie exclaimed. "It was a hit from the right rear, from above, from the book warehouse. Hell! We know that! No shot could have come from the front. The backward movement of the head was a natural consequence of ballistics; the back pressure of a bullet passing through an enclosed space. To that you can add what I would call a form of optical illusion. You see, Zapruder was panning in his camera from his left to his right and he was keeping the President in the center of his viewfinder. For an amateur, he did a good job. That made it look like the limousine was moving along at a fairly steady pace. When you concentrate on the main subject, the President, it's easy to forget to notice the background. That's the key to the whole deal—the background. When the limousine slowed down, you can see more detail in the grass because the panning action slowed down. But as the limo sped up, the cameraman panned right trying to follow the President. You can see the change in speed by noticing how blurred the grass gets. There's no detail.

"The driver slowed down just an instant before John fired," Charlie droned on. "Then, at the same instant, the shot hit, the driver hit the gas, and the limo shot forward. Remember, the President was in trauma from the neck wound, and he was wearing a back brace. He lost control of his motor action when the head shot hit, and as the limo lurched forward, that and the back-pressure caused his head to pitch back. It could be mistakenly said that the head was driven backward. Most people only had access to still photos rather than Zapruder's film, and still shots aren't as dramatic as the movie. When all the attention is focused on the President, the background is simply overlooked. So you have back-pressure amplified by the forward thrust of the car. Try it sometime. And there's that awful burst of brain matter, it definitely explodes *to the front!*

"And remember what Joe said, there was no frontal shot, and we all know that for a fact!"

"If this is so simple, Charlie, why hasn't it been publicized so people can understand it and get over it? Then they can stop all that talk!"

Charlie grinned, shaking his head, and answered the simple truth. "Because they don't want the truth, It won't serve their purposes!"

The Old Man was truly absorbed, and wanted details. "Charles, are you saying—"

"Because of how people are," Charlie pontificated. "Those who know it was a rear shot don't require proof. Those who believe it was a front shot don't want and won't accept proof. People will be arguing that point years from now."

"Yes, I suppose that's right. Some people simply will not accept reality if it's in opposition to their beliefs. Uh, anyone else while we're on this?" the Old Man asked, looking about the room. "Have we any problem regarding some claims that two rifles were found in the Book Depository rather than only Oswald's? John didn't leave his, surely!"

I had the answer. "No sir, there was only one rifle: Oswald's. What happened was a deputy constable or something, anxious to get into the act, was talking when he should have been listening. At first glance, he called it a German rifle, a Mauser, because it didn't look like it was an American make. He didn't pick it up or examine it, and he's not an expert on guns. But a closer examination by the crime lab people confirmed that it was actually Italian, a Mannlicher-Carcano. This is a case where a hasty and wholly uninformed guess made by someone speaking out of turn was picked up and passed on as gospel truth. Then, when the correct information was offered, conspiracy buffs decided that the truth was just another attempt at a cover-up. So to have something to talk about, those people used the error as an opportunity to advance their positions: conspiracy. To have something to talk about they contend the President was killed with a German rifle, but that Oswald's Italian rifle was switched later so Oswald could be framed."

"I wonder if anyone has guessed what really happened." Tony mused. "I wonder if anyone has even come close?"

"Let's hope they haven't!" I said. "This has become something like a nightmare. I still wake up sometimes in a cold sweat. It's still so unreal, even after so long a time! How did we ever get into this? Have any of you thought back on—"

"Hush, Dave!" the Old Man admonished. "Your feelings are understandable, but entirely too dangerous. We must steel ourselves to the reality of our venture and move on. It was nasty, but it was necessary. Our society, our very existence, was in deadly jeopardy from that fanatic despot. We could not have survived another five years of him, much less his dynasty."

Joe took another glance at his watch. It was ten o'clock. How much longer would it be? Although he still had at least two hours free time, he was becoming quite anxious. The energy drain had affected his appetite; he was suddenly aware of his stomach's growing plea for nourishment.

The Old Man must have been a mind reader, for he interrupted Joe's thoughts, asking, "What would you boys say to a bit of a snack? I'm beginning to feel peckish."

This seemed strange, because the Old Man was a stickler for habit, and wasting time on food was not one of his usual indulgences. He picked up the house phone and directed his attendant to bring some food. While they waited, I made another pot of coffee.

The room had become stuffy. The fire had burned itself out, and the atmosphere had become as weighted as our thoughts. Taking our fresh coffee in hand, we found ourselves strolling back to the veranda. The sharp coolness of the autumn night was almost overwhelming, the air, intoxicating.

"This kind of night gets me to thinking football," Joe commented wistfully. "It's the kind of night to be watching the Redskins beat the cleats off the Cowboys, eh, Dave?"

"Yeh, I guess so, only I haven't thought much about football lately," I lamented. "Since I didn't go to college I don't follow football, but it is a relaxing pastime. I like to watch the game in the den with a couple of beers and something to munch on. I don't really like the idea of all the hassle that goes with going to the Cotton Bowl and then trying to go home in a traffic gridlock."

"Man, you're lazy!" Joe sighed.

"No, he's only showing his age!" Tony corrected.

I went with the subject, "Age? You're a fine one to talk. Age? Look in the mirror sometime."

"I was thinking about a little deer hunting, myself," Tony continued. "It's that time of the year. Deer hunting, Thanksgiving, Christmas, then—Do you realize that in just a little while it's going to be 1965?"

"This fresh air reminds me of camping out. We used to get away at least once a year for a few days and camp in the mountains," Charlie remembered. "I think I like the Smokies best. I guess 'cause they're close to Washington. But when you cross the mountains and drop back into Cade's Cove, you're a hundred years back in time. It's so quiet and peaceful. I don't know, though. Last time we were there, it was so crowded. There's always been a mob in Gatlinburg. But now it's crowded in the woods. I guess everybody's started going camping now. You guys notice how many recreational vehicles and—"

"Everybody's trying to run away. That's what it is," Joe put in. "Things are too busy-busy nowadays. Everybody's in a mad rush to get somewhere, but when they get there, that really isn't where they wanted to be after all. So they rush somewhere else because somewhere else has to be better. It just goes on and on. People always seem to be looking for 'somewhere' but they never seem to find it. I wonder if *somewhere* even exists?"

"If what exists?" I asked.

"Somewhere," Joe repeated. "People have been looking for it ever since I can remember, but I never heard of anyone who found it."

"Joe! I didn't know you were such a philosopher!" Tony teased.

"Philosopher's left foot!" Charlie scolded, "Can't you hear anything? The poor guys homesick."

The Old Man had been standing off to one side, looking over the railing into the darkness. He had remained out of the conversation; it was ours, and he was content to listen. It pleased him that "his lads" were able to relax. He felt guilty at ending the session but he was mindful that Joe had to leave pretty soon, and it was getting late for him, too. Seeing that his attendant had placed some sandwiches on the table and had departed, he took an unaccustomed deep drag on his cigar, pitched it out into the night, mused at the arcing trail of faint, lacy red sparks, then turned to the group.

"My lads, I do hate to interrupt good conversation, but our food is ready. I suppose we should partake and see whether we can conclude tonight's business." We flipped away our cigarettes, mumbled some closing words to each other, and turned away from the night.

Resuming the agenda, the Old Man consulted his list, then turned to me and said, "Let's talk about Mr. Ruby again. So far, we have received no bill for the services of an attorney. Now quickly Dave, we promised that man an attorney, and we owe him that. Do you have any idea what the status is in that regard?"

"No sir, not really," I answered. "The first two lawyers went to him. He kept one for a while, and then Melvin Belli entered the picture. I understand that Belli was his brother's idea, Ruby's brother, Earl, I think. I understand he made contact with Belli, and then Belli called in the others. Actually, except for Don Thomas's brief services, Ruby hasn't hired a lawyer. At least, not outright. Of course, Belli and those lawyers he brought in, Hanna and Simmons, they're going to cost a bundle. But I would guess there's some kind of book deal in the mill. Belli is a writer as well as a lawyer, and Ruby's caper will make a cinch book deal, and my bet is that Belli and the rest will be paid out of the proceeds. So far, I've heard nothing about a bill to anyone for legal services."

"You remember, Dave, we have an obligation to him, and we must keep it. You be certain that he knows that he has not been forsaken. Will you do that, please, Dave?"

"Yes, sir, certainly."

The Old Man scanned his list again. Joe fervently hoped it wasn't long. "There have been suggestions that Oswald wasn't actually Oswald. How solid are we here?"

Oh God, Joe thought. *How many more times are we gonna go over this!*

"Actually, it doesn't make any difference," Tony said. "Whoever he was, if he wasn't Oswald, he's dead and gone now. Whether he was Oswald, Tom Thumb, Jack the Ripper, he—"

"I must differ with you, Tony!" the Old Man interrupted. "I feel that any and all weaknesses in the investigation and solution of the assassination pose a potential threat, because it attracts attention, critical attention. I would prefer that the commission's report be accepted and the entire matter be permitted to die a natural death. For as long as people pry into this, there's the risk that someone might stumble onto something."

"I'm afraid you can forget about that, sir," I disagreed. "Forget about it dying a natural death. It's been almost a hundred years since Lincoln was killed, and there are people who are still trying to conduct new investigations into who was involved. Was it only John Wilkes Booth? Did the Surratts and the others have anything to do with it? Certainly this one's no different. In fact, with more and greater means of collecting and distributing information, this one will be even more speculative. Scholars and nuts will have a field day for years to come. In the year 2000 there will still be conspiracy buffs looking, people who weren't even alive in 1963."

"Nevertheless, we should be diligent," the Old Man persisted. "We've come too far and we've done too well to become careless now. Since we have no crystal ball, we must use our wits to assess every possibility and be careful to lay contingency plans. Are we sure we have the right Oswald?"

"We're as sure as we can be, within reason. We used the usual means for making identification. We took his fingerprints and checked them with the FBI and New Orleans. They checked out with ours. It's pretty certain, he was one and the same man."

"We took it a step further," Charlie added. "We checked the deceased's dental records and blood type with Oswald's Marine Corps dental chart and medical records. They confirm the identification."

"Those things can be faked, can't they, Tony?" the Old Man inquired. "That's one of the oldest tricks, isn't it, arranging false identification?"

"Yes sir," Tony conceded. "It isn't always the easiest thing to do, and it can be done, but I rather doubt it in this case."

"Why?" the Old Man asked, dryly. "Why couldn't he be a Russian agent who was substituted for the real Oswald? I'm not arguing with you, Tony. I'm being the devil's advocate. This surely wouldn't be the first time some enemy of our country planted a spy in a government activity. Now if Oswald, or that is, the substitute, was in fact a Russian agent wouldn't they have moles in our agencies, Charlie, who could've made substitute records? Couldn't they have switched dental charts and fingerprint cards?"

"You've raised a big issue, sir. Let me see how I can best explain it. If the guy we buried as Oswald really was a mole, he waited a long time for his assignment. Usually, when a mole comes in for a mission, he scores, and then he splits, unless he's a deep mole; one with real high status; a long-term assignment. You see, even though he can fool a lot of people, he can't trust being able to fool everybody indefinitely. And there's Mrs. Oswald to consider; his mother. She accepted this corpse as her son."

"But what if they were holding her son prisoner in Russia? Couldn't they intimidate his loved ones, make them go along with the switch by threatening the hostage's life?" the Old Man countered.

"Yes, sir, that's possible." Tony was a little exasperated.

"But that doesn't fit in with his mother," I observed. "Mrs. Oswald is a strong-willed person. I don't think she would go along with a deal like that. Not indefinitely. I think she would start raising some kind of a storm. She'd want her son back. I don't think she would have waited more than two years without doing or at least saying something—demanding the government do something! And now that the subject is dead, she would most certainly be clamoring for the real Oswald's return. She would threaten to blow up the Kremlin."

"Who says she doesn't know something?" the Old Man retorted. He was into it again; Joe was going to miss his plane.

"You've got a point," Tony conceded. "Let me go at it this way. I don't think Oswald fits the role. Remember, he went to Russia in the fall of 1959, five years ago. He stayed there through the spring of 1962. That's two and a half years."

"They could have developed a substitute twice in that time, couldn't they?" the Old Man asked. No doubt his imagination was conjuring a lot of plausible intrigue.

"Yes sir, but that would be highly unusual," Tony replied. "I believe that the original Oswald is the same one who went to Russia, who married the Russian girl. They had a baby, and then returned to the States."

"Now there's a second child. I mean, after all, Oswald, the recent Oswald, didn't seem to be very close to his family, not overly fond of them. Somewhat like he was acting out a role. And for someone who was very close to his mother before, Oswald didn't seem to be as close later. Doesn't that look like someone who might have been an imposter?" the Old Man picked away at his theory.

"Yes, sir, but if Oswald's wife was going along with the deal, I don't know why," Tony continued. "If she's an unwitting participant, the Russians would be taking a big chance on a failure; they just don't play that way. If she is an agent—well, they're going real far out to actually marry and have babies, just to have a front. If they kidnapped the real Oswald after he married her, the Russians could have simply said that she didn't want to come to the States, or that the Ruskies wouldn't let her leave. No need to add another actor to the script, one who couldn't even speak English. No, there's no need for her to be here unless she is the real Oswald's wife and the dead guy is the real Oswald."

"But let me give you the best reason," Tony smiled. "Our boy Freddie could never have played cat and mouse with an agent trained and assigned by Moscow. They would have rapped Freddie in a New York second. Their 'Oswald' would have pulled a reverse on Freddie. They would have had all the facts on what was happening. I don't know just how they would have handled it, but they wouldn't have sat back and done nothing if we were messing with their man."

"Couldn't his wife be here to take suspicion off Oswald or who ever it was? Make him more real, I guess? Or maybe she's an agent too. Isn't she related to some kind of colonel or something?" the Old Man kept probing.

Joe was now fidgeting dangerously. He cast pleading glances, but Tony obliviously slogged on.

"I'm sorry, sir," Tony said in frustration. "I thought I just answered that question. I don't know how to handle this. I'm trying to explain but—"

"Now, Tony, please remember, I said I am only playing the devil's advocate," the Old Man replied soothingly. "Please continue. I'll try not to interfere. However, I do want to feel that our position in all this is safe and solid because we have done our homework. Now, please go on."

"And on, and on, and on," Joe moaned discreetly. My heart went out to him. He should have long since bailed out of this mess.

"It's true that Oswald stayed pretty much alone, and that's typical of an agent. They don't get too close to people. But Oswald was pretty much of a loner *before;* all his life. His and Marina's relationship with the Russian group wasn't typical of agents."

"What if that was how he met his contacts and—I'm sorry. Please continue, Tony."

"Yes, sir, that's possible, too," Tony replied. "But I don't really think so.

"Let me touch on another thing. While the descriptions of Oswald and the 'other' Oswald might have had a few discrepancies between them, there is one means of identification most people are unaware of—the ears. If you study pictures of the real Oswald, and concentrate on the ears, including photos of him as a child, you can see positive identifying characteristics. Then study photos of the later Oswald, those close-ups in jail. The middle of the front of the ear is easily identifiable and so are the earlobes.

"While the ears can be doctored, they usually aren't, unless there is a pronounced difference between subjects. Anyway, had there been an operation to surgically alter the ringer's ears, the scars would have been noticed by the doctor during the postmortem. In Oswald's case, there's no mention of evidence of plastic surgery. I believe there was a reference to some slight wrist scars where Oswald supposedly cut his wrist in a phony suicide attempt when they were going to make him leave Russia not long after he got there, but that's all."

"Are the ears really that reliable, Tony?" the Old Man interrupted. "I'm serious. You mentioned that most people don't know this. I surely didn't."

"Yes sir," I said, preempting Tony's monologue. "While it isn't scientific like blood or fingerprints, it is obvious to the professional observer. Of course, a lot depends on the uniqueness of the features."

"By the way, the early and the later Oswald had the same blood type, for what it's worth," Charlie volunteered. "But it was 'O-positive,' which is so common it's possible that Oswald and his double could have both had the same type without too much coincidence. Anyway, it was the same. I'm pretty confident that the right Oswald is buried there in Fort Worth. I'm not sure much would be learned if they exhumed the body. It isn't too likely that they'd do that. That would involve a lot of red tape, legal hassle and family consent. And we don't want further interest.

"Most of all, remember Freddie. He couldn't have played games with an agent. Not like he did with our Oswald."

"What about Ruby? Is there anything more we should discuss here?"

I took the question. "All he wants is a new trial and a chance to exonerate himself. He only lives to become what we've offered him the chance to be: a hero. What's more, he knows that if he talks, let's say, out of turn, he'll lose the whole bag. He's got a lead pipe cinch for a new trial. Staying away from the psychomotor gibberish, he should get a jail term after which he knows he can collect. While he doesn't always seem real bright, he's a long way from stupid.

In fact as a survivor; he's real smart. However, his condition is something I'll have to keep tuned in on. If anything looks like it's going sour, I can't say what I might be able to do. I'll stay close to things and sound off if I see any problem."

My statement set well with the rest: none could offer any better ideas so the subject was considered settled, or so we fervently hoped.

"Tony, I know I've asked you before, more than once, but what about John and Freddie?" the Old Man wheedled. "I simply cannot overcome a gnawing uneasiness where these people are concerned. Perhaps it's because I never met them. I've never done serious business with anyone about whom I didn't know all that I needed to know. And that has nothing to do with my confidence in you, Tony. I know you, and I know that your knowledge of these people should suffice. But for some reason, well, as I said, I can't shake this gnawing feeling."

"Yes, sir, I've sensed your feelings! And I'm at a loss to explain to you my reasons for trusting John and Freddie in any other terms than those that I have given before. They were available because they have proved themselves in action. I didn't get them out of a Sears catalog or from a bar on skid row. Really, sir, they're pros! I know that doesn't mean a lot to you, not in your line.

But this *is* my line, in a way. That is, I'm not involved in something like this every day. But this wasn't the first time and it might not be the last time. I know my business, and they know theirs. What else can I say?"

"I understand," the Old Man said without offering further resistance. Then he removed an antique gold watch from his vest pocket, extended his arm as far as its gold chain would permit, and observed the time. "Gentlemen, it's past eleven. Joe has to leave, and I'm sure we are all quite tired. Suppose we wrap this up. I hadn't wanted to make this an endurance contest, but we had much to cover, and I don't think we should see each other more than necessary. We've covered the most often mentioned points of contention, regrettably some more than once, and I feel that they are adequately answered, disproved, or that they will not likely lead to anything of a serious thereat or consequence to our group. In closing, let me ask for this last consideration. Do we have any weak link? Dave, how is your friend doing?"

"I don't think we have anything to worry about," I assured him. "He's a real solid type. In fact, he might be retiring before too much longer. He has his 'twenty' in, but he's a couple years short of turning fifty and he won't be eligible to draw his pension until then. He has wanted to go into the construction business, but he hasn't been able to get enough ahead to feel safe making the leap. You can get mighty comfortable with the security of a civil service job, but you can't be too comfortable on the results."

The Old Man sat quietly for a moment. Then, just as the others were noting a twinkle in his eyes, he commanded. "Davey, you tell him to do it! He'll have his backing. You just tell him to get moving. I won't go into details, but it will be arranged. A lawyer will work out the details so that help will not be conspicuous on his records, but he will have his backing. And I will arrange for his mortgage financing. He will have a market for his notes. We certainly owe him that.

"While we are on the subject I will mention something we've never discussed before. I feel obliged, no, privileged to compensate each of you handsomely. I realize you did this for your love of country, but you deserve more, much more, than your country's unspoken gratitude. You shall each be rewarded. Again, I won't go into details. I haven't worked things out fully in my own mind yet. But you, each of you, have earned more than my gratitude. As God has blessed me with prosperity, I will arrange for your fortunes. As you are well aware, it would be unwise for any of you to suddenly become wealthy; things must be worked out. I won't discuss amounts, I don't wish to insult your integrity. But you will each be accommodated equally in a quiet and inconspicuous manner. You, in turn must conduct your lives so that you may grow into your wealth without arousing suspicion. Let me say this much, however. Neither you nor your immediate families shall ever suffer want so long as you retain a life of dignity. And I have no fears in that regard. God knows you have acquitted yourselves with the highest degree of integrity, discretion and control. In fact, I feel it a distinct privilege to have known and worked with you, and to be able to express my gratitude in this way.

"I will arrange for your individual, confidential trust funds when I return to Dallas, but please let me remind you: make no sudden changes in your respective lifestyles. Stay in touch with one another, be loyal to one another. Coordinate your actions so you arouse no suspicion."

A hush came over the room. The group seemed to realize, each at the same time that, while we knew we had been associated with a man of immense personal wealth, none had given any thought to receiving anything for what we did. Certainly, not for such largesse as the Old Man suggested. Ours had been acts of dedication. We had simply believed that our deed was necessary for the future of our nation. The thought of compensation never occurred.

The Old Man's last statement left us numb. We attempted to demur, explaining that no such recognition was expected or necessary, but the Old Man was quietly adamant. We would receive tokens of his gratitude. The revelation clearly gave him a genuine sense of pleasure, but we noted a moist shine in his eyes, a tremor in his voice, and his message had the tenor of a requiem.

"Do we have anything else to discuss? It's almost eleven-forty-five. Joe needs to get away by twelve or he might miss his plane."

We looked about to see whether one of the others would speak. There were no further comments.

The Old Man then arose and stepped forward. "While I've never given it conscious thought, I suppose we've known all along that this hour would one day come. And now it has. Lads, we are adjourned. And barring some serious emergency, we'll never meet again. In fact, for practical purposes, we have never met. Except for the tokens of my gratitude, *we* never existed."

Taking out his notes again, he lit them, held them until they were well ablaze, then dropped them into the embers on the grate in the fireplace. "Good night," he said. "God bless you and keep you. Good bye."

As we got up to shake hands and exchange personal expressions of feeling, it became obvious, the Old Man wasn't the only one with wet eyes.

A little recovered now from the stupor of tedium, Joe was given the opportunity to leave first. As soon as he had said his farewells he was gone, relieved that he would just be able to make the earlier flight. He couldn't remember when he had been so tired, but he was amazed at how light and breezy he was beginning to feel as he headed for the airport and hopefully for a less complicated future.

As Tony was about to step away from his last handshake, the Old Man quietly instructed him to linger until the rest had gone.

By twelve we had reached the veranda again. Instead of the welcoming feeling it had offered before, it now offered no feeling at all. It was just a front porch from which we were about to step out into the night and hopefully into a new and better tomorrow. We were unable to believe that anything could go wrong. From here on it would surely be downhill with the wind at our backs.

At the last moment, Tony said, "Hey, I better go to the john. Don't wait for me. I'll be in touch!"

As we became red tail lights barely visible in the distance, Tony rejoined the Old Man in the lodge. He later confided in me that the Old Man had given him one last assignment.

"Tony, I didn't want to alarm the others needlessly, but we do still have a problem. No matter how hard I've tried to understand your vote of confidence for John and Freddie, I can't. Tony, listen carefully, for this is my last word and my last assignment for you. We cannot risk the continued presence of John and Freddie. Do you understand what I mean?"

It took but an instant for his instructions to register. "Yes sir, I understand."

"And Tony—no outsiders."

"Yes, sir."

With that, the Old Man gave Tony a pleasant parting smile, turned and departed through the rear door. That was the last time Tony would see him.

* * *

I covered the first miles without a conscious thought. I made my last turn from the back roads and was on the main highway for several minutes before it struck me. *It's over! It's over! Thank God it's over! When had it started? Was it a year ago? Two years?* It seemed more like ten or maybe a hundred.

From the first, it had seemed unreal. Now, it still seemed unreal, a fantasy. For such a long time I had prayed for a good night's sleep, that I might waken from this chronic nightmare. *Now, it's all over. We're through! Praise the Lord! It's done. We're through with it. Oh God, don't let anything go wrong! Oh, no! And please, dear God, please, no more!*

In a brief moment, my anxiety gave way to nervous excitement. My usually conservative driving reflected my newfound mood. The accelerator had unwittingly reached seventy. When I noticed my speedometer, I burst into foolish, even giddy laughter. I let up on the throttle and held my speed at a bit over fifty. I wanted to get home.

I saw the moon for the first time since I couldn't remember when. Rolling down my window I inhaled deeply of the sharp autumn air. Even the chill felt good to me. Oh, did it ever feel good. And I saw that there were stars in heaven. In fact, it seemed that there were a great many more than there had ever been before.

Where could they have come from? Where had they been? I was aware of a sudden wave pulsing through my body. It was a grand feeling. I was finally aware that I was grateful to be alive.

* * *

I reached home in much less time than ever before. Turning into the driveway I could see a light in the living room. Mary never sat up in the living room. Why was she in the living room? It was a little past one o'clock. It's December first. Could something be wrong?

As I shut down my car and hurried toward the house the front door opened. She stood there, dressed for bed but fully awake and smiling. I paused a few moments, then continued up the steps and started to speak, but she spoke first.

"Hi, honey. Welcome home!"

Could she know? How could she know? It's uncanny! There's no way she could know! Before I could regroup my thoughts, she had stepped forward with her arms outstretched. Without speaking we told each other how we felt.

She said, "You look great!"

"Oh, God, do I ever feel great. And it's great to be home! It's great to be alive!"

EPILOGUE

About three weeks later a Miami newspaper carried a brief inside article about a body found in the bay. The man had apparently drowned while fishing. The notice did not mention his line of work, nor did it mention his name, Freddie.

* * *

A week later on the West Coast a man entered the hospital with severe stomach cramps. He had complained of having nasty ulcers but this was not just an ulcer problem. In fact, the doctors weren't sure just what it was. Food poisoning? Maybe botulism. But all the tests were negative or inconclusive. He lapsed into unconsciousness and died in less than a week. The cause of death was not fully known. Official cause of death was described as severe stomach disorder complicated by ulcers. Pathologists did not detect a minute dose of a rare poison derived from the castor bean. No mention was made of his profession or his alias, John.

* * *

The years 1965 and 1966 were comparatively uneventful. The media supported the Warren Commission's account of the assassination. Lyndon Johnson moved into the presidency in his own right. The war in Vietnam, space exploration, student protests, and civil rights made headlines. It seemed that I might have been wrong when I predicted that the books would never close on the assassination: it seemed they had.

* * *

Jack Ruby was granted a new trial in October of 1966. That amounted to nothing, however, for in that same month he was admitted to Parkland Hospital with inoperable cancer. He remained under arrest until his death on January 3, 1967. The conspiracy theorists were on hand to suggest that "they" had injected him with live cancer cells to kill him and shut him up because "they" were afraid he would reveal "their" identity as the conspirators in the assassination of President Kennedy.

* * *

Shortly after he retired from the CIA in 1965, Tony's often strained marriage ended in a messy and vindictive divorce. A few weeks later he took a sudden and unscheduled fishing vacation.

He never returned from his first day out on Chesapeake Bay. His rented boat offered no clues as to what had happened to Tony. Some say it was an accident. Others aren't so sure. We wondered just how much his strenuous assignments with the group played in his misfortune. He was declared legally dead in 1975, but his body was never discovered. During the ten-year period, his ex-wife and his heirs were well-provided for by an unknown benefactor. After being declared legally dead, his old and unchanged will was probated. His family received a most generous estate.

* * *

The Old Man was a hardy breed. He continued to prosper, and he kept his word. His lawyer set up the trust funds and maintained them as he had promised. He never saw any members of his group after that last night at the lodge. He continued to develop his great wealth and used it to support conservative candidates, office holders, and causes. In his later years, he began making generous contributions to charitable causes, mostly those concerning higher education for the less fortunate students. In the summer of 1981, he died peacefully in his sleep.

* * *

Jerry retired and entered the building industry and enjoyed better than modest success. He almost never thought of the assassination. He died of a stroke in August 1980, leaving his heirs well off.

* * *

Joe left the Secret Service "for health reasons." Then he took a position with a major petroleum corporation. The opportunity came as a complete surprise. He didn't even use their brand. They had obtained his name, but they never said where, only that he had been highly recommended. He retired in 1978 and died in 1979. Again, his heirs were well off.

* * *

Charlie left the FBI and opened his own law practice. He did quite well. The retainers he received from a couple of large organizations helped him get started. Those clients and others had walked in within the first month. They never did say why they chose his firm. Business and investments increased his wealth. He was killed in 1982 when his private jet crashed over the Rocky Mountains while returning from Los Angeles where he had just engineered a merger between two major national corporations. His attorney-sons assumed control of the firm.

* * *

Eventually, I retired. My lifestyle never changed. I have taken care that nothing about me suggested that privately I am a wealthy person. I have provided for Mary and my family to be as comfortable as they possibly can. I am satisfied with my success as a person. I am satisfied that I did what it was necessary to do, and I did it the best way I knew how. On this, a rainy winter morning in January 1983, I feel death to be very near so I will sign off and make arrangements for the future. I am the last survivor of our group, and I feel quite alone. As bad as it was, we did what we truly believed had to be done. Now I must arrange for our story to be told, but not until it can do no harm to the surviving family members of our group. I will entrust this journal to a man whom I trust to carry out my wishes. May God and history forgive us.

* * *

The foregoing is Dave's journal just as he wrote it. It was with reluctance and trepidation that I decided whether to honor my promise to Dave. Then I realized, Dave was its publisher, I was his agent, and had given him my faithful word.

Time proved his predictions to be true. The assassination investigation didn't die a natural death. Each year seemed to generate a new crop of "experts" determined to find something all the others had missed. Each placed his critical significance on the most trivial detail. Some twisted the truth to serve their purposes while others invented new "truths." And then there were others who mostly guessed at it.

Some have come frighteningly close, but proof eluded them. Now they know.

THE END